DEEP BLUE

Elune lay prone, her body half submerged in the pool, her limbs spread-eagled, each firmly tied to a weight far too heavy to shift. Daccombe Bay provided everything Juliana's fertile brain could desire. She could hear them discussing the next stage of her punishment as they searched for things to use.

'Perfect!' Juliana declared. 'How many are there?'

'Seven, I think,' Thomazina declared.

'Good, I will start.'

Elune listened as Juliana approached her. A shiver went through her as Juliana's hands found her pubic mound. She felt a finger burrow into her, then another. Elune squirmed and wriggled her hips for more, only for the touching to stop as quickly as it had begun. 'Not yet, little one,' Juliana chided. 'We must allow the full indulgence of your senses.'

'I've brought all seven crabs,' Thomazina said suddenly. 'One's an edible.'

'Then give that one to me,' Juliana ordered. 'We'll spare her face, but not those darling little titties.'

GH00758768

DEEP BLUE

Aishling Morgan

This book is a work of fiction.
In real life, make sure you practise safe sex.

First published in 2001 by
Nexus
Thames Wharf Studios
Rainville Road
London W6 9HA

www.nexus-books.co.uk

Typeset by TW Typesetting, Plymouth, Devon

Printed and bound by
Cox & Wyman Ltd, Reading, Berks

ISBN 0 352 33600 5

Deep Blue is dedicated to James Marriott, for the original inspiration, to Hilary Wade, for allowing me to use her character, Nich Mordaunt, and to Sigodin-Yth/Txcalin, just in case.

One

Her bikini must have belonged to a ten-year-old sister. For certain it was never meant to hold what she had, which was plenty. Boobs, for one thing, big, round globes of creamy girl meat squashed in behind two tiny triangles of bright-blue material. They were real, too, quivering as she walked, the nipples showing, stiff beneath the ridiculous bikini.

Joe shifted his weight in the grass and made a tiny adjustment to his binoculars. The girl was walking along the beach, carefree and relaxed, indifferent to the indecent display she was making of her body. Most of her boobs showed, and the minuscule pants were pulled tight into the groove of her pussy. Long hair of the deepest possible black, pert features set in an easy smile, a firm rounded tummy, full hips and long, long legs completed her look; near bare and by far the most attractive girl he had seen while spying on the beach.

There were others: smart young professional women who could afford the cost of the island's holiday homes; older women, rich in their own right or with affluent husbands; one or two who might have been nannies or day trippers like himself. Most were scantily clad, one or two even topless, and his cock had been stiff in his pants for some time. None of them compared to the girl in the blue bikini, who made the best of them look poor, artificial and contrived, despite fashionably slim bodies and designer costumes.

She stooped as he put his eyes back to the binoculars. For a moment she was in profile, showing the rear curve of a truly glorious bottom barely constrained in her pants. She picked up a shell, spent a moment admiring it and put it back on the sand, once more displaying the side view of her bottom. Joe swallowed and reached down to squeeze his cock, hot fantasies running through his head as he imagined stripping her, pulling off her tiny blue bikini and bending her over, fucking her from behind as he fondled her huge, dangling boobs.

He was desperate to come, but a glance at his watch showed that the hydrofoil returned to the mainland in less than half an hour, and with a grunt of annoyance he pulled back from his hiding place. A quick check showed that the cliff path was deserted and he started back, nonchalant to all outward appearance, but burning internally with images of half-naked girls, most of all her, the beauty in the blue bikini, the innocent tart, the one who showed it all and just didn't care.

As he walked back he thought of how it might have been. If only he'd had a chance to talk to her, if he'd had enough money to stay on the island, if he'd been rich or famous, somebody she would want to talk to, somebody she might even go to bed with. It was impossible. For all his wishful thinking he knew she would never be interested. Doubtless she was rich, although with a figure like hers she was no catwalk model and with her air of innocence it was difficult to think of her as a businesswoman. Probably she was the daughter of some stuck-up banker or tycoon, and rich enough to be truly carefree. In any case, she was hardly likely to be interested in a delivery boy.

His feelings of lust and resentment lasted as the hydrofoil took him back to the mainland, leaving the island behind, a low bulk of faded grey-green, highlighted with the paler colours of the beaches and houses. Seen from afar, it had always projected an air of mystery, of being unobtainable, a place where he would never fit in, never be welcomed. Having visited and spent a day spying on girls, the sensation was stronger than ever, with a good measure of envy thrown in.

On shore it was worse, with the colourful bustle of Tawmouth tawdry and cheap beside the affluence of St

David's Island. The beach was crowded, mainly with families and groups of teenage friends, so noisy that they came close to drowning out the tinny pop music that drifted from the pier. Beyond was the sea, sparkling and blue in the sunlight, bobbing with heads and the colours of lilos and beach balls. Further out two ships were visible, a china-clay coaster making for the river mouth and the French ferry.

Joe shrugged, then smiled as his eyes came to rest on the chubby bottom of a pretty young blonde in a pink bathing costume. As he admired her the irritating exclusivity of St David's began to recede and he set off along the front, once more intent on his favourite pastime. However ordinary the Tawmouth girls might be, there were plenty of them, in every shape, size and colour, none bare, but with enough tit and bum spilling out of swimming costumes to keep his cock near to erection in his trousers.

His intention had been to find somewhere private on St David's and come in his hand over what he had seen. The girl in blue had distracted him, and as he feasted his eyes on the Tawmouth girls his urgency became stronger than ever. Jerking off was impractical with the crowds around him. Chatting up a girl was out, too, the process of finding her, flirting with her and hopefully enticing her into taking his cock in her hand or mouth too slow and too uncertain. For a moment he considered a visit to the town's massage parlour, where hand relief was rumoured to be available for twenty pounds, only to abandon the idea as too sordid.

With a sigh of regret he decided to return to his flat and employ a well-thumbed pornographic magazine to ease his tension. After that he could turn his full attention to finding the girlfriend he so badly needed. Reaching the pier, he turned towards the town only to stop as his eye caught a flash of bright blue on the beach beyond. She was walking out of the sea, the same gorgeous girl he had watched on St David's, her overstretched bikini bulging with girlish flesh, wet and tighter than ever.

He found himself licking his lips, his cock stiffening to full and embarrassing erection. She was glorious,

3

irresistibly glorious, and, although sure he would be rejected, he knew he had to try. Willing his all too obvious erection to go down, he made for the steps to the beach, struggling for a good opening line as he went. She was walking up the beach, wearing the same happy smile she had before, her huge boobs bouncing with every step she took. Trying hard to look casual, he angled towards her, praying she was not going to join one of the families on the beach or, worse, one of the other single men.

She did neither, but made for an ice-cream van on the front. Joe followed, coming close behind her as she reached the steps. Climbing up, he found his face level with her magnificent bottom, the two plump globes of flesh moving inside her hopelessly inadequate bikini in a way that set his cock to a rigid bar of flesh. Most of her bum was out of her pants, two heavy, cream coloured hemispheres, with the scrap of blue material caught between them. Some hair even showed, down between her thighs, along with a shallow V of flesh above the waistband, the top of her split. He could even smell pussy.

His eyes stayed fixed to the motion of her bottom until she reached the top of the stair. From below he could see the groove where her bikini pants were caught between her pussy lips, and was imagining her stripping, pulling down her pants for his enjoyment. Swallowing hard, he came up behind her, joining the queue for ice cream. Standing close, he caught the scent of sea water from her hair, which was so dark that the sunlight struck a sheen of deepest blue from her crown. She was quite small as well, several inches shorter than he was, although she had seemed taller on the beach and not quite so wonderfully busty. Her small size increased his confidence.

'Great day, huh?' he managed.

She turned and smiled, showing none of the wariness or dislike he had expected, her large, dark-green eyes innocent and wide.

'Neat swimsuit. Is it designer?' he asked and immediately regretted the boldness of his remark as her expression turned to puzzlement.

He opened his mouth to make an apology, only for her to turn as the ice-cream man asked what she wanted. Cursing himself, he let his eyes wander down her bare back to the swell of her bottom and the inch of soft crease where her bikini failed to cover her big cheeks.

'Ha'penny cornet, please, mister,' she said in a voice that belied her obvious maturity.

Joe looked up, surprised by the girlish voice but also by what she had said. She was holding a coin out, a bronze one, green with verdigris.

'You taking the piss, love?' the ice-cream man demanded. 'A cornet's a quid, a quid fifty for a double.'

'One pound?' she asked.

'Yeah, a quid. You foreign?'

'Oh dear.'

'Here, I'll get it,' Joe cut in, holding out a five-pound note over her shoulder. 'Make it a double, with flakes and chocolate sauce. The same for me.'

The ice-cream man grunted and turned into the interior of the van. The girl turned, her smile broader than ever and pathetically grateful. Joe smiled back, deciding that she obviously was foreign, perhaps French, although her accent was more like the local Devon, stronger if anything.

'Thank you, sir,' she said. 'You are so kind.'

'No problem,' he answered. 'Fancy a walk?'

'A pleasure,' she said.

Her voice had changed, now less girlish, more confident. Taking the ice creams, Joe gave her one. As they began to walk she took his arm in an unconcerned gesture, leaving his heart pounding at the feel of her flesh. Elation was swelling inside him, made stronger by the envious looks of other men as he walked along the front, arm in arm with a girl who might have walked straight from the pages of a dirty magazine.

'What's your name?' he asked.

'Thomazina,' she answered, then paused. 'Maybe Tammy?'

'Tammy's easier,' he said, 'and nice, too. I'm Joe.'

'Pleased to meet you, Joe.'

5

'Where do you come from then?'

'Across the sea, France.'

Joe paused. He wanted to talk more, but everything he could think of seemed stupid, while he was sure that what he really wanted to say would get his face slapped. She seemed happy in any case, licking her ice cream and looking around, indifferent to stares, whether jealous, admiring or disapproving. His cock was still hard, and he knew it showed, praying she would not notice, only for her to look down at his crotch. The blood rose to his cheeks as he prepared for the string of angry words, only to hear her giggle.

'Would you like to put him inside me, your man?' she asked.

'Jesus, you bet,' Joe answered, taken aback by her bluntness but determined not to chicken out from the offer of a lifetime.

'I beg your pardon?' she answered.

'I'd like to,' he stammered. 'I'd love it. I wanted to from the moment I saw you. Come on – my place is just up the hill.'

'By the sea,' she answered, shaking her head.

'We'd be seen!' Joe protested, gesturing at the beach, less crowded than by the pier but far from empty. 'I don't know where you come from, but in England you can't just fuck on the beach. We'd get arrested!'

She nodded and took his hand, pulling him forward. Joe followed, eager to take what was being offered but certain it would all fall apart before he got his cock sheathed inside her gorgeous body. Yet she seemed as eager as he was, breaking into a run and laughing as he followed, along the course of the sea wall where the railway swung in from the town.

Joe let his eyes feast on Tammy's body as she ran, admiring the way her hair swirled and the movement of her bottom in her bikini pants. Before, she had been gorgeous, a beautiful, unobtainable thing, far beyond his reach. Now she had offered herself and the fantasies he had been building up, of stripping her and having her flaunt her

6

naked curves for him, had become a very immediate reality.

Once before he had walked to the end of the sea wall, where a headland pushed out to the sea with the railway running beneath it. The last part of the beach was a jumble of huge red boulders, with coarse sand and rock pools between them. He imagined this to be where Tammy intended to go, out of sight behind a rock for a quick knee-trembler. Instead she kept on, scrabbling out among the rocks in her bare feet, indifferent to the slimy weed and the splash of the waves. Joe followed, determined not to seem a spoilsport, around the headland to a tiny cove of fine red sand beneath towering cliffs of the same dark, rich red. Tammy was already on the beach, sitting cross-legged with an arch look on her face. Joe approached her, his heart pounding, wondering how to start without looking clumsy or inexperienced.

She reached out, grinning openly, and caught hold of his zip, tugging it down. Joe could only stare as she reached into his fly and pulled his cock free of his pants, tugging at the shaft, then leaning forward to take it in her mouth. He moaned as her soft lips closed on his penis, trying to blank his mind to stop himself coming in her mouth and spoiling it. Looking down he found her eyes shut in bliss as she sucked on his penis, clearly enjoying it, far more so than either of the two girls he had previously talked into blow jobs. Nor was she inhibited about her body, with one hand already down the front of her bikini pants, massaging her pussy.

'Jesus, you French girls are hot,' he moaned. 'Come on, get those gorgeous big tits out.'

Tammy went on sucking, but put her hands to her bikini, tugging the cups up over her breasts to let them spill free, huge and firm, the nipples sticking up, rose pink and hard. Joe knelt, pulling his cock from her mouth, caution set aside in the face of her obvious willingness. Placing his cock between her breasts he began to fuck them, at which Tammy giggled and obligingly pushed them together. With his erection sliding between them he once more felt the urge to come, spraying sperm over her huge boobs and in her pretty face. Holding back with an effort, he stood away.

'I can't wait,' he stammered. 'Sorry, but I've got to fuck you now.'

'How?' she asked. 'Like the dolphins, or like the dogs on the beach?'

'Doggie,' he gasped. 'Jesus, Tammy, you're so fucking sexy.'

She had turned, lifting her bottom in open invitation, her knees wide to show her sex, hidden only by the tiny scrap of blue material, her back pulled in to leave her big cheeks high and wide. Presented for rear entry, her bottom was more wonderful than ever, big, female and firm, a magnificent moon of pale flesh, with what little the bikini concealed his to expose. She was flawless, too, creamy and smooth, ivory pale, with a small, octopus design tattooed on the tuck of one plump cheek to add a daring touch to her rude display.

'I'm going to pull your pants down,' Joe grunted. 'I'm going to pull your pants down and I'm going to fuck you, like the dogs on the beach, just like the dogs on the beach.'

He took hold of her bikini pants and pulled, exposing her bottom and pussy, the lips full and pouted in a nest of jet-black fuzz, her anus a tight pink dimple between the lush cheeks. She giggled, then sighed as his cock nudged her sex. Joe pushed, taking her by the hips as his erection slid into the warm depths of her vagina. Tammy sighed again, then hung her head and began to pant as her body jumped to his first push. Joe reached forward, mounting her and taking her big, dangling breasts in his hands, fondling them as he fucked her.

'You're so fucking sexy,' he repeated. 'You look like butter wouldn't melt and you're so fucking hot. Oh, your tits feel good. I've never had such a big pair. And your bum, so big, so wobbly. Jesus, you're lovely, Tammy, you hot, dirty bitch. I'm going to spunk in you right now, right up your hot little pussy. It's happening. I've come in you Tammy, I've come up your pussy. Oh, Jesus, you're hot.'

Joe sank back, his cock pulling from her hole. For a moment he expected her to be angry at what he'd said, and for the way he'd fucked her so crudely and so quickly. Tammy gave no such reaction, but let her face and breasts slump forward into the sand, reaching back to find her pussy. Joe stared, open-mouthed, as she began to masturbate, panting and moaning with her knees wide and her fingers working in her sex, a display more lewd and abandoned than anything he had imagined. His come was running from the open hole of her vagina, down over her fingers as she rubbed, smearing the thick white mess over her wet flesh. The hole began to contract, squeezing out more come, her anus also, opening and closing as if winking at him. Her moans became more urgent, changed to short, frantic gasps and then a long, ecstatic sigh and he realised that she had reached orgasm, masturbating in front of him in a display ruder by far than anything he had seen in person.

'Jesus, Tammy,' he managed as she rolled on to her back with a happy sigh.

She smiled and gave a little purring noise, stretching her body on the sand. Lost for what to say, Joe climbed slowly to his feet, only to be forced to jump forward as the wash of a wave came close to his shoes. Tammy took no notice, neither troubling to cover herself nor move when the water touched her foot.

'That was good,' he managed, sure he ought to say something. 'Thank you.'

'A pleasure, sir,' Tammy answered.

'We don't really say "sir" any more,' Joe laughed. 'All that formal stuff went out years ago. Nobody ever called me sir before, anyway!'

'You say "mister"?'

'No, just Joe's fine, especially when we've just, you know, fucked and all.'

'I understand.'

'Anyway, we'd better get back. The tide's coming in.'

Tammy nodded but made no move to get up.

'Look, are you around at all?' he asked. 'Are you staying in Tawmouth?'

9

'No . . .'

'Oh, right . . . It's just that, you know, it would be nice to see you again. You're really cute and everything. I suppose you're going back to France on the evening ferry.'

'No. Perhaps we may meet on the beach again. Or at the solstice party at the Wythman?'

'Party, what party?'

'There will be a party on the solstice, at the Wythman. It will be such fun.'

'That's that mound on the big hill, isn't it?'

'Yes. I'll be there.'

'Great, I'll keep an eye out. Look, we've got to go before we get cut off.'

'You go. I need a swim.'

'You're going to get one, longer than you bargained for!'

'I will be well.'

'Well you're a big girl, but if you end up spending the night halfway up the cliff don't blame me!'

'I will not. You must leave, Joe. Thank you for tupping me.'

'Sure, see you again, yeah?'

Tammy nodded and Joe made for the headland, where the waves could be seen, breaking perilously close to the cliff face. Twice he looked back as he went, finding Tammy first standing, in the act of removing her bikini, then half immersed in the water, stark naked as far as he could tell. When he reached the tip of the headland he turned once more to wave, but found her lost to view. A large wave broke against the rock he was on, splashing him and increasing his urgency to get to safety. Hurrying on, he reached the beach, wading the last few yards to leave his legs wet from the knees down.

As he climbed to the sea wall he shook off a trace of worry. Tammy had been so confident that she was safe, and the worst that would happen was for her to have to shelter a little way up the cliff for the night or to swim around the headland. Neither choice would have suited him, but he was sure that if he'd pushed the issue it would have put her off, while as it was there seemed every chance of having her again.

Walking back along the front, he felt thoroughly pleased with himself, whistling and running over what had happened again and again. It was all great, from the first peep of her body in the overtight bikini to watching her come under her own fingers. It had been hard to talk to her, but she hadn't minded his talking dirty, which put some girls off. She'd been well up for it, too, really keen and really dirty.

One thing was odd. She had been at St David's and at Tawmouth, so she must have come back on the same hydrofoil, yet he definitely hadn't seen her. Then again, all it meant was that she had a private motor launch, or had come back on someone else's, so it wasn't such a mystery.

Ed Gardner stood looking out across the sea, watching the French ferry as it swung slowly in towards the dock. A good number of passengers were visible on the open decks, apparently a typical range of French and British tourists, arriving for and returning from holidays respectively. With luck there may be a few who looked disreputable enough to search, and perhaps he would find a little cannabis or ecstasy. There may even be the chance to have a pretty girl or two body-searched, which always gave him pleasure. Even though it was against regulations to do the job himself, it was worth it just to see the looks on their faces when they realised they would soon be bending for the insertion of well-greased fingers into their vaginas and bottom holes. It was great afterwards, too, watching the shame and anger in their expressions.

The dock quivered as the ferry bumped into place, and Ed set his jaw and folded his arms across his chest as the bow door began to open. Passengers appeared on the footway, a cluster of French schoolgirls, a family in loud holiday clothes, a single man in a neat white suit. Ed considered the man, watching his face for any trace of unease or hint of sweat. None was evident, merely a natural arrogance that made his opinion of customs officials very clear. For a moment Ed considered stopping the man, only to abandon the idea as too likely to lead to trouble. Still, the single, haughty glance had pricked his pride and his determination to take his feelings out on a more vulnerable passenger increased.

More came, mainly holidaymakers, families who were French, British and from elsewhere in Europe, none of whom seemed worth stopping. Only when the initial press had died to a trickle did he allow the stern expression on his face to briefly twitch into a smile. The man was perfect, an obvious libertine, and more than likely to be carrying drugs, possibly even something hard. In height he was perhaps a touch under six foot, two inches shorter than Ed. He was slim in proportion, slight even, with bright-red hair tied back into a thin ponytail. Black jeans and a black top seemed normal enough, but black nail polish definitely was not. His shoes were also suspect, the thick heel at least three inches in height. Worse still were his earrings, cheap gunmetal set with crimson enamel in an eight-pointed design, which in Ed's book made him definitely weird and probably homosexual.

'Excuse me, sir, might I see your passport?' Ed asked as his target came close.

'Certainly, officer,' the man answered, his educated and somehow condescending tone setting the final seal on Ed's determination to have him searched.

Ed took the passport as it was offered, opening it to find a clear picture of the man obviously taken at most a few weeks before.

'You are Mr Mordaunt?' Ed asked. 'Mr Nicholas Mordaunt?'

'Nicalo,' the man replied.

'Could I ask you to step this way, sir?'

'Why?'

'Just a routine check, sir.'

The man followed him into the interview room, apparently with no great surprise, which further increased Ed's suspicions. Two cases were surrendered without argument, a large travel bag and a briefcase, both black. Within the bag were clothing and a few essentials, nothing more. The briefcase proved more fruitful, containing a magazine illustrated by a picture of a naked woman entwined in the tentacles of an octopus, stylised but of an undoubtedly sexual nature. Flicking it open, he discovered further drawings, some with sexual content, some without, apparently illustrating text, which he didn't bother to read.

'Are you aware that it is an offence to import pornography into this country, sir?' he asked, keeping his voice cool and level although thoroughly pleased with himself.

'Pornography?' the man demanded. 'What pornography?'

'This pornography, sir,' Ed answered, turning the case to display the cover of the magazine.

'That's not pornography,' Mordaunt retorted. 'It's a learned work!'

'Pornography,' Ed repeated.

'Nonsense!' Mordaunt insisted. 'It is a treatise, to do with pre-Celtic imagery.'

'Really, sir?'

'Yes, really. For goodness' sake, do I look like the sort of man who smuggles in dirty magazines? And if I was, do you think I'd have left it on top of the papers in my briefcase?'

'I really couldn't say, sir. We get all sorts. The girl is naked, she's getting off. In my book that's pornography. And it's perverted.'

'Philistine!'

'I could have you arrested, sir.'

'Officer, the paper is a work of scholarship. Much of the original work was done in this town, towards the middle of the nineteenth century, also in London, where it was published. Can it be illegal to bring back something that was published in this country?'

'It's pornography. You get a straight choice. I confiscate it and that's that or you get shirty, I arrest you and we can work it out in court. What's it to be?'

For a moment Mordaunt looked as if he was about to answer, then his jaw set into a hard line, his eyes meeting Ed's. They were green, the colour of virgin olive oil, and disconcerting, but Ed returned the stare until Mordaunt at last gave a hiss of frustration and began to repack his bag.

Ed held his stern expression until Mordaunt had left. Smiling, he tossed the magazine to one side, hoping it would make good reading later. Women with octopus was weird, too weird, but there had to be other stuff, hopefully some bondage. He glanced at his watch and his smile grew broader as he thought of the end of his shift. He was meeting Lily, a girl he had been out with twice. She was an archaeologist, in Tawmouth for a year to study for a master's degree, blonde, small-breasted, with a pouting, heavy little bottom that wiggled as she walked. Quiet, sensitive and intellectual, she was also easily dominated. He had discovered this on their first date, bullying her into hasty sex on the floor of her room and surprised to find that she didn't resent the act. On the second occasion he had persuaded her to perform a striptease while he watched. She had been clumsy and embarrassed, but her nervousness and her blushes as she peeled nude had made the act far more exciting than any professional strip. This time he hoped to push it further, maybe to tie her hands, maybe more.

In her tiny room above a dockside fish-and-chip shop, Lily Tompkins lay on her bed, naked under a short bathrobe. A book lay open in front of her, a work on prehistoric sites in south Devon. Her attention appeared to be on the page, but she was finding it impossible to concentrate. Despite every effort, her mind continually drifted to the coming evening and what she might expect of Ed Gardner.

She knew he was a bully, and part of her hated him, yet it was impossible to deny her own compulsion towards being sexually bullied. Alone in the town, and never having found friends easy to make, she had gladly accepted his initial offer of a date. He was good-looking as well, tall, muscular and handsome in a rather craggy way, with a firm, square jaw that projected all the confidence she lacked. It had been easy to let him make the decisions, to control her, taking her to an Italian restaurant, then a pub and finally back to her room. He had more or less invited himself up for coffee, which had turned to kisses, to

14

fumbles and to the removal of her knickers from beneath her dress. She had taken it placidly, accepting his cock in her mouth before being rolled up on the floor and entered. A few dozen hard pushes had taken him to orgasm, withdrawing at the last moment to come over her belly and dress. He had wiped his cock on her discarded knickers and finished his coffee, leaving her to clean up. Afterwards, when he had gone, she had masturbated to orgasm, not over him as such, nor over their sex together, but over the crude, casual way he had wiped up his come and her own juices, using her most intimate garment as a rag.

Her intention had been to refuse a second date if he asked, but when the time came she had found herself mumbling assent. They had eaten fish and chips on the quay, then returned to his house. He had made her drunk on cheap lager, then put on some dreadful music and told her to do a striptease. She had obeyed, blushing furiously as she did her best to dance and undress at the same time. As her clothes came off it had been impossible not to think of herself as a stripper, doing it for money: Lily Tompkins BA, stripping to music in some seedy bar. By the time she was nude she had been shivering with embarrassment. She had been wet, though, wetter than she could remember.

Ed had made her kneel, sticking her bottom up in a thoroughly vulgar pose and entering her from the rear. Being aware of what she was showing had added to her woes as he had grunted his way towards orgasm, and when he had pulled out and deposited his sperm over her naked buttocks and down in her crease she had been near to tears. Later, back in her room, she had masturbated again, and done it kneeling, her nightie off, sobbing with humiliation as she brought herself to climax. Now it would happen again, or something worse. She knew she would do it, though, and cursed herself for being weak even as she anticipated the pleasure of the orgasm she was bound to take afterwards.

After pushing herself up from the bed, she began to dress. A rebellious voice in the back of her head told her to choose the plainest possible clothes: white knickers and

15

bra, jeans and an old T-shirt. Half an hour later found her in a knee-length black cocktail dress, black silk culottes, hold-up stockings and no bra, with three-inch heels to complete a look that she knew Ed would appreciate but that she personally felt made her look like a call girl, albeit an expensive one.

Feeling resentful, and weaker than ever, she set off for her rendezvous, hoping that Ed would at least have the decency to provide something less basic than fish and chips before seducing her. He was waiting in the square, casually dressed, standing by the fountain in a nonchalant pose that made the best of his lean, muscular figure. Lily felt a warm flush at the sight and found herself smiling and allowing him to kiss her, then to squeeze her bottom as he began to steer her towards the front.

He proved in generous mood, selecting a good restaurant and ordering oysters, then Dover sole, washed down with Muscadet. Lily quickly found herself becoming tipsy, also both nervous and excited at the prospect of what was likely to follow the meal. Ed talked, his normal mixture of right-wing politics and stories about his work, to which she listened politely with no more than the occasional noncommittal comment. Within she was thinking of having to strip for him, lifting her little black dress to show her underwear and naked breasts, easing down her culottes with her bottom stuck out, burning with embarrassment as he commented lewdly on the sight of her bare bottom . . .

She shivered, then looked up to see if he had noticed, a coy glance to which he failed to pay any attention whatever. Instead he signalled a waiter, ordering lemon cheesecake to be followed by strong Irish coffees without troubling to consult her. She sighed, unable to deny the pleasure in being under his control but still wishing she had a more assertive personality.

They finished the meal, the whiskey-rich coffee leaving her unsteady on her feet when they rose to go. Ed put his arm around her, supporting her, then letting his hand wander lower to take hold of her bottom and squeeze, indifferent to the busy evening crowds. Lily said nothing, but let him lead her, through the town centre and up the hill to the Edwardian terrace where he lived. As the door closed behind them she felt a sensation of having been cut off, of having lost her last chance to back away.

Ed took her hand, leading her up the stairs to his room, an austere, masculine chamber with a great iron-framed bed at the centre. Lily found herself shivering, awaiting his orders, to strip or pose, to suck his penis or part her thighs for him.

'Climb on the bed,' he ordered, 'arse up.'

Lily obeyed, her jaw shaking as she crawled to the middle of the bed and adopted the rude pose he wanted. Kneeling, bottom lifted, she felt the blood rush to her cheeks, blushing with embarrassment.

'Cute,' Ed drawled. 'Now put your hands out. Take a grip of the bedstead.'

Looking back, Lily again did as she was told, stretching her arms forward until they met the iron bars of the bedstead. Ed moved to one side, pulling open a drawer, lifting out what she realised was a skipping rope. For an instant she wondered if she was going to be made to do exercises in the nude, only to realise the significance of her position. Her jaw started to tremble as she realised she was going to be tied up, both in anticipation of what he might do once she was helpless and from the knowledge that she was about to take part in an act of kinky sex.

'No, Ed, please,' she managed, but she didn't move, holding passively to the bedstead as he came to kneel beside her.

'Relax, babe,' he told her. 'You know you love it.'

Lily found her breath coming faster as the rope was looped around her wrists, pulled tight into a figure of eight and knotted off on the bedstead. She was helpless, tied in place, his to use, with her bottom raised and vulnerable, a dirty pose she was holding because she'd been told to. Her teeth met her lip, biting, holding back the tears that threatened to well up in her eyes, even though she could feel the warm dampness in her culottes. When they were pulled down, as she knew they would be, the full, embarrassing extent of her excitement would be revealed, her swollen, ready sex.

He turned his body, pushing his crotch close to her face, his hand going to his fly. Lily watched, unable to take her eyes away as he slid down his zip, delved inside and pulled out a dark, heavily hooded cock. She swallowed and closed her eyes as his hand took her hair, pulling back her head. Her mouth came open, wide, gaping for his penis despite her reluctance and the shame of committing what she had always been told was a dirty thing to do. It went in, filling her mouth with the salty, male taste, and she was sucking, whimpering in her throat, close to tears, but sucking nonetheless.

'That's my little girl,' Ed breathed from above her. 'You love a good big cock to suck, don't you? Come on, get it in deep, make me hard.'

Lily gulped in as much as she could, until the rapidly swelling head was pushed against her tonsils. She began to gag and tried to pull back, only for the grip in her hair to tighten and stop her.

'None of that, girly,' Ed chided. 'You've got to show some respect for your man, take his cock right in your throat and swallow it if he wants to come in your mouth.'

Trying her best, Lily let the head of his penis squeeze deeper into her windpipe, until she began to choke and was forced to pull back. Ed laughed, took a firm grip on her head and began to fuck her mouth, sliding the now erect shaft of his penis in and out. Lily opened her eyes, unable to resist the awful sight of his hard cock shaft, glistening with her own saliva.

'You're a natural,' Ed drawled, 'a real little cocksucker, a little cocksucking tart.'

A bubble of shame rose in her throat at his words. It was true: she was sucking his penis and she was enjoying it, and it was all the better for having her wrists tied to the bedstead, leaving her helpless in his power. He was fully erect, solid, meaty and male in her mouth, and she wondered if he was going to carry out his threat, come down her throat and make her swallow it.

'Right, let's have the dress up,' he drawled. 'Let's see what you've got on underneath. Something special, just for Ed, I'll bet. Keep sucking while I do the business.'

Lily obeyed, sliding her lips up and down on his penis as his hands went to her dress, then lifting her knees one at a time to let him pull it up. It came, eased up her legs, tickling the backs of her thighs.

'Stockings, nice,' he said, continuing to pull, lifting the dress up over her culottes to expose the tight seat. 'Fancy French knickers, too. My, but you *are* a treat, dolled up like a right little madam. Now let's have those little titties out.'

She groaned deep in her throat as the dress was pulled up, revealing her braless breasts. They swung loose, feeling heavy and blatantly rude, huge and prominent despite their small size.

'You ought to get a boob job,' Ed grunted, taking one breast in hand and rubbing his palm over the nipple. 'I like big ones, big, fat knockers. Right, that's enough sucking, I'm ready for your tight little cunt.'

He pulled back, leaving Lily shivering, the tears brimming in her eyes but her bottom held high, ready for stripping. Ed came behind her, took hold of the waistband of her knickers and down they came, exposing her bottom, the open, naked cheeks, the tiny dimple of her anus, the lips of her sex with the thick puff of pale hair below. The first tear rolled from an eye as she thought of what she was showing and she let out a faint sob.

'Nice arse,' Ed told her. 'I like them big and round. Nice cunt, too, good and hairy, shows you're a real blonde. You're well wet. Eager little tart, aren't you?'

Lily closed her eyes, squeezing tears from the rims. Her bottom wasn't big – she knew it wasn't, not really – but lifted and spread to his lecherous gaze it felt huge and incredibly rude, a fat, wobbling, bulbous thing with every dirty detail on show. His cock bumped her sex, rubbing in the wet and nudging her clitoris to make her gasp. Despite herself she pushed her bottom up for more, only to have his penis slide up her vagina, filling her hole with meat and filling her head with shamefaced ecstasy.

She was tied, being fucked, dress up, knickers down, showing everything with her wrists strapped in place and a penis in her sex. Nor could she hold herself, but started to grunt and squeak as he fucked her, panting out her ecstasy despite the tears of shame running down her cheeks.

'That looks good,' Ed panted from behind her, 'my cock, right in your little cunt, splitting the lips with your big arse spread and your little rosebud showing. I'm going to fuck you in that one day, Lily, my cock right up your tight little arsehole. You'd love that.'

Sobbing at the crudeness of his words and grunting from the effect of having him pushing inside her, Lily could do no more than shake her head in a vain attempt to reject his claim that she would enjoy being sodomised. Yet she was tied and she knew that if he wanted to try to force his cock into her rectum there was nothing she could do about it.

His shoves were getting firmer, jamming her into the bed and making her grunt, then cry out. Ed responded with yet harder shoves, until Lily could only squeal breathlessly into the bed.

'That's right, come on my cock, you little tart,' Ed growled and once more pushed himself to the hilt in her vagina.

She gasped even as she heard him grunt, and his cock jerked from her hole. A moment later she felt something warm and wet splash on the bare skin of her bottom and knew he had come over her. She moaned, burying her tear-streaked face in the pillows as he finished off over her bottom, ejaculating twice more in small spurts and smearing what remained on his cock down between her buttocks.

She could feel it all, and imagine how it looked. A long streamer had been laid across her bottom, bridging the cheeks and hanging over her crease. More was on her left cheek, lower down, on the fullest part; yet more was between them, soiling her anus with come. It was too much, too dirty, too obscene to be denied, and as she lifted her face from the damp pillow she knew she was going to truly disgrace herself.

'Make me come,' she panted, begging. 'Rub me, Ed.'

'You dirty little bitch!' he snapped. 'You come on my cock girl, that's all. Show some respect.'

Violet laughed, throwing back her long purple hair in a gesture of open, uninhibited amusement. Yasmin responded to Violet's laughter with a wicked grin, then raised her glass to her black-painted lips. Around them the Black Joke pub was packed with Tawmouth's wilder set, goths like herself, black-clad, adorned with exotic jewellery and piercings, New Age types and pagans, nondescripts, a group drawn by their fascination with mysticism and the great long barrow on the top of Aldon Hill.

The door opened, admitting a newcomer, a lean young man, black-clad from head to foot, his startling red hair tied back in a severe ponytail. On seeing the crowd he gave a satisfied, somehow proprietorial smile, which held as he walked to the bar. Violet glanced at him, then again, recognising his face.

'That's Nich Mordaunt,' she hissed, leaning forward to make herself heard above the noise.

'Who?' Yasmin answered.

'The guy at the bar,' Violet went on, 'with the red hair. He's Nich Mordaunt, the guy who writes that occult stuff, you know, with the freaky rituals.'

'That stuff you showed me with the candles?' Yasmin answered, half turning.

Violet nodded and sipped her drink, pretending not to stare and thinking of how it had felt to lie spread-eagled as she fed a thick, crimson candle into her vagina, her head spinning with alcohol and cannabis. Yasmin had watched as Violet masturbated, indulging in a ruder and less formal version of a fertility rite penned by Nich. It had been exciting, exotic and free, ending with the two of them in bed together for a night of kissing and pussy licking, drunk and stoned, every last inhibition abandoned.

'Come on, let's chat him up,' Violet suggested. 'He's that freaky he's got to be worth knowing.'

Yasmin nodded, her eyes glittering with mischief as she slid from her bar stool. Violet went first, approaching Nich with an unabashed smile. He responded, admitting who he was, more than happy to discuss his beliefs and work. Violet found herself fascinated, by his openness, by the conviction with which he believed in those things she was eager to accept, by the rich green of his eyes. When another friend joined them and Yasmin became distracted she paid little attention, soaking up Nich's words and feeling more and more eager for sex.

By closing time there was no doubt. Yasmin was lost in the crowd, Violet and Nich rapt in each other's attention. Together they walked through the town, neither questioning what was to happen as they made their way to the attic flat she and Yasmin had hired for the summer. Inside they shared wine and sweet biscuits laced with cannabis, sipping from either side of a carved horn goblet before letting their lips meet, touch, then kiss, Violet's mouth opening beneath his.

When they broke apart it was for her to stand. She shed her clothes as he watched, letting them fall to the floor around her until she was nude. Nich nodded, allowing his gaze to linger on her hair, the fine, pale features of her face, the amethysts in her ears, her nose, the purple glass of the Lavabell in her belly button. Her pubic hair was dyed, the same rich purple as her hair. A single tattoo marked the gentle lower curve of her belly, three purple letters in cursive, Grecian script, I, O and V.

'Ianthe,' Nich said softly. 'Your matron deity?'

Violet nodded and smiled, delighted that he should know, and understand. Sinking slowly down, she set her knees to either side of him, pressing her sex to his crotch as his arms came around her back. He kissed her mouth, her neck, her nipples, taking each breast in turn and sucking gently until Violet had begun to sigh with pleasure and dig her nails into the material of his top.

'The daughter of the sea,' he murmured. 'You must know, then. He must have called you here, but for now you are mine.'

Violet barely heard him, lost only in the pleasure of her body and of knowing she had found somebody who could

22

accept her, who understood without her needing to explain. Lifting herself, she reached down, easing his fly open and freeing his penis. He continued to kiss, brushing her skin with his lips, on neck, chest and nipples. She took his erection in her hand, rubbing the head to her clitoris, exciting herself, rising, lowering her body on to his shaft, taking it inside. His hands were behind her back, stroking her neck and the gentle groove of her spine, working slowly lower, to the swell of her bottom, taking each cheek, lifting her to her own rhythm as she moved on his erection.

A finger found her anus, tickling the tiny hole and making her sigh. His lips were on a nipple, his teeth holding the firm bud of flesh just on the edge of pain. Rising, she let his penis slip from her vagina, only to settle on him, her sex pressed to his erection, her clitoris hard against him. She began to squirm, moving her hips to wriggle her bottom in his hands and bump her clitoris on his penis, over and over, bringing her ever closer to orgasm as he teased her breasts and anal ring. She cried out as she came, calling on Ianthe, pressing Nich's head between her breasts and writhing her underside on his penis as wet come erupted on to her tattooed belly.

Two

Lily awoke to Ed's grumbled demands for coffee. A hour later he had gone to work, leaving her propped up in bed. Her feelings were mixed, and while it was impossible to deny that she had enjoyed the sex, even being tied, the underlying shame and guilt were too strong to be denied. Ed made her feel protected, and wanted, also used. Having refused to help her to orgasm, or even accept her need, he had untied her and quickly gone to sleep, leaving her frustrated and ashamed.

Shifting in the bed with an irritated grimace, she looked around for something to read, hoping to take her mind off Ed and the memory of being so rudely enjoyed. Several magazines were stacked neatly in a rack, but investigation showed them to be either tedious men's magazines or about guns. A voice in the back of her head was telling her that if there was a genuinely dirty magazine she would read it, but to her relief there was nothing overtly sexual. What there was, at the bottom of the pile, was a publication faced with a beautifully executed pen-and-ink drawing of a woman entwined in the tentacles of an octopus and apparently in a state of ecstasy.

Surprised, shocked, but intrigued, Lily extracted the magazine, taking care not to disarrange those above. The picture was terrifying, yet horribly compelling, also totally out of place with what she knew of Ed's character. It was impossible not to be fascinated, and she found herself tiptoeing guiltily back to the bed with the magazine in her hand. Glancing at the cover once more, she saw that there was no title, only the scribbled legend 'Laverack, 1963. £2.50'.

With no idea of what to expect, save something pornographic and bizarre, she was surprised to find a frank, but hardly salacious, discussion of the octopus as a motif in sexual imagery, tracing it back to an eight-armed pre-Celtic deity. Other pictures showed women copulating with octopus, squid, even a cuttlefish, but interspersed with photographs and sketches of places, including the Wythman barrow on Aldon Hill, which was relevant to her own research.

She read on, fascinated but disturbed. The text was so open, so rational, as if for a woman to have a sexual experience with an octopus was not only possible, but a perfectly reasonable thing to do. Nowhere was there a hint of the monstrous perversity of the act, or any moral comment whatever, save a condemnation of those who had defaced ancient carvings and persecuted pagans. By the time she had finished she was shaking her head in a vain attempt to rid her mind of the images she had seen and the astonishing insouciance of the text. That Ed should read such a thing seemed impossible, a complete contradiction of his chauvinist and Christian beliefs.

Despite a resolve to dress and go back to her room, she found herself making another coffee and returning to the bed to study the thing in greater detail. Given what was happening to them, she had expected the women in the pictures to show horror and revulsion. The truth was the opposite, their expressions of pleasure, ecstasy, even a serene, enraptured bliss. Most were stylised, even reduced to the form of an icon, those intended for recognition by initiates. Some showed more detail, one even illustrating the entry of the beast's sperm arm into the woman's vagina.

By the time she once more put down the magazine her mind was reeling with the impact of what she had seen. For one awful moment she imagined herself in the same position, gripped in tentacles, a fat, rubbery sperm arm invading her body, only to pull her thoughts away. It was hard though, and she found herself wishing she could surrender to her feelings as the women seemed to be doing, taking pleasure without guilt or shame, allowing the dirty, dark part of her mind to overcome her reserve completely.

She had to masturbate, and it had to be as rude and open as possible, really dirty, otherwise she knew she would risk letting her mind slip to the cold embrace of the octopus. Ed's old shirt came up, baring her breasts, the nipples pushing up, high and hard to betray how excited she was. Her hand slid down the front of her culottes, finding the puffy, swollen flesh of her sex, wet and open. Two fingers slid into her vagina, her thumb cocked back to find her clitoris and she let her imagination go, her inhibitions fading with her rising pleasure.

He was with her, Ed. She was bound hand and foot, kneeling, her bottom thrust high and helpless, spread bare. He was behind her, the cock she had just sucked erect in his hand, inspecting her rear view in minute detail, his gaze taking in the fullness of her bottom, the way her sex lips pouted from between her thighs, the wetness of her vagina, the tight pink ring of her anus. She would be looking back, watching as he came forward, groaning as her vagina filled with cock, panting like an animal as she was fucked. He would take her by the hips, feeling her flesh and watching his cock slide in and out of her body. She'd expect him to come, but he wouldn't, instead pulling out and climbing from the bed.

He would leave her, tied up in the nude, nursing his erection as he walked from the room. She would hear him in the bathroom, see him return, now with a tube of lubricating cream, and as he climbed back behind her she would know what was going to be done to her. Helpless, unable to do a thing to stop him, she would beg and plead, promise to suck his cock until he came, to strip for him nightly, to get in any rude pose he wanted, anything other than sodomy.

Ed would laugh at her, well aware of the hollowness of her voice, of the insincerity of her pleas. He would grease

26

her bottom, smearing cold cream between her open cheeks, rubbing it into her anus, pushing a finger into the tiny hole. She would be sobbing and shivering, tears running down her cheeks as she pleaded for him to leave her anus virgin. He would only laugh the louder and his finger would pull from her ring, leaving her greasy and open, vulnerable to the erection being pointed up between her buttocks. She would feel it touch, the firm, round head pressed to her, but not to her vagina, not where it was supposed to go, but to her anus, to the tight little hole that was never, ever meant for a man's cock but that so many dirty bastards seemed to want to use. She would cry out as he pushed, a final plea to spare her the degradation of sodomy, but he would simply push harder, straining her poor little hole until her ring popped, his head went in and she was being sodomised, buggered, used in her bottom, with a long, fat cock sliding up her overstretched hole . . .

Lily came, letting out a great, broken sob as the head of ecstasy that had been building up inside her burst and her mind flooded with guilt for what she had been thinking of. Yet still, as she slumped back among the bed sheets, she knew that if Ed just pushed her hard enough she would let it happen.

Thomazina lay inert in the water, her body moving to the gentle rhythm of the waves. The buzz of sound from Tawmouth seafront could be clearly heard, music blending with the chatter of many voices and the distant rumble of a train. She watched, looking at the clothes of the people on the front. Most were in beachwear, much like her own, if generally more modest than what was worn on the island and the French coast. Others wore the popular blue trousers, including many of the women, along with colourful tops. Hats were rare, dresses common only among older women and female children, although many younger girls wore skirts, often short enough to leave most of their legs showing.

Closer, beneath the loom of Aldon Cliff, the beach was almost deserted, the river mouth cutting it off from the main front. Those few who had troubled to take the little ferry that crossed the river were well spaced out, seeking privacy for one reason or another. Thomazina scanned the beach. A group of girls lay basking in the sun, face down, their bikini tops undone to leave their backs bare. An older man sat on a rock, puffing a pipe and staring out to sea. Two family groups stood among the boulders below Aldon Head, the children with nets to dip into the rock pools.

Her gaze went back at a movement. A single girl was coming out of the tunnel that led to the beach, a girl of about her own height, dark-skinned, wearing tight black trousers and a black top holding in breasts only a little less large than her own. Thomazina watched as the girl looked left and right, choosing the empty piece of beach between the tunnel and where Ness Head thrust out into the flow of the river. She carried a rug, which she spread out on the sand when she had reached the end of the beach.

The girl undressed with a minimal show of modesty, pushing down her trousers to briefly display small white drawers before her top fell back in place. Shoes, socks and trousers were kicked off, the drawers tugged down in the shelter of the top and replaced with a pair of brilliant-yellow swimsuit bottoms. The top went next, revealing an ample white bra. This was unclipped and let fall, exposing big, dark breasts topped by yet darker nipples. Thomazina watched for a while, fascinated by the colour of the girl's skin and the size of her nipples, then began to paddle in towards the river mouth.

The girl was intent on swimming, walking down the beach with a single, self-conscious glance towards the other people in view. She had chosen a good place, a piece of calm water sheltered by the sand bank that curved out from Ness Head. Thomazina knew it would be shallow and warm, the perfect place to bask, and was sure the girl would take her time swimming.

Pushing hard against the current of the river, she swam to the level of the Head and pulled herself out among the rocks. Boulders sheltered her from view as she approached the place where the girl had undressed to find the rug spread out as she had first seen it, the clothes scattered carelessly across it. Peering from the shadows of a great tumble of sandstone, she watched the girl swim, waiting until she was hidden from view. With her lips set in a mischievous smile she darted out, snatching up the black trousers and top, the drawers and bra, the socks and shoes. Nipping quickly back into the shelter of the rocks, she ran to the water's edge and slipped in.

Violet stirred lazily, wondering if by sucking Nich's cock she would be able to tease him back into life. He was asleep, as he had been for the hour since she had woken up, and so far she had been reluctant to wake him. Yasmin had been gone when Violet woke, leaving a note to say she was swimming at their favourite spot on Ness Beach. Violet knew the note had been left in the hope that she and Nich would follow, but had lacked the energy to comply. Now, with two cups of strong coffee inside her, she was beginning to feel herself once more, also a pleasant, lazy arousal.

Nich had been great, coaxing her to orgasm three times with considerable skill and care. He had also been a lot less selfish than most men, concentrating on her pleasure as much as his own, if not more. True, when the time had come for his second orgasm she had knelt for him and allowed him to enter her from behind. Even then he had used the head of his cock to excite her clitoris in between periods inside her, and she had come before him. Now, with his body naked beneath a thin covering, she was tempted to pay back some of his consideration, allowing him to wake to the feel of her mouth around his penis.

The temptation was too strong. Gently she lifted his cover, revealing his slight frame with his good-sized penis lolling against his thigh. She licked her lips in anticipation but reached for the matches that lay on a nearby table, striking one to light a scented candle. She was already pantiless, and the act of peeling her T-shirt over her head left her nude. She curled herself beside his body, a position that meant he could reach under her belly for her pussy if he wanted to. As the rich scent of orange began to drift through the air she took him in her mouth, taking the whole of his cock and sucking lovingly.

He groaned, stirring as the blood started to swell out his penis. Violet began to suck harder as his hand found her hair, stroking with a gentle, sleepy motion. As his cock began to stiffen she found her own excitement rising and cocked her leg up, making what she knew was an open display of her sex to him. He touched her thigh, his long fingernails moving on her flesh, scratching gently down the sensitive skin. Her thighs came further apart, wide, offering herself like a cat hoping for a tickled stomach. A knuckle found her sex, brushing the lips, nudging her vagina, the finger uncurling to allow a nail to tickle the wrinkled bud of her anus.

Violet moaned around her mouthful of cock, taking him in her hands, one to cup and squeeze his balls, the other to circle his shaft and masturbate him into her mouth. He continued to tickle her anus and stroke her hair, the ball of his thumb finding the damp flesh of her vulva and starting a rubbing motion, firm against her clitoris. She tugged harder, knowing what he was doing would soon bring her to orgasm and eager to take his sperm in her mouth at that instant. His nails found her vagina, tickling the mouth, a finger slipping inside. Her anus had begun to contract, her buttocks tightening to the ecstatic, agonising feel of having the tight hole of her bottom teased as she was masturbated. He moaned softly and her tugging became frantic, a desperate jerking as the muscles of her vagina began to squeeze on the intruding finger.

His cock jerked and she found herself mewling deep in her throat as sperm erupted into her mouth. She swallowed, gulping it eagerly down, revelling in the sensation of having him ejaculate in her mouth as her own climax broke in a wave of ecstasy, her thighs clamping tight on his hand as his finger slipped inside her anus at the very peak of her pleasure. It was slow, her thighs and bottom squeezing over and over as the orgasm ran through her head. All the while she sucked on his erection, draining the sperm and at last pulling it from her mouth, giving the head a parting kiss and rolling on to her back.

They lay still for a while, Nich's hand still clamped between Violet's thighs, a finger in each hole. She was purring, a contented, catlike sound, torpid and happy. Only when the door slammed did they move, coming apart to stretch and shake themselves.

'Bastards!' Yasmin's voice sounded from beyond the door.

'What's the matter?' Violet demanded, moving quickly around and pulling the coverlet over both Nich and herself.

'Some bastard stole my clothes!' Yasmin exclaimed as she pushed the door open. 'Hi, Nich.'

Violet suppressed a giggle. Her friend was wrapped in a blanket, clasped firmly to the front to keep her big breasts hidden but open lower to show the yellow triangle of her bikini pants.

'On the beach?' Violet asked.

'Yes, I had to walk through town like this!' Yasmin answered. 'That old git who runs the ferry was really leering at me.'

'Didn't you see who it was?'

'No. There was nobody else there, not near me. I reckon it was this old bloke I saw, but he didn't have them on him and he swore blind he hadn't nicked them. I'm sure he had, the old perv. My other stuff wasn't taken, not even any money. Just everything to make sure I had to go back topless, so it must have been some pervert.'

'At least you had the rug.'

'Probably kids playing a practical joke,' Nich suggested.

'Maybe,' Yasmin answered, 'but they might have left my stuff where I could find it. I searched everywhere.'

She left, walking into her room, still reviling the thief. Nich stretched and yawned, indifferent to his nudity as he climbed to his feet. Violet followed suit, padding quickly into the tiny bathroom before Yasmin could take it. She showered, feeling pleased with herself and wondering what she should wear to make a good impression on Nich. Ready, she gave up the bathroom to Yasmin and returned to her room to find Nich, still naked, sprawled on the mattress with one of her books open in front of him.

31

'Last night,' she said, voicing a question that had been niggling at the back of her mind, 'you said I must know. Must know what?'

Nich turned, frowning slightly.

'What?' Violet demanded.

'Sigodin-Yth,' Nich answered.

'What?'

'Have you been getting unusual dreams recently?'

'No more than usual.'

'Then you don't know.'

'Know what?' Violet demanded. Nich went quiet, his frown deepening. 'Come on,' she urged.

'What is your attitude to Christianity?'

'Paternalistic rubbish. Why?'

'I shall tell you,' Nich answered. 'Will you walk up to the Wythman with me?'

Violet nodded eagerly, fascinated and impressed by the absolute seriousness of Nich's tone. She began to dress, choosing purple underwear and a long, simple black dress that could easily be pulled up if the occasion demanded. Nich gave an approving grin at the sight and made for the bathroom as Yasmin left it.

On learning that they intended to visit the barrow Yasmin insisted on coming, and Nich, after asking a few questions, agreed. They set off, through Tawmouth and across the river by ferry, then up the steep path that led to the crest of Aldon Hill. The conversation remained neutral until they found themselves alone, Violet only then demanding Nich's explanation.

'You mentioned that you came down to attend the solstice festival,' he began, 'and as a devotee of Ianthe, I imagined it meant more to you than to most.'

'It does. Most of the people who come now are just there to party.'

'You've been before?'

'Yeah, most years since it started.'

'It started earlier than you might think,' Nich answered, 'but certainly it has been growing with the resurgence of paganism. What do you know of the barrow?'

32

'It's a Bronze Age burial mound, the biggest in England, for some great king, I suppose.'

'No king, a god.'

'The name you said earlier?'

'The name is Sigodin-Yth, yet I doubt that is the original. It has a Celtic feel, even Norse, while Wythman is a corruption across at least three languages. Still, gods may be named by believers, in the very nature of gods, so Sigodin-Yth will serve.'

'I thought the name of a god was really important, sacred maybe,' Violet answered.

'In essence a god is the product of human thought,' Nich explained. 'Real, be assured of that, but dependent on the belief of worshippers. The name may well be regarded by the worshippers as a sacred thing in its own right, being created by them, along with the god, as part of their belief system.'

'So what's he a god of?'

'Protection, life from the sea, abundance, fertility, possibly. I am uncertain. The only extant legends are Celtic but the barrow is pre-Celtic. The origins of the belief are completely lost; all we have is an eight-armed symbol representing Sigodin-Yth, possibly an octopus.'

'Chaos?' Violet queried.

'Not at that date.' Nich laughed. 'Although – who knows? – the symbols may be related. No, the Celtic image was of an octopus-headed man, which has inspired artwork across the centuries, including Lovecraft's Cthulu, which you may have read.'

Both girls nodded.

'Also a great deal of erotic art,' Nich went on. 'I picked up a treatise on the subject before I left London, but some ignorant jerk in customs confiscated it.'

'A Bronze Age god, cool,' Violet whispered. 'So you thought I knew and had come to dedicate myself to him?'

'Not exactly,' he answered. 'Most gods of the time are forgotten by man and so no longer exist. Sigodin-Yth is not forgotten. Quiescent yes, insensate I suspect not.'

'Great Cthulu dreams,' Yasmin recited.

'It must be remembered that the Cthulu mythos is a work of fiction, nothing more,' Nich answered. 'Still, it seems certain that Lovecraft must have known of Sigodin-Yth. The calling dreams, the representation in the ritual of summoning, both present parallels too close to be mere coincidence.'

'Calling dreams? Like the nightmares in *The Call of Cthulu*?' Yasmin queried.

'Not exactly,' Nich answered. 'Lovecraft, for reasons of his own, imbued what is essentially a beneficial deity with horrific characteristics. The Celtic legends talk more of compelling, urgent dreams with a strong erotic element. This is why I am down here.'

'Explain,' Violet demanded.

'Certainly,' Nich answered, 'on your word that it will go no further, at least not until after the solstice.'

'Absolutely,' Violet assured him, Yasmin nodding acquiescence.

'A paper was drawn to my attention recently,' Nich began. 'It was an indictment of pagan beliefs by a Christian psychiatrist, a quack in my opinion, using science as a tool to justify his prejudices, but no matter. He was endeavouring to prove that paganism can be damaging to mental health. In support of his theory he cited Tawmouth, linking the growing popularity of the Wythman solstice parties with a rise in reports of disturbing dreams in the town.

'The fool attempted to link this to drug taking, ignoring the facts that only females had the dreams and that no such phenomenon has been reported at the much larger pagan gatherings at Stonehenge and Glastonbury. Knowing the Sigodin-Yth legend, it occurred to me that the Wythman barrow might not be a burial mound at all, but the remains of a temple much like the one in Brittany I visited recently. Sure enough, I discovered that the barrow had been opened towards the middle of the nineteenth century, and, sure enough, carvings had been found of the eight-armed symbol. Yet I could find no evidence of strange dreams in Brittany. Could it be that Sigodin-Yth sleeps beneath the Wythman?'

'Wow,' Violet said.

'The psychiatrist also failed to do his research properly,' Nich went on, 'or he would have discovered that odd dreams at Tawmouth are not a modern phenomenon. I have found references to supposed possession, to women drawn to walk up to the barrow in the night. I'm hoping to find further examples among local records, but it would seem that Sigodin-Yth has maintained himself across the centuries by the projection of dreams, generating sufficient belief to remain extant if not active.'

'And now, with all the people going up for the festival, he'll be growing stronger?'

'No. As you said, those who attend the festival are not necessarily pagans, still less believers. They may be drawn by the god, but they do not know of him. The first festival was in '89, a rave organised by three men. Only women are drawn to Sigodin-Yth, besides which I have spoken to them and they know nothing of the god. No, this year there may be over a thousand people at the festival, but they know nothing of Sigodin-Yth.'

'You're planning to enlighten them?' Violet queried.

'Exactly,' Nich responded.

The shop door clicked shut as Mr Hobbers pushed the till drawer back into place. His podgy face had been set in a friendly smile as he wrapped the set of medals he had sold and took the money, but the smile became smug with the customer gone and the not inconsiderable profit safely his. Turning to his back room, he gave the shop door a last, nervous glance and settled into his armchair, out of sight of the shopfront but in easy hearing of the doorbell.

Reaching down beneath the chair with one short, plump arm, he drew out a magazine, his perpetual smile taking on a new and lewd quality as he viewed the cover. It showed a girl, perhaps eighteen or nineteen, well fleshed, her pretty face set in an angry, sulky pout. The reason for this was clear. She was bent across a tennis net, racket in hand, looking back over her shoulder as a tall, steel-haired man pulled up her short white skirt. Her panties were showing, pure, fresh white and taut over a chubby bottom.

His tongue flicked out, moistening his lips in an automatic response to the picture. Opening the magazine, he quickly found the central spread, a two-page colour picture of the same girl, but now in a seriously awkward position. She was across the man's knee, on a chair by the edge of the court, her skirt now all the way up on to her back and her big white sports pants pulled down into a tangle around her thighs. Her buttocks were red from spanking, her face set in an expression of consternation and misery, his hand raised to deliver the next slap. Everything was showing, the full spread of her naked bottom, the lips of her fleshy teenage fanny, even her anus, visible as a dark-brown dimple between the curves of her ample cheeks.

Mr Hobbers swallowed, wishing that it was he giving the pretty young tennis player her punishment, panties down across his lap, kicking and squealing as her naked bottom was slapped to a glowing red. His cock was beginning to stiffen, threatening embarrassment should another customer come in. Reluctantly, he closed the magazine and put it down, trying to think of anything except reddened female bottoms but failing until the chime of the door brought him back to reality with a start. He rose and shuffled quickly into the shop, finding a young woman admiring a picture of an English man o' war.

'The *Redoubtable*, Captain Warrender's ship, painted in Tawmouth harbour, 1842,' he said. 'They don't make them like her any more.'

'No, she was beautiful,' the girl answered.

'So what can I do for you, my dear?' he asked.

'I was wondering, sir, if you would like to buy a coin, an old coin,' she replied.

Hobbers paused, rubbing his chin before making an answer. Her accent was Devon, strong Devon, her words polite, far more formal than he would have expected to look at her. She was buxom, in overtight black jeans stretched around broad hips and a fleshy bottom, a black

T-shirt, also a little small across more than ample breasts made to look larger still by her tight waist. Only then, as his eyes ran down her figure, did he realise that her clothes were wet.

'You're soaking,' he said in surprise. 'Are you all right?'

'Very well, thank you,' she answered. 'I slipped when I found the coin. It was in the water.'

'I'd be happy to look at it,' he said, 'but wouldn't you rather get into some dry clothes first?'

'Might I?' she answered. 'Here?'

'Here?'

'I would be no trouble, I assure you. Perhaps in your back room?'

Mr Hobbers found himself swallowing, imagining her undressing in the back of his shop, stripping all the way. Once she was in a towel or a dressing gown he would make her tea, talk to her while her clothes dried. Maybe he could risk a peep, catching a glimpse of her beautiful bottom or the huge breasts her top did so little to hide.

'If . . . if you're sure,' he stammered. 'I . . . I'll close the door.'

'Thank you, sir,' she answered. 'You are most kind.'

She stepped around the desk and into the back room. As he leaned in to pull the door closed she had already started to undress, unbuttoning her jeans and pushing them down, giving him a hint of wet white panties that set his heart fluttering. He shook himself as the door latch clicked into place, wondering if he was the victim of a trick. If so he was not sure it wouldn't be worth it, and with a guilty glance at the shopfront he dropped to his knees, putting his eye to the large keyhole in the rear door.

The girl was in the act of pulling her trousers clear of her ankles, a pose that left her bottom stuck out with the wet white panties clinging to her lush curves. She was truly magnificent, her bottom plump and heavy, yet without a hint of sag, perfect spanking material. With her jeans off she put her hands to her top, tugging it high to reveal huge breasts spilling from an overtight bra. It too was wet, and as she turned he could see the darker rings of her nipples quite clearly through the material.

The door chimed and he looked up with a start, expecting to see some rough young men, accomplices of the girl. Instead an elderly lady entered, enquiring the price of a figurine in the window display. He responded, only then remembering that he had put his spanking magazine down on the floor, forgetting to tuck it out of sight under the armchair. A ghastly feeling of embarrassment welled up inside him as he realised that it would be in plain view of the girl, yet he could do nothing, only answer the old lady's questions. When she finally left he was red-faced and wringing his hands, imagining her angry accusations, of perversion, maybe even of trying to trick her in some way. Yet he could hear nothing.

Praying that she had somehow failed to notice the magazine, he stepped quickly to the door, turning the sign to CLOSED despite the half-hour or so until his normal lunch break. Returning to the door, he knocked.

'Are you decent? May I come in?' he asked. 'There's a towel by the wash basin if you need it.'

'I have it, thank you kindly,' she answered, which he took as assent for him to enter.

He pushed the door open, only to stop, his face reddening. She was in his armchair, wrapped in the towel, his dirty magazine open in her hands. His hand went to his face, preparing for the flood of abuse and complaint – but nothing came.

'Thank you, you are so kind,' she said. 'This young lady, why is she being punished?'

There was no antagonism in her voice, not even sarcasm. She was holding the magazine out, displaying the extraordinarily rude centre spread of the girl getting her spanking, a picture he was sure would send any real girl into furious indignation. Was she simple, or really so innocent that she didn't realise the sexual implications of the picture? The former seemed the more likely answer, and went with her wandering around in wet clothes and agreeing to strip off in the back of a strange man's shop. The idea that her lack of guile might be taken advantage of entered his head unbidden, to be pushed down immediately with a stab of guilt. He might like the idea of girls being spanked, but he was no abuser.

'Um . . . She was naughty,' he answered, reaching out for the magazine.

'In what way, to need to be beaten so sternly?' the girl asked. 'With a stick and by hand. I am afraid I cannot read well, hardly at all to be truthful.'

She was simple, she had to be, he decided as he took the magazine. His fingers were shaking hard, and it was impossible not to glance at the deep slice of cleavage and ample expanse of smooth thigh showing above and below the towel. She paid no attention, clearly waiting for him to answer her question. He flicked the page over, showing pictures of the hapless girl stripping and touching her toes for the cane, then back, to those of her playing tennis with her panties showing as the skirt rose and of her being taken by the ear before punishment. Sure that if he created a fuss she would be more likely to tell somebody, he could think of no answer other than the reason given in the photo-story.

'She was supposed to be revising, not playing tennis,' he said quickly.

'Revising?' she answered.

'Studying,' he said, 'working for her exams, to try for university.'

'I understand: the book gives moral advice. She looks very funny, but it must have hurt so dreadfully. I always laughed when my sisters were spanked, and I know it was cruel, but they would laugh when it happened to me.'

Mr Hobbers could find no answer. Having the beautiful, near-naked girl confess to getting spanked, and in front of her sisters, was as much as he could bear. It was impossible not to think of her, bent across her mother's knee, perhaps with her jeans pulled down, maybe even her panties, her sisters giggling as her bottom was slapped to a glowing pink. The temptation to ask for more detail was strong, almost overwhelming.

'The waiting was the worst bit, really,' she went on, apparently indifferent to his red face and quickening breathing. 'We would have to kneel on the settle with our dresses turned up to show our bottoms. We were supposed to think on our transgressions. I never did: I always thought of how much the punishment was going to hurt.'

'Did . . . did it happen often?' he asked, failing to keep the catch from his voice.

He had given in, telling himself that just talking could do no harm and that he was unlikely to have such an opportunity ever again. His cock was stiff in his trousers as well. Resistance was no longer possible, not just because of what she was saying, but the way she was saying it, pensive yet gay, recalling the pain and indignity of her punishment, yet without rancour, in fact almost playfully.

'Not so often,' she answered, 'at least not to me. Emily was the naughty one. Sometimes I think she did it on purpose, just so everyone would pay attention to her, even if it was to her bottom.'

The girl giggled, making her breasts quiver. Mr Hobbers swallowed, wondering if he truly had the willpower to keep his hands to himself. It would have been so easy to reach out and tweak the towel open, exposing her lovely big breasts, the soft swell of her belly, the little furry triangle that would show between her thighs . . .

'Tell me about when it happened to you,' he demanded, abandoning the last pretence of disinterest.

'I was the eldest,' she replied, still quite casual. 'Oh, I do beg your pardon, I haven't introduced myself. I am Thomazina.'

'Frank,' he answered weakly, 'Frank Hobbers. Go on.'

'I was the eldest,' she repeated, 'and I suppose I was the best behaved. At least, I would like to think so. I was forgetful sometimes, though, and that was why I was spanked, the last time. It was after milking, and I was taking the cows back when I met Jan Raxun in the lane. We were courting, in a way, so we walked together. I was much too fussed over him to mind my business, and I didn't shut the gate properly, so all the cows went out, down along the lane. Mother was furious and told me to get on the settle right away, while she fetched a stick. I made a dreadful fuss, saying I was too old to be spanked and that at least Emily and Jane should be sent out of the house, but Mother would have none of it. So up I went, on to the settle with my skirts turned up high and my poor bare bottom stuck out to the fire. Emily and Jane giggled like anything, and teased me about being so hairy below. Mother gave me twenty cuts and I was howling by the time it was over, but I was made to stay there while they all had tea.'

Mr Hobbers suppressed a groan. Thomazina's voice was merry, chattering, a girl describing a funny but somewhat embarrassing experience, with none of the resentment and hurt he would have expected in a spanked girl's voice. From what she said it was also obvious that her panties had been taken down, leaving her bare in front of her sisters. His hands were trembling, and his cock felt like an iron bar in his trousers.

'You are very excited,' she said, pointing to the bulge in his trousers. 'Is it because I have no clothes on under my towel?'

'Yes,' he sobbed, 'and because of what you've been saying.'

'About being spanked?' she giggled. 'I remember the boys liked to watch if they could, and it made their little men hard too, because they had seen our bottoms. Afterwards they would show us and make us touch them if they could catch us. I liked that, it always seemed to make the spanking hurt less.'

'You wouldn't . . . I mean, I don't suppose you'd like to do it now, to me?' he managed.

'Why, certainly, Mr Hobbers, and I shall show you my bosom. The boys always liked my bosom.'

'I'm not surprised,' he groaned as her towel dropped.

They were truly enormous, great fat globes of girl flesh, wobbling gently as she giggled at his reaction. Her nipples were rosy pink, quite big and stiff. Beneath her breasts her waist was tight, flaring to broad hips still hidden beneath the towel, her tummy a small, soft bulge, dimpled at the centre by a neat tummy button. He could only stare, his blood pounding as he took in her beauty, a sight he had never expected to see again, at least not outside the pages of a magazine.

'I shall take him out for you. Would you enjoy that?' she asked.

He nodded, watching transfixed as she leaned forward. Her fingers went to his fly, fumbling at the mechanism, then pulling it down. His cock pushed at the opening and she giggled as her hand brushed the hard flesh through his underpants. Then they had been pulled open at the front and his erection was out, in her hand. She began to masturbate him, tugging his cock towards her body in a determined, matter-of-fact way as if she thought nothing of taking an old man's cock in her hand.

'There we are,' she said. 'Is that pleasant?'

'Beautiful,' he groaned, 'and so are you.'

'Why, thank you.'

She continued to masturbate him, although his legs were beginning to hurt and his cock to fail in response. Thomazina said nothing, but let go, lifted her breasts and folded his cock and balls between them, rubbing the plump meat into him. He groaned and began to push himself into her cleavage, fucking her breasts, only to find the pain in his legs growing worse.

'I must sit, my dear,' he groaned. 'I fear that at my age this is a little much.'

'How thoughtless of me!' she answered. 'Certainly you must sit, and I shall sit on your knee.'

She stood, letting the towel drop away without thought for the consequences. Hobbers lowered himself into the armchair and made a knee for her, his eyes fixed on the plump swell of her sex. He desperately wanted to ask her to show him her bottom, even if he might spank her, but his fear of breaking the moment overcame his need, and as she settled herself on to his knee the chance was gone. She leaned close, placing an arm around his shoulder and making herself comfortable, her breasts pressing to him as she once more took his cock in hand.

'There we are. Now you will soon be off,' she announced cheerfully and went back to masturbating him.

His let his hand stray to her bottom, taking one chubby cheek and moulding the flesh, still half expecting her to protest. Thomazina made no objection, only giving him a playful squeeze and tugging a little faster on his cock. He was nearly there, his eyes fixed on her body, watching her breasts and tummy wobble to the rhythm of her furiously jerking arm, his head full of images of her being upended and spanked in front of her sisters.

'Tell me again,' he groaned. 'Tell me how you were spanked, about how mother pulled your panties down.'

'Drawers do you mean?' she asked.

'Yes, but say panties, please say panties.'

'Oh, we didn't wear those,' she laughed. 'Just a dress and petticoats, two for Sunday best.'

'No panties?' he breathed.

'No panties,' she answered. 'It's a lot more comfortable, you know. I like to go without, but I know girls are supposed to wear them, and with skirts so short nowadays . . .'

'The spanking, tell me about the spanking.'

'Oh, sorry, silly me. So I was spanked in front of Emily and Jane, with my skirt and petticoat up on my back so my poor bottom stuck out. They laughed so much at the sight Mother threatened to give them the same if they didn't stop. That shut them up, but I still howled, and then I had to stay like that right through tea, with my bottom showing and feeling thoroughly sorry for myself . . .'

Hobbers came, his sperm erupting from his cock as Thomazina squeaked in surprise. Immediately she ducked down, catching the second ejaculation in her face. She took his cock in her mouth, sucking and swallowing to drain his sperm, all the while looking up into his face with one big, deep-green eye watching him and the other closed, shut by a blob of sperm. He let her suck, lost in ecstasy as he imagined the sight of her, kneeling bare-bottomed while her mother and sisters casually took tea. Only when he had begun to go limp did she stop, pulling back to once more settle her fleshy bottom on to his knee.

'You should have said,' she chided. 'It is always much better to let the girl take it in her mouth. Otherwise it gets all messy. A boyfriend told me that after I'd made a mess of his car seat, and look what you've done to your nice clothes!'

He was still puffing and could find nothing to say, but only lie back as she took a tissue and cleaned the mess from her face and his trousers. As before, she was quite casual, indifferent to her nudity as she mopped up. He felt guilty, sure that he had taken advantage of a simple girl, also worried, thinking of angry parents or a boyfriend. Yet in many ways she seemed anything but simple, merely extraordinarily innocent and utterly immoral. Through thirty-five years of marriage, numerous prostitutes and a handful of early girlfriends, he had never before met a woman who approached the task of masturbating him in so easy a manner. Some had been eager, more reluctant; Thomazina had been breezy, as if hanging the washing out, or making a bed.

'My coin, I must show you my coin,' she said, moving towards where she had laid out her jeans in his tiny kitchen.

She bent, clearly visible through the door, making a prime display of her ripe bottom and even giving him a glimpse of plump pussy lips in dark hair.

'Quite,' he managed. 'How are your clothes?'

'Still wet, I'm afraid,' she answered. 'Ah, here it is.'

Hobbers reached out, expecting some ordinary pre-decimal piece but determined to break the habit of a lifetime and pay her a decent amount. Even if it was worthless he intended to make a fuss, only to be brought up short as she passed him a large, very obviously gold coin and sat back on his knee. He looked at it, trying to ignore the feel of her naked bottom on his leg.

'Portuguese,' he remarked, peering close. 'Be a dear and pass me my lens. There, by the books.'

Thomazina moved, again giving him a flash of spread bottom as she reached down for the lens. Despite his recent orgasm he found himself blowing out his cheeks and wondering if her casual attitude to dispensing sexual favours extended to being spanked. She had been punished, and she didn't seem to find the pain and indignity too unbearable . . .

'Is it of value at all?' she asked, breaking his train of thought as she once more settled herself on his knee.

'Yes,' he admitted, 'it is a standard piece, struck at Porto in 1642. Would you accept three hundred pounds for it?'

'Three hundred pounds? Why, sir!' Thomazina answered.

'Four hundred?' Hobbers answered quickly, thinking of soft, fleshy bottoms and her firm hand on his erection.

As Nich explained his intentions Yasmin felt a rising sense of mischief, also a touch of jealousy that Violet had managed to bag him so quickly. Not that she would necessarily be excluded, as they had shared boyfriends before, yet there was definitely something proprietorial about the way she had held his hand as they climbed the slope of Aldon Hill.

They had reached the top, an area of rough furze around the barrow itself. It had always given her a feeling of mystery and power, much as she felt at Stonehenge or when she and Violet had visited the Grey Wethers. Now it was stronger, and although she found it impossible to accept all of what Nich was saying, there was no difficulty in believing that the great low mound of earth had once been the site of pagan rituals in Celtic and pre-Celtic times.

Since her rejection of the religion into which she had been born, she had come to embrace more and more of modern paganism, finding it free and inspiring to her femininity as against the moral restrictions her parents had tried to force upon her. Nich's words filled her with rebellious joy, a pleasure akin to what she felt during sex or even swimming topless, acts that would once have been regarded as grossly insubordinate.

'The Brittany temple is open, and faces the sea,' Nich was saying. 'I suspect the same is true here.'

He angled to the left, moving to the front of the Wythman and climbing the narrow path that had been worn in the long grass. Yasmin followed, her sense of the

45

mystical increasing. Nich performed a quick gesture, making a half-bow to the sea which Violet hastened to copy, Yasmin also. The top of the Wythman was flat, an expanse of tall grass some ten yards wide by close to a hundred long, sultry and warm in the hot sunlight, strangely quiet, with no sound but the gentle hum of insects.

'I shall sunbathe, starkers,' Violet said suddenly. 'That's if it wouldn't be sacrilege and if Nich would be a sweetie and keep an eye on the path.'

'A pleasure,' Nich answered, giving Violet the same formal bow he had made towards the sea. 'As to sacrilege, I imagine having a naked woman lying on top of his barrow would be entirely in keeping with Sigodin-Yth's ethos.'

'Then I shall do it,' Violet said. 'Come on, Yasmin, keep me company.'

Violet peeled up her dress, revealing purple panties and bra, which she quickly shrugged off with no more than a glance at where the path came up from below. Yasmin followed suit, her sense of mischief growing as she peeled, making a point of going all the way. She was quickly naked, doing her best to seem casual about the display of her body in front of Nich. He had squatted down, folding his legs beneath him so that he could see the slope of the hill while both girls were hidden in the grass.

With the hot sun on her bare skin and the faintest of breezes ruffling her hair and making the grass stir around her, Yasmin felt both happy and pleasantly naughty. She was nude in the open, a sensation she loved at any time, better still when it involved showing off to a man.

'Rub some cream on my back, Nich,' Violet said, her voice lazy and sensual.

Yasmin turned to watch, propping her head on a hand. Violet was face down, her eyes closed, her long hair held up to leave her back exposed, her slim body gently bowed to where her rounded bottom rose, her long legs straight out and slightly apart. Nich began to apply cream, massaging it into her back with his fingers until Violet had started to make soft purring noises. He reached her bottom, smoothing the cream into the cheeks as she pushed it up with a contented sigh. Yasmin bit her lip, wishing it was she who was being massaged and wondering if Nich would take advantage of Violet's sleepy arousal.

He made no move, creaming the full length of her legs with slow, deliberate motions until Violet's skin gleamed from neck to toes. Yasmin's nipples had gone hard, tempting her to touch them and reminding her that while Violet and Nich had spent the night in each other's arms she had slept alone. Violet was still purring, while Nich moved slowly back up her legs, rubbing the cream well into her thighs, lifting her bottom as his hands cupped the tuck of her cheeks.

'Fuck her, Nich, that's what she wants,' Yasmin suggested, thinking that it was also what she wanted, badly.

Nich returned a grin of pure mischief. Violet pushed up her bottom still further, making herself available. Nich glanced once to the slope and put his hand to his fly, easing it down, opening the button and freeing his cock, already close to erection. Cocking his leg across Violet, he knelt over her, tugging at his penis as his eyes feasted on her naked rear. Yasmin reached out, unable to help herself, took Nich's cock and began to stroke the shaft, then to rub it between her friend's cream-slick buttocks. He sighed, allowing her to do it, Violet giving a pleased moan in response. In moments he was hard, the head of his cock moving in the greasy valley of Violet's buttocks, rubbing her soft flesh, touching her anus to draw a squeak of either expectation or alarm, moving lower to find the entrance of her vagina.

Yasmin let go as Nich slid into Violet. He began to fuck, holding his body up on his arms and bouncing on her upturned bottom. Watching his shaft going in and out between Violet's slim cheeks, Yasmin gave in to her own feelings, taking her breasts in her hands and starting to massage. Nich turned to grin at her and she held them out, then rolled over on to her back, intent on masturbating in front of them while they fucked.

Violet's eyes were open, her mouth, too, watching in breathless pleasure as she was fucked. Yasmin spread her thighs and put her hand to her pussy, in full view of the others as she began to stroke her clitoris. Violet stretched out an arm, touching Yasmin's thigh, then the curve of her bottom. Yasmin groaned as a finger found her vagina and slid inside. Nich was going faster, moving on Violet's bottom, his front slapping against her cheeks with each push. His head was turned, his gaze fixed on where Violet was now masturbating Yasmin freely. He grunted, pulling sharply back to spray sperm over Violet's bottom, a sight that was too much for Yasmin. She came, grabbing her breasts to squeeze both plump globes hard as her pussy burned under Violet's touch. Her head was swimming, lost in ecstasy and the exquisite sensation of doing something so wonderfully, openly improper.

By the time her senses recovered it was to find Violet turned beneath Nich, her thighs high and wide, sucking on his penis as he lapped at her pussy. She was coming, her legs crossed over his back, pulling his face into her sex, releasing his penis at the last moment to lick at his cock and balls as she rode her orgasm. Yasmin watched, happy in the afterglow of her own climax, delighting in her friend's uninhibited ecstasy until they at last relaxed and rolled apart.

'You can do my front now,' Violet laughed as Nich sat back.

'By all means,' Nich answered, 'although I can see somebody over towards the cliff, a blonde woman, with a severity of dress that suggests disapproval of nude sunbathing.'

'I suppose we'd better put our knickers on at least,' Violet said.

'Perhaps,' Nich answered.

Yasmin turned, pulling her knickers out from among her other clothes and slipping into them as Violet did the same. Returning to sunbathing, she felt content in the knowledge that, however Violet's relationship with Nich went, she would not be entirely excluded.

* * *

Lily stood looking out to sea, feeling embarrassed and slightly irritated. After reading the treatise on erotic octopus art it had been impossible not to visit the Wythman barrow. Not only was it one of the most important Bronze Age sites locally, but the treatise had suggested the discovery of an octopus carving when the barrow had been opened, a fact she had been unaware of.

She had hoped to be able to explore and photograph the site in peace, only to discover that not only was there somebody there, but that from the sound of things they were having sex. Determined not to be put off, she had walked to the cliff edge and stood gazing out over the sea while she waited for them to finish.

Finally she became tired of waiting, telling herself that she had as much right as they to be there, more, considering what they were doing. Walking back towards the barrow, she saw somebody rise, a man, then another, a young woman in what was presumably a purple bikini but looked like bra and panties. Ignoring them, she walked to the board where a somewhat defaced map showed the site, along with text recording it as a pre-Celtic burial mound. As she read it she heard voices behind her, a woman asking a question, a second female voice adding to it and the man answering.

'This is certainly the prime site,' he was saying. 'The Brittany site is no more than half the size, although completely excavated. This map must be based on the nineteenth-century excavation, but is basically speculation. The dig was only done by the local vicar and some workmen after all, and even then archaeology was pretty primitive in 1850.'

'Eighteen fifty-three,' Lily said quietly, unable to resist showing off her more detailed knowledge, 'by the Reverend Clerebold Wilmot, the Vicar of Abbotscombe.'

'You have studied the Wythman barrow?' the man demanded.

'I'm in the middle of a degree on Bronze Age sites in south Devon,' Lily answered, feeling the blood rise to her cheeks and wishing her shyness wasn't so obvious, 'but it's not technically a barrow, according to some references. It's said to have been some sort of temple, to an octopus deity of all things.'

'So it is,' he answered. 'You seem remarkably knowledgeable. I don't wish to push, but I don't suppose you have any papers relating to the site?'

'Nothing in particular,' she answered, unable not to feel flattered by his response to her knowledge. 'Actually, I've only seen the temple reference in one paper, and that was on art and not really scientific at all. I may be quite wrong.'

'No, no, you are right, be sure of it. This paper, it wasn't by somebody called Laverack, Theo Laverack?'

'Yes, that's it.'

'You have a copy of Laverack, with you?'

'Yes, I mean no. It's really my boyfriend's.'

'A student too?'

'No, he's a customs officer, actually.'

Three

Ed Gardner took a last drag on his cigarette and stubbed it out in the ashtray. Sitting outside the Ferryboat, he had been drinking since after work, along with several colleagues and the two policemen who had been on day duty at the ferry terminal. All but one of the others had left, mostly returning to families, leaving him in increasingly drunken conversation with the police sergeant, Jeffrey Perkins. When his companion had pointed out a particularly attractive woman at the bar, he had begun to talk about Lily, boasting of his conquest.

'Fucking gorgeous, I tell you,' he was saying. 'Bob-cut hair, blonde, real blonde, her muff and all. Only twenty-one.'

'Nice,' Perkins answered.

'One of these shy types,' Ed continued. 'Wouldn't say boo to a goose, but she fucks like a rabbit. It's a laugh actually. She makes out she hates it even when she's really loving it. Three times she came off last night, tied to the bed, the kinky bitch.'

'Nice.'

'It's great. She'll do anything, anything I tell her. I even told her I'd put it up her arse, and what d'you know, she loved it.'

'Yeah?'

'Yeah, dirty bitch, like I said. You know, she'd do anything, anything, just because I tell her. Not for anyone else, just for me. She's that gone on me.'

'Sure, Ed.'

'I'm not joking, Jeff, anything. She'll do striptease, she'll suck and swallow, kneel down so I can have her doggy, anything.'

'Sure, Ed, that's nice, but that's normal stuff. I bet she squeals if you do have her up the arse.'

'Sure she'll squeal, she squeals about fucking anything. Doesn't stop her doing it, and I've had no complaints afterwards. That's what matters, Jeff, not what a woman says before, what she says after. They're always coy before, just to keep us interested, but after eight inches of cock up the cunt it's a different story.'

'Up the cunt, yeah. Up the arse is different. Sure, you get a few dirty ones, but most of them don't like it.'

'Not my Lily, she'll do as I say and love it.'

'What if you told her to suck some other bloke off?'

'Yeah, I reckon. She'd hate it, because it wasn't me, but she'd do it.'

'Yeah, right.'

'She would. Sure she'd make a big fuss and beg me not to make her and that, but it'd just be for show. She'd do it.'

'Twenty says she won't.'

'How d'you mean?'

'Twenty says you can't make her suck me off.'

'You dirty bastard, you're just after a cheap blow job!'

'Thought so, when the money's down you soon change your tune.'

'No, no, I'm for real. I just . . .'

'Yeah, Ed. You're full of shit!'

'No one calls me a liar, Jeff.'

'Then put your money where your mouth is.'

'All right, all right, you dirty bastard. Make it a fifty and you're on.'

'Fifty it is. Drink up, then.'

'What, now?'

'Yeah, now, Ed.'

Ed swallowed his pint. His head was reeling with drink, his cock stirring in his trousers at the thought of Lily. As the idea of making her suck the sergeant off sank in it

52

became more appealing. He knew it would get to her, really get to her, and that in the end she'd love him for it. Treat them rough and they'll crawl to you, his father had said, and he'd been right.

Lily was sure to be in her flat. She never seemed to have had much of a social life anyway, and now she was with him she didn't need it, so unless she had let herself back into his place she would be there. They set off, doing their best to look sober as both were still in uniform, cutting around behind the docks to the shop above which Lily lodged. Sure enough, she was there, answering the door with a worried expression when she saw the police uniform.

'Don't worry, babe, this is my friend Jeff,' Ed assured. 'Now run along and get us a beer.'

Lily made for the kitchen, sent on her way with a slap of her rear. She was in white jeans, the tight denim making the best of her full bottom, and Ed shared a knowing leer with his friend as she scampered into the kitchen, her bottom moving enticingly behind her.

'Nice,' Jeff remarked, 'very nice.'

'You ain't seen nothing,' Ed answered, 'and you may as well hand over that fifty now.'

Jeff grinned and shook his head, but said no more as Lily came back into the room carrying a four-pack of beer. Ed took it, handing two to Jeff and placing the remainder by his chair.

'I didn't know you were coming, or I'd have picked up a bit,' she said apologetically.

'No problem, babe,' he answered, tugging her down on to his lap.

She went with the pressure, settling herself uneasily on his knee and making no resistance as his arm curled around her waist. He cupped a breast through her jumper, briefly feeling the rounded swell of it before she pulled away with a squeak.

'Hey, hey, babe, be cool,' he chided. 'Jeff's a friend, he doesn't mind if I cop a bit of a feel while we have a beer. Here, give me a kiss.'

He pulled her in, easily overcoming her resistance until her lips were pressed to his. She met his kiss reluctantly, pulling back, only to let her mouth open with a sob as he applied more pressure. Their tongues touched and he felt her body start to relax, at which he once more took hold of her breast and began to knead. He felt Lily start but kept his hold, fondling her and stroking his fingers across the swell of her breast until the nipple went hard.

'Ed, please,' she said. 'Not now.'

'Relax, babe,' he answered. 'Come on, let's have these out.'

'Ed!' she squeaked, but too late as he whipped up her top and bra, spilling her breasts free and catching her arms up behind her to leave them sticking out, bare, the erect nipples pointing high as he pulled her body back into a tight arch. He could feel her shivering and felt his cock twinge in response to her, to her nakedness, to her helplessness and to his control over her body. She was whimpering softly to herself, but said nothing and made no effort to escape his grip. He took his time, teasing her, sure she would soon be excited enough to do as she was told. With both nipples rock-hard and her breath coming in little ragged pants, he decided she was ready.

'Good girl,' he soothed. 'See, Jeff, she needs to be taken in hand, but she loves it. Now, Lily, I owe Jeff here a little favour, so you're going to get down on your hands and knees, crawl over to him and give him a nice, long suck, just like you give me, eh?'

'Please, no,' Lily sighed, but her voice was broken and he was sure she would do it, just with a little more pressure.

'I didn't ask you,' he said. 'I told you. Still, I know it's hard, so let's give your cunt a little frig to get you in the mood.'

He put his hand to her jeans button, and hers closed on top but without force. She sobbed as the button popped, then again, louder, as her zip slid down and the front of her knickers came on show. Ed slid his hand down them, finding her sex moist and ready.

'You're soaking, you little tart,' he laughed. 'So let's not have any more shit. Come on, get your mouth round Jeff's prick. It's for me, right?'

Ed gave her a gentle push and she slid to the floor, moving to all fours as she had been ordered and crawling to Jeff. He grinned, gave Ed a last look and pulled down his zip, flopping his cock into his lap. Lily looked at it, then at Ed.

'Suck it,' Ed ordered. 'Get it in your mouth and suck it until you get a mouthful. Come on, Lily, babe, for me, for your lover.'

Lily didn't move, her eyes pleading, large and moist, her lower lip pouted and trembling.

'Suck it,' Ed growled. 'Come on, do as you're told or it could get worse.'

Lily swallowed, closed her eyes and leaned forward, opening her mouth to take in Jeff's flaccid penis as he offered it to her. He gave a contented sigh as her lips closed on his shaft and her head began to move, up and down, her lips pursed to make a slide for his penis. Ed gave a chuckle of satisfaction as he found that watching her suck on another man's penis gave him no jealousy whatever, just a wonderful feeling of power.

Jeff was soon erect, half his cock standing free of Lily's mouth, the other half inside. Lily sucked with her eyes shut, her face set in an expression of utter misery as her lips worked up and down on the policeman's cock. Her bottom was stuck out behind her, flaring from her hips to a tempting ball of flesh within her tight white jeans. With the button undone they had already come down a little, and Ed determined to increase her embarrassment by pulling them down all the way, making her show her knickers while she sucked cock, maybe more.

'Let's have a bit more out,' he laughed. 'That juicy arse for a start.'

He came behind her, tugging her jeans down around her thighs. Her knickers came with them, leaving her bottom showing. It looked good, framed by the top and the dishevelled lower garments, her cheeks slightly open to show a puff of pale hair and hint at the area around her anus. She kept sucking, obediently bobbing her head on the stiff penis in her mouth as Jeff watched her stripped.

'Tits too, I reckon,' Ed drawled, 'not that she's got much, but it's good to see them swing. Come on, babe, get them out.'

Lily hesitated only a moment, then tugged up her top over her breasts, leaving them hanging. She was nude from chest to thighs, everything that mattered showing, and Ed's cock was hard in his trousers. He stood back, admiring the way the outer lips of her sex pushed out between her thighs with the soft pink of her inner lips showing between them. Lifting a foot, he trod lightly on her back, forcing her to dip low and spread her buttocks, revealing more of her sex and the tight spot of her anus.

'I'm going to fuck her, Jeff,' he slurred. 'Hold still, you little bitch, and keep sucking. Push that big arse out, spread it.'

She obeyed, shivering hard as she lifted her bottom, reached back and pulled open her cheeks, her anus stretched taut between them, her pussy moist and ready below. He knelt, tugging at his belt to get his trousers open. For a moment he was tempted to try to bugger her, only to decide to postpone it and enjoy the easier, more natural hole, at least for the moment. She was wet, and too tempting to be ignored.

'She fucking loves it, like I said,' he announced. 'Her cunt's dripping like a tap.'

His cock came free as he pushed down his trousers and underpants, pointing up, directly at the damp folds of Lily's sex. Taking her by the hips, he moved forward, his cock nudging her pussy, finding the hole and sliding inside. He grunted as his length slid inside her.

'Keep them held open,' he ordered. 'I want to see it go in and out. I want to see your arsehole.'

Lily made an odd choking noise in her throat, but kept her bottom spread, an awkward position that forced her to suck Jeff's cock by bobbing her head up and down on his erection. Ed watched his cock, admiring the spread of

Lily's bottom and the rude contrast straining anus and open, cock-filled hole made with the demure knickers and smart jeans he had pulled down to get at her. She looked so sweet, so innocent, which made it so much better to get her stripped down with a cock in each end. It made him want to soil her, to leave her stripped and filthy, and as Jeff began to groan with his approaching orgasm Ed knew what he wanted to do.

'Do it in her face,' he grunted. 'She loves that, right in her face.'

Jeff reached out, grabbing Lily's hair. She went with the pressure, his erection slipping from her mouth, wet with saliva, a single strand still hanging between the glossy head and her lip. He took it, jerking the shaft as Lily tried to turn her head, too late, as he ejaculated a thick mass of come full into her face. Her mouth came open in wordless protest, only to receive his second spurt. His grip tightened and he pulled her head around, pushing his erection back into her mouth to finish off, fucking her throat as she gagged and jerked on his cock.

'Nice,' Jeff groaned as Lily struggled to accommodate him.

'Swallow it, you little bitch, swallow it all,' Ed grated, feeling himself start to come as Lily pulled slowly back from Jeff's cock.

He saw her throat work and knew she had done it, swallowing her filthy mouthful in meek obedience to his order. Reaching out, he grabbed her hair, pulling her around even as his cock slipped from her slimy vagina. She turned, her soiled face screwed up, her eyes shut, her mouth a tight line with sperm bubbling from either side. He put his cock close, pressing it to her lips and they came apart, revealing the interior of her mouth, sticky with strings of white sperm. Jerking hard, he aimed his erection at her open mouth, felt himself come and saw it spurt from the end in an arc of viscous white, catching one eye and her nose as well as going into her mouth. As Jeff had done, he thrust his cock inside as he came, finishing off in the warm, wet cavity of her throat and ignoring the bubbling, choking noises she was making as he did it.

She was filthy, utterly soiled, her lips pouted around his shaft, still sucking it. Come smeared her face, one thick blob shutting an eye, more smeared on one cheek, thick streamers of it hanging from her nose and chin, her hair dirty, her top fouled. Ed grinned, a feeling of raw power running through him at what he had made her do, at how he had controlled her and made her suck two cocks and take two men's sperm in her face. Only as he stood back did he realise that she had begun to masturbate.

'Get your fingers out of there, you little tart,' he growled.

It was too late. Lily was coming, sobbing brokenly in her ecstasy. Ed slapped her face but her moans only deepened while his hand came away sticky with his own come. She was sobbing and whimpering, crying too, thick, oily tears squeezing out from her eyes to add to the filthy mess of her face as she came, over and over, whispering his name in a hoarse croak again and again.

On a bench overlooking the sea, Thomazina sat, happily munching fish from an open newspaper. The chips she flicked away, over the sea wall to the beach, where a group of seagulls had gathered to enjoy her bounty. The tide had just begun to ebb, coloured lights reflecting from the calm surface of the sea, showing Tawmouth front in distorted mirror image. To her left the pier pushed out into the sea, ablaze with light, the music of the amusements and arcades blending to discordant noise. A couple approached, whispering urgently, only for their conversation to pause as they passed her. For a moment the man's eyes met hers, moving quickly to her breasts to earn a mild rebuke from his girlfriend. Tammy smiled and took the last bite of her fish.

She rose, stretched and pushed her newspaper into a litter bin. Her face set into a determined frown as she studied a poster plastered to one of the lamp-posts that illuminated the front. It showed a picture of the Wythman, or what she supposed was intended to be the Wythman, along with dancers and symbols. It announced the solstice party and also a name, DJ/MC Topher Knight. Clearly he was someone important, and the girl she had asked had said he was most likely to be found at the Black Joke pub.

Making her way through Tawmouth, she found the Black Joke in a street behind what had been the harbour before the modern docks were built. It was familiar, the black beams and high gables provoking a sense of nostalgia, a sense destroyed the instant she pushed open the door. Noise hit her, conversation blended with loud music, also the scents of sweet-smelling smoke, perfume and beer. The single long room was crowded, filled to capacity with young people, clad in black like herself, in rich dark colours, in drab khakis and greens.

Pushing her way to the bar, she drew one of the notes Mr Hobbers had given her from her pocket, holding it up in imitation of the man beside her. One of the barmaids approached, the man calling out a request for beer. Thomazina watched and listened, noting the way the beer was served. As the barmaid returned with the man's change, Thomazina caught her eye.

'A pint,' she called out, 'and please could you tell me where I might find Mr Knight, Mr Topher Knight?'

The barmaid gave her a peculiar look but shouted back over the noise as she took Thomazina's money and jerked her thumb upwards.

'Upstairs bar, black guy with the locks.'

Taking her beer, Thomazina made for the stairs, wondering what part of her behaviour had caused the barmaid surprise. The stair was to one side, rising to a room much like the one below, if marginally less noisy and crowded. Nobody was black, nor was there anybody with locks, although one or two had chains. One man, however, had skin of a dark, glossy brown and hair set into thick strands, not unlike the tentacles of an octopus, a style she felt appropriate for the solstice organiser. He was clearly of some importance anyway, lolling back in an armchair and very much the centre of attention of a group.

As she approached, she realised that the girl to his left was the one whose clothes she had taken. Telling herself that it was hardly an unusual style, she kept on, approaching the man and returning his questioning look with her brightest smile.

'Mr Topher Knight?' she asked.

He nodded, his eyes meeting hers, flicking down to the broad expanse of her chest, then up again. His smile widened and he patted a stool to one side, asking her name.

'Tammy,' she answered.

'Topher,' he answered, 'but I like "Mr Topher Knight" – it sounds good. Maybe I'll use it.'

'May I ask if you are the organiser for the solstice party?' she asked.

'Just the MC, darling.'

'MC?'

'I'm on the mike. Ronnie here's your man.'

He nodded to another of the group, a tall man, thin, with a sharp face and sandy hair. Thomazina smiled again and shook the offered hand.

'I would like to make a request, if I may,' she said. 'Here is something to pay for perhaps some cider, or beer if you prefer, and some friends and I would like to dance on the barrow.'

'The local Bill want to keep us off the actual barrow,' Ronnie began, then stopped as Thomazina spread a fan of twenty-pound notes out on the table.

'Bill will understand, I'm sure,' she said. 'Doesn't he like dancing?'

'Not Sergeant Perkins,' Topher put in. 'He's a regular, grade-one arsehole.'

'He did his best to close us down,' Ronnie added. 'Still, maybe later on. How many of you are there? What are you actually going to do?'

'We will be four,' Thomazina answered. 'The dance is for the pleasure of the crowd, like a music-hall dance, a burlesque.'

'Like an old-fashioned cabaret?' Ronnie queried. 'That's not really our –'

'Let her do it,' Topher cut in. 'What, so you dress up in cancan gear?'

'No, no,' Thomazina answered. 'We must be naked.'

60

'Naked! Hey, can you see Jeff Perkins's face?'

The others laughed and Thomazina smiled in response.

'Do it!' Ronnie called. 'I reckon they'll find a way to ban us next year anyhow. Let's go out with a splash!'

The others chorused agreement, Ronnie taking up the money from the table and asking for fresh orders from the bar. Topher made introductions, including the girl whose clothes Thomazina had on, Yasmin, who responded with an uncertain smile.

Lying in Nich's arms after being brought to orgasm beneath his tongue, Violet felt tired and content. She was drifting towards sleep and wondering if she would dream of his god. It was early, yet after an evening of vigorous sex both had decided on sleep, with the unspoken expectation that the night may bring more than simple rest. Now, with her body absolutely at ease, her senses slipped slowly away, her last thoughts of the warm breeze on the barrow, Nich's embrace, and sea stretching away to the horizon, twinkling blue in the sunlight, cool and welcoming . . .

When she turned, the barrow was there, as before, only open, with men standing around a wide black aperture that led down into the earth. She walked forward, puzzled, addressing a question to a man in clerical dress, his face red and half hidden beneath thick whiskers and greying hair. He answered her in outrage, pointing to her purple underwear, calling her a harlot and a temptress, demanding that she kneel, that the other men around take her and beat her.

She responded in anger, accusing him of hypocrisy, of seeking to deny her sexuality, charges that only led his face to grow redder as a half-dozen brawny workmen closed in on her. They took her arms, pulling her back as the priest drew a slim black volume from his pocket. She was pushed to the ground, forced into a kneeling position, face to the sea, her back and outthrust bottom towards the open mouth of the barrow.

The priest began to chant, sanctimonious words, begging for her forgiveness from his god and her acceptance of what was about to be done to her. Rough hands took her bra, wrenching the strap until it broke and her breasts fell bare into the bright sunlight. Laughter greeted the sight, earning a rebuke from the priest and the instruction that although it was right to strip her for the sake of her shame it should be done with decorum. Violet protested, calling them abusers, only to have her arms twisted yet more tightly and the grip in her hair redouble, forcing her to push her bottom out.

A tight grip fastened in her panties, too, at either side, holding them so that she knew they could be tugged down at any instant. The men began to count, one, two, three, and her panties had been wrenched down, baring her bottom as the priest once more chided the rough men for taking too much pleasure in their work. The biggest of them made a gruff apology and began to loosen his belt, then to pull the thick strap of blackened leather slowly from his trousers.

Kneeling, held, naked bar the pathetic scrap of purple cotton that linked her thighs, Violet struggled to free herself, finding her limbs sluggish, reluctant to move, let alone break the powerful masculine grip that kept her in position. She was to be beaten and she could do nothing, not even hide the rudeness of the view she was presenting to the men. The man with the belt walked around her, lifting it, chuckling as he watched the fear and panic in her eyes.

It came down, slapping on her naked flesh, making her body jerk again and again as she was beaten to the droning chant of the priest's voice. She tried to cry out, to beg for mercy, to apologise, swearing she would have dressed properly if only she had known, demanding to know why her underwear was so indecent anyway. They took no notice, laughing at her as her buttocks danced to the smacks of the belt, the priest no longer interceding, until her will broke and she began to scream and writhe, her body still refusing to obey the commands of her mind.

The priest stopped chanting, and as he did so the whipping stopped, leaving her sweaty and dishevelled in their grip, panting and groaning in her pain. He gave her a smile, cold and tight, with neither warmth nor pity, coughed and in a quiet, half-ashamed voice stated his intention of turning his back while the workmen raped her. She screamed, writhing in futile effort against their strength, cursing the priest, naming him a hypocrite, a violator, a torturer, cursing his religion and calling on the barrow god in a voice cracking with despair and self-pity.

A cruel smile twisted the face of the man who had beaten her. Taking her hair from his companion, he forced her head up, making her watch as he began to unbutton his fly. His trousers bulged beneath it, hinting at genitals of obscene, monstrous proportions. Her gaze went up, meeting his eyes, hoping for some faint spark of human decency but finding only cruelty and lust. He laughed down at her, the sound broken by a wet smacking from behind and cut off abruptly. His face changed, harsh, merciless passion vanishing to an expression of terror, of blind panic as he stumbled backwards, tripping, to run screaming as something firm and wet touched Violet's naked bottom . . .

She woke with a start, gulping in air and fighting down the urge to scream. The realisation that it was only a dream came quickly, and with it the memory that she had hoped to dream, only a dream very different from the ghastly nightmare she had experienced.

Yasmin let her weight lean on the arm on Topher Knight, her pleasure rising at the feel of his firm muscles. She was giggling with drink, full of arousal and mischief at the prospect of what was doubtless in store for her. Nich had asked her to do her best to gain the man's confidence, but from the moment she had met him she had been determined to take it further. It had begun well, Topher responding coolly but enthusiastically to her open flirting, only for the girl Tammy to appear and quickly draw his attention. She had known he preferred full-figured girls and had thought her own voluptuous curves would give her every advantage, but Tammy was yet more curvaceous, certainly bustier and perhaps with a narrower waist.

She had risen to the challenge, kissing Topher and stroking his thigh, only to have Tammy do the same but allow her hand to stray to the crotch of his trousers. He had refused to show favour to either, revelling in their attention and the all too obvious envy of the other men at the table. Yasmin had quickly realised that his intention was to get them both into bed at the same time, and with that had come an idea for how to get her own way.

Leaning close, she had whispered into his ear that she would be more than happy to have a threesome, knowing full well that her willingness to accept the idea would give her an unassailable advantage over her rival, whatever really happened. Having gained the advantage, she had leaned across to Tammy, putting the proposition in Topher's hearing range. Twice she had tried the trick before. Both times her rivals had been shocked, leaving them looking prudish and winning her the man. Tammy had smiled and kissed her.

Realising that he was going to get what he wanted, Topher had acted fast, walking from the Black Joke with an arm around each girl and leaving a trail of envious stares in his wake. Now, in the cool night they were walking through the streets of Tawmouth, the girls nuzzled to his sides as he led them along the front. His hotel proved to be the Royal, once fine, now somewhat decayed, which they entered at the back, giggling guiltily as they climbed the stairs to his room.

Inside she threw herself on to the bed, her head spinning. Topher moved to the bar, Tammy coming beside Yasmin, kneeling and pulling up her top. The bra came with it, revealing huge pink breasts considerably larger than her own and crowned with big, rose-pink nipples. Topher gave a grunt of appreciation as he stood from the bar and Yasmin quickly peeled up her own top, determined not to be outdone.

'You are beautiful,' Tammy said as Yasmin peeled. 'I love your skin.'

Tammy reached out, stroking Yasmin's flesh, on her neck, down one breast and on to a nipple, making the bud stiffen in response. Yasmin shivered, fighting down a touch of shyness. Tammy was looking down at her with obvious pleasure, feeling a breast, a gesture that made it very obvious their sex would not be confined to satisfying Topher.

He was pouring drinks, spilling some as he watched the two topless girls. Yasmin's breasts were in Tammy's hands, both nipples hard. She sighed, arching her back to push them out, her last reservations vanishing in the pleasure of having her breasts felt with such casual intimacy. Tammy giggled and came down, their mouths meeting in an open kiss, big, soft breasts pressing together, their arms going around one another.

'Hey, wait for the man,' Topher demanded as he reached the bed, setting the drinks down beside it.

Yasmin reached a hand out and squeezed his crotch, finding a bulge of satisfying size beneath the denim. He grinned as she began to tug down his fly, Tammy turning to watch. His shirt came off as his zip slid down and her hand burrowed into his fly, pulling out a thick, dark cock. Shuffling forward, he offered it to her mouth, only to have Tammy gulp it quickly in and start to suck. Yasmin pressed her face close, kissing his cock where it disappeared between Tammy's lips. Tammy pulled back, letting the thick, rapidly hardening penis slip into Yasmin's mouth.

For a while they shared, stroking each other's body as they sucked his cock, stopping only when he was rock-hard, his erection rearing from his fly, a good nine inches of fat, black penis. Yasmin took it in hand, finding to her pleasure that her fingers failed to meet around the shaft. Tammy had knelt back and was undoing her trousers, fumbling with the button in her haste.

Together, Yasmin and Topher watched Tammy strip, revealing broad hips, a softly rounded belly and a thick bush of jet-black hair between chubby, girlish thighs. Her flesh was ivory-smooth and very pale, in keeping with her complexion, making Yasmin wonder just how old she was. Nude, Tammy crawled up the bed, reaching for the cock that Yasmin had been stroking as she stripped. Yasmin let go, making short work of her own trousers and panties while Tammy kept him ready.

Both naked, they rolled together, feeling the full curves of each other's figures, exploring plump breasts and bottoms, kissing mouths and nipples as Topher rapidly completed the removal of his clothes. Yasmin was beneath Tammy, two huge breasts lolling in her face, her hands on the girl's bottom, feeling the full, meaty cheeks and holding them wide, knowing that it made a thoroughly rude and tempting display of both pussy and bottom hole. Tammy responded, sinking into Yasmin's embrace with her bottom lifted, an obvious target to which Topher was not slow to respond.

He came behind Tammy, entering her as Yasmin held tight. The sensation of holding a girl who was being fucked was wonderful, not just sexy but protective, hearing Tammy's groans and gasps as the big penis worked inside her and knowing that she herself would shortly be getting the same treatment. Sure enough, once Topher had taken his fill of Tammy he withdrew, took a hold on Yasmin's ankles and tipped her up. She was entered, her legs high, her thighs pressed to the soft flesh of Tammy's bottom. He began to fuck her, moving in long, slow pushes, her vagina feeling wonderfully full with his big penis inside.

She began to suckle Tammy's breasts, taking each nipple in turn and pressing her face to the heavy, hanging globe of flesh. There was something wonderful about sucking a girl even bigger than herself, and one who took such obvious pleasure in her ample curves. Like her, Tammy thought nothing of flaunting the size of her breasts and bottom, wearing tight clothing to enhance her figure, doubtless equally aware of just how much such a display of female flesh turned men on, real men.

Certainly Topher was enjoying it, taking turns with their pussies, never too long in either girl, but just enough to leave each sighing and moaning before once more putting his cock to the other hole. Yasmin let him do it, her pleasure rising as she was entered again and again, or as Tammy grunted and shivered in her arms. He was holding back, she knew, eager to take his fill of two willing girls, never going too fast until at last his resolve broke and she felt Tammy's body jerk to harder, firmer pushes. He groaned and she felt something wet on her belly, his sperm, spilling out from Tammy's overfull vagina.

Even as he pulled out Tammy had begun to turn, and before Yasmin could make a choice she had a full, opulent bare bottom over her face and a head buried in her pussy. Tammy was licking, working eagerly on Yasmin's clitoris, seemingly desperate to bring her to climax. It was impossible not to return the favour, reaching up to take Tammy by the hips and pull her bottom down into her face. Tammy went with the pressure, spreading her thighs over Yasmin's face and pressing her pussy to her mouth. Yasmin began to lick, her eyes glued to the pale skin of Tammy's bottom and tight hole of her anus.

Topher had stood back, sipping his drink and watching the girls lick, his big cock hanging half limp over his balls. Yasmin could taste his sperm, salty and male in Tammy's vagina, filling her mouth as she licked, smearing her chin and nose as she rubbed her face in her lover's sex. He began to masturbate, watching, obviously enjoying the view despite his recent orgasm. Yasmin felt a finger touch her pussy and slip inside; another touched her anus, tickling the tight hole, and she was coming, full in Tammy's face, licking Topher's sperm up as her orgasm hit her, a long, glorious climax to leave her lying back in bliss.

Tammy's response was a grunt of frustration and to sit up, smothering Yasmin's face. Yasmin began to lick once more, her nose pressed to Tammy's bottom hole as she did it, uncertain if she wanted to be queened so blatantly in front of Topher but with little choice in the matter. Tammy squirmed it in Yasmin's face, groaning aloud. Hands went to Yasmin's breasts, feeling them eagerly, then slapping, making her jump as she felt the first contractions of Tammy's vagina. The smacks stung her breasts, making her want to spread herself, bare to the girl she was licking, an unfamiliar but lovely feeling that went with having her nose rubbed in a girl's bottom hole as her face was used to come on. Not that it mattered what she thought, with Tammy sitting on her face, gasping in ecstasy as she came, crying out loud and finally slumping forward and to one side.

Four

'If it happens again I'll know to call on Sigodin-Yth earlier!' Violet laughed, doing her best to make light of the nightmare that had left her shivering and frightened in the night.

'It will happen again, I'm sure of it,' Nich answered.

He had been doing his best to show concern, but she knew it hid excitement. She had described her dream on waking, then again in the morning, leaving Nich with his fingers steepled and his brow furrowed in thought.

'I had imagined something less traumatic,' he admitted after a pause. 'A calling, a compulsion, something serene and mystical. Still, maybe I am simply trying to impose a modern ethos on an ancient god, which could never be valid. Let us consider the Bronze Age equivalent. What might a Bronze Age woman have feared? Wild beasts? Raiders of some sort? So she meets her fear and is protected if she calls on the god.'

'That works,' Violet answered. 'I'll tell you something, private. My parents were very religious. We used to go to church every Sunday, say our prayers before bed, the works. I started to rebel at thirteen and church was the thing I hated most of all. My parents were tolerant at first, condescending actually, saying it was just a phase and that I would grow out of it, all that crap. That just made me worse. I had my ears pierced when I was fourteen and I started getting into pagan jewellery designs for my earrings, chaos symbols, little ankhs and things, which really pissed them off. So they tried to stop me and the more they pushed the more I pushed back. I started reading pagan stuff, including some of yours. It was great, it made me feel I could be myself and not worry about sinning and doing as I was told all the time.'

'Thank you,' Nich cut in. 'Allowing people to escape the restrictions of the Lah religions has always been important to me. I'm glad I helped. Go on.'

'When I had my nose pierced they really freaked,' Violet continued. 'They sent me to this priest. Syrupy Sam we called him, because of the way he talked, really oily. He used to play the guitar and make us sing and tell little stories he called parables to make us behave properly. I hated him. I've never hated anyone so much in my life!'

'Was it him who came to your dream?' Nich asked.

'No, Syrupy was tall and sort of fleshy faced. The priest in the dream was much older, with big white sideburns and that. Syrupy wouldn't have had me beaten for being outdoors in bra and panties either: he'd have taken me aside for one of his "quiet words".'

'He wasn't a molester, then?'

'Not physically; mentally I felt violated.'

'And you fought?'

'I had my tummy button pierced, got my Ianthe tattoo and turned up in a crop top.'

'Fine.'

'I got a quiet word. You see, he wouldn't believe I'd done it because I had different beliefs, or even because I was an awkward little cow. It was because I didn't understand the truth of his rotten god. In time I would see the light. He was sure of it, so were my parents.'

'Incorrectly.'

'They still reckon I'll change, but last year Mum gave me a big amethyst geode for my birthday. The thing is, there's nothing like Christianity to put me on the defensive. I suppose my attitude is much like a Bronze Age girl would have felt about wolves or whatever.'

'It fits,' Nich agreed. 'I wonder if your priest was the image of the Reverend Wilmot, taken up by Sigodin-Yth as an image of antagonism. There might be an early photo of him, with luck, then we'll know for sure you are being called.'

Violet swallowed, unable to deny the excitement Nich so obviously felt, yet still fragile from her nightmare. Still, before she had doubted Nich's word, seeing Sigodin-Yth as conceptual but no more. Now she found she shared his belief if not his absolute certainty, yet she knew that would come if the man from her dream proved to be the Reverend Wilmot. Wanting some time to think, she went to make coffee, only to be interrupted by Yasmin.

'Did I do it or did I do it!' Yasmin declared, her face one huge smile as she greeted Violet.

'Do what?' Violet demanded. 'You've been to bed with this Knight guy, haven't you?'

'Yup,' Yasmin answered, 'and not just me: this other girl, too! It was well wild!'

'You slut! What did you do? Tell me!'

'What *didn't* we do? Five orgasms I had, five! Topher's great. He's got this thing, right, where he holds your legs and rubs his prick on your clitty in between putting it in. That was good, so good. He's big, too, not so much long, but thick, really thick!'

'Wow! So what about this other girl?'

'Tammy, she's great, really dirty, worse than me! She sat on my face! She's got huge boobs, and this really cool tattoo, an octopus, right on one bum cheek!'

'An octopus?' Nich asked from the door of Violet's room.

'Yeah, in green, with red eyes. Look, I was going to say. Your part of it didn't go so well. Tammy was after doing some sort of cabaret at the festival, actually on the barrow. She'd got it all fixed before I had a chance to talk to Topher alone, and once we were in bed, well you know, I just never got around to it.'

'A cabaret?' Nich asked.

'Sort of,' Yasmin answered. 'I didn't get the details, but it'll be four girls, nude!'

'Neat,' Violet put in.

'That's not a problem,' Nich said thoughtfully, 'especially if you got in with Knight. I wonder, do you know where this Tammy lives?'

'No.' Yasmin shrugged. 'We talked a bit, in between sex. She sounds really posh even though she's a dirty bitch. I think she's from France, or maybe Spain. Her hair's darker than mine, real glossy black. I did ask where she got the tatt. She said from a sailor, some place in behind the docks.'

'Shouldn't be hard to find,' Violet said.

'It was pretty faded. I was telling her she ought to get it filled in. Maybe the bloke's not there any more.'

'Worth a look. I might get something done myself.'

'Do that, if you're of a mind,' Nich put in. 'I have some research to do and I also hope to retrieve my copy of Laverack.'

Thomazina walked from the door of the Royal. Her head hurt and she was grateful for the cool weather that had come in from the west during the night, bringing a fresh wind and showers. Crossing the formal gardens that separated the beach from the buildings of the front, she leaned against the railings, looking out over the sea. The beach was deserted, the waves tumbling in, high and fretful against the sand, cold and welcoming, stretching away to where St David's Island was no more than a dull loom against the grey horizon.

Shaking her head, she chided herself for pouring rum cocktails on top of beer, then smiled at the memory of indulging herself with Yasmin and Topher. Starting to the east along the front, she quickly passed the town, walking on by the railway until she reached the headland, against which the waves were breaking in angry splendour, sending spray into her face and across the tracks.

Her clothes were wet, her top plastered to her breasts, her jeans uncomfortable between her thighs, and as she reached the shelter of the boulder patch she began to undress, stripping nude before burying her clothes beneath a cluster of rocks. With a quick glance along the beach, she

71

went down to the water's edge, walking out into the waves without hesitation to slip into the cool, comforting embrace of the sea.

With vague thoughts of the stacks to the west of St David's Island she struck out, swimming easily and coming to the surface only for the occasional breath. Tawmouth quickly became blurred, no more than a jumble of grey shapes in the rain, with even the high red cliffs to either side of the town losing their colour. Above her the sky was broken, a ragged tumble of cloud, with odd shafts of sunlight striking down on the western horizon. Vague thoughts of rest stirred her mind, along with contentment and self-satisfaction.

On finally reaching the biggest of the stacks, the Ore Stone, she made for a sheltered gully on the eastern face, a favoured place, out of the west wind, its angle making it invisible from the island. The water was calmer, the surface moving to the heavy swell but oily smooth, broken only by the spatter of raindrops. An object moved as she approached, black and glistening for a moment, before slipping beneath the surface. She paused, checking the sea around for signs of floating tar even as something took hold of her ankle and she was wrenched beneath the surface.

She went down, struggling to reach her leg, pulled under in a swirl of bubbles, twisting and kicking to break free. Kicking out with her free leg, her foot struck something that darted away, then took hold, clutching at her leg. Green water swirled around her, darker below, where something pale moved beyond the black swirl of her floating hair, and more, deeper. Reaching, she grabbed, pulling until the grip on her legs gave and her body pressed to another, cool and soft. Arms encircled her waist, squeezing her, a hand slipping down to cup the turn of her bottom, another sliding up her back. A face appeared in front of her, neat, piquant features in a pale oval, small and delicate, an instant before they broke surface.

Thomazina shook herself, gasping in air as the impish face in front of her broke into a happy smile. Once more she began to swim, hurriedly, into the shelter of the gully, where she pulled herself from the sea on to a sloping ledge, and composed herself just beyond the reach of the waves.

Her companion followed, easing a small, slender body on to the rock, entirely naked. Like Thomazina, her hair was true black, showing a blue-green sheen in the dull light. Otherwise she was quite different, tiny, svelte, her breasts no more than gentle swells, her hips subtly rounded, only the tangle of curls over her sex showing her maturity. Lying full length beside Thomazina with her feet on the wet rock, she let her breath out in a long sigh.

'You, Elune, need to be introduced to a man I have met,' Thomazina stated. 'He is keen to place wayward girls on a straight path.'

'Tell me,' the other demanded.

'In time. Have you been yet?'

'Last night, when the tide was low. And you?'

'I have been here three full days, although I spent the first basking. I have allowed a lecherous little Peeping Tom to seduce me. I have enjoyed a strange and wonderful man with dark skin, in company with a similar girl. I have met an old man who likes to smack girls' bottoms.'

'And doubtless done nothing to ensure the success of the party?'

'Not at all. All four will be helpful. Well, the Peeping Tom perhaps no more than a little and the girl was just along for the ride. The old one and the dark-skinned one will be useful. So I have done a great deal, more, in any case, than you. Where have you been?'

'Inishmaan, lately, with a mad old fool who thinks I'm a pixie. He is rich, though, and generous, and dirty.'

'What does he do? Tell me.'

'He likes to watch me pee, and best of all he likes me to do it in my pants, little white pants he buys especially.'

'How strange. Is it much fun?'

'It feels warm and wet and heavy. It drives him to a great passion, especially if I am in those blue trousers, jeans, and undress in front of him to show what I have done. The feel is nice, but he is sure I hate it and will buy me ice creams and chocolate afterwards, so I always touch myself later, when he is not looking. Except when he makes me do it in front of him, which he still thinks I hate. What of you?'

'I have been in Brittany and down to Oléron, eating oysters and lobster and teasing the boys. Twice I came up, once to live with a painter in Rouen. He was full of passion, but angry. When he couldn't sell his work he would hit me, so I jumped into the Seine, from a bridge. He thinks I drowned.'

'Thomazina!'

'Perhaps he will be kinder to his next girl. The second was with Juliana, who I met on Karrec-Hir. She wanted to see Rome again and I went with her as far as the mountains. There is a long lake, the Drac, where I lived with a man who made honey, but it wasn't the same.'

'Is Juliana here, or Aileve?'

'Neither. They will come.'

'They will. But tell me of the man who likes to smack girls' bottoms. Is he dirty, or cruel, or only strict?'

'I suppose he must be cruel, to so enjoy a girl's suffering, but he did not seem so. Certainly he was dirty, and not strict at all, although I thought so at first. He had a periodical, with pictures, showing a man beating his daughter for playing at lawn tennis instead of studying. I thought it was for instruction, as it seemed to show the way to punish the girl, but when I told him how my sisters and I were beaten he became very excited. I pulled his little man for him and afterwards he gave me money for a coin I took from the *Sao Joao*. More than he should have, I am sure.'

'Money is difficult. The boys on Inishmaan have a trick which is both cruel and dirty. Shall I show you?'

'What is it?'

'Don't be silly, that would spoil the fun. Just lie and bask, face down.'

Thomazina turned on her front, watching Elune sidelong, uncertain as to her feelings and remembering one or two of the small girl's other tricks.

'Shut your eyes, silly,' Elune laughed. 'Pretend you are a pretty Irish girl, asleep on the beach in your bathing suit, dreaming of handsome young men and pretty frocks.'

74

'I have no bathing suit.'

'Imagine one, very cheeky, bright red and hardly covering your great big bottom. Come now, don't be dreary.'

Thomazina pouted but shut her eyes and turned her face to the rock as she heard the gentle splash of Elune's body entering the sea. She waited, listening to the sounds of the sea and the cry of gulls, feeling her fatigue despite her worry. Half asleep, she never heard Elune emerge from the water, but felt something soft and wet pressed gently between her legs where her buttocks met her thighs. It had a rubbery texture, like kelp stem, yet she could imagine the horrible embarrassment of a girl on a beach waking to the feeling and thinking she had somehow soiled her bikini pants in her sleep. It was cruel, and dirty, even for Elune, who took a delight in mischief. Still, it didn't really work on her, not when she had known something was going to happen.

She stayed still, sure that refusing to respond would be the one reaction that thwarted Elune's wicked humour. The thing was pressed tight in between her thighs, touching her sex, rather like a cock just about to be pushed inside her. It seemed to be moving too, very slowly, running like treacle. For a moment she wondered if it was not kelp but a lump of tar, which was bound to catch in her hair and force her to shave herself. Anger at Elune welled up inside her, only to be replaced by shock as the thing squirmed against her, now definitely moving, sucking to her leg and swelling against her sex lips. A hot stinging sensation started at the mouth of her vagina as she reached back, grabbing at the thing. It was squashy and wet, hard to grip and stuck to her thigh, forcing her to stick her bottom up and cock her legs apart, an act that drew a peel of high-pitched laughter from Elune.

Thomazina turned, finding Elune perched on a rock with her legs pulled up to her chest, her face set in an expression of glee. The thing came loose, sucking at her leg as it pulled away. Looking down, she found herself with a big, green-purple anemone in her hand, a snakelocks, its tentacles already pulling back. Flicking it hastily into the water, she turned on Elune, whose eyes were bright with mischief.

'Could you catch me you might whip me!' Elune laughed. 'But you won't: you are too slow, too big, like all your sort!'

The small girl darted away as Thomazina grabbed for her, laughing merrily as she skipped out of reach. Safely clear, she turned again and made a face and a gesture of her hands, signifying the contours of Thomazina's body in farcical exaggeration. Thomazina started forward, only to see Elune pull herself up a rock face with quick, easy motions she could not hope to emulate. Her sex seemed to be on fire, a hot pain of maddening intensity, and her anger was real, if tempered by an understanding of the other's character. Certainly Elune knew what to expect if she was caught.

'Come up!' Elune taunted. 'Teach me my place! Smack my bottom like your old man!'

Thomazina turned away, refusing to answer. Once more she lay down, stretching herself on the wet surface of the rock, turning her face seawards with feigned indifference to Elune's continuing taunts. Presently there was silence and a while later the sun broke through the clouds, warming her back. She yawned and stretched, shutting her eyes with a sleepy smile.

For a while she basked, trying to ignore the hot sting of her sex and the need to scratch and rub at herself. She knew full well that, if she allowed the irritation to drive her to masturbate, Elune's amusement would know no bounds, so she held herself immobile until the faintest of sounds caught her attention. Peeping through her eye-lashes, she watched Elune creep closer, impish face set in a manic grin, fingers carefully holding a yet larger snakelocks anemone. With every muscle limp, Thomazina judged her moment, grabbed and closed her fingers on Elune's ankle. Elune squeaked in shock and kicked out, but Thomazina had already found a hold in her hair, twisting the long black locks hard into her left hand.

'Let go, let go!' she squealed. 'I was playing. I didn't know he'd sting, I didn't!'

'Big and slow I may be, but I am not stupid,' Thomazina answered. 'Now come down to your knees.'

'No, please, I am delicate, very delicate!' Elune begged. 'You know how delicate I am!'

'You should have thought of that before,' Thomazina answered and pulled the small girl's face down towards the rock.

Elune went into a kneeling position. With a sudden flick, she tossed the anemone towards the sea, but Thomazina had expected the move and caught it, quickly turning the stinging tentacles downwards to save her hand. With Elune's face to the rock, her bottom was pushed high, the cheeks well apart, her sex on full display, also her anus. For a moment Thomazina paused, unsure if she could perform so cruel an act, but the hot pain in her own sex stiffened her resolve. Pressing the fat body of the anemone to Elune's vagina, she squeezed it into the tiny hole, ignoring her victim's kicking legs and repeated pleas for mercy.

'Oh, you wicked, fat monster!' Elune cried as her vagina closed on the anemone's body. 'Ow! Thomazina, please, it is beginning to sting!'

'Good,' Thomazina answered. 'Now come here.'

She pulled, dragging the squealing Elune up the gully to where the rock closed overhead. The falling tide had left the gully floor exposed, showing green, weed-encrusted rocks and the thick, brown stalks of kelp. Thomazina chose one, as thick around as her wrist at the base and some four feet in length, twisting it from the rock.

'No!' Elune squeaked. 'Not that too! My fanny burns, Thomazina, have mercy!'

Thomazina ignored Elune, twisting her grip to force the small woman to bend, bottom high, legs set apart. She could see the anemone, a circle of purple-green flesh within the pink of the vagina, two tentacles hanging out, squirming slowly against the tender flesh. Grinning, Thomazina brought the kelp stick down hard across the girl's helpless bottom. Elune kicked and squealed, jumping on her feet as the whip struck home, her tiny buttocks bouncing to the impact.

'Fat, rotten monster!' Elune squeaked, then squealed louder still as the kelp stalk slapped down across her upper thighs. 'Ow! Please, Thomazina, that hurt!'

Thomazina placed another smack across Elune's bottom, bringing the thick brown kelp fronds down hard to spray seawater over both of them. Again Elune danced and kicked, her little body moving in frantic response to the pain of the beating. Thomazina found herself grinning, unable to hold back her enjoyment of her victim's helplessness and nudity. Twisting her hand hard into Elune's hair, she delivered eight hard blows in succession, leaving Elune dancing and gasping for breath with her tiny buttocks jiggling crazily up and down in her pain.

'Beast!' Elune gasped as she fought to recover herself. 'I shall pee on you! I shall give you to Juliana!'

'Juliana is more likely to take my side,' Thomazina answered, drawing a miserable sob from Elune, then a squeal as the kelp frond lashed down once more.

'Beat me, then!' Elune snapped. 'Beat me well, you horrid, fat beast, and just for a little trick! Oh, he stings so! I can feel him moving, Thomazina! Ow!'

'Then push it out,' Thomazina answered.

Elune said nothing, but braced her legs, offering Thomazina a fine view of spread pink bottom, dimpled anus and open sex, the anemone's full set of tentacles now dangling from the sore, red hole like an absurd beard. They were moving, writhing against the tender skin of Elune's sex lips, some even moving up to her anus, turning the skin at the centre of the tiny hole an angry, swollen red. In response, Elune's muscles twitched, making her anus pulse and her buttocks jump and shiver. Thomazina's own sex still stung and she could feel for the small girl's pain.

Smiling, she lifted the kelp and once more brought it down, the anemone retracting suddenly into Elune's vagina at the impact. Thomazina went to work, methodically thrashing Elune with hard, rhythmic blows, watching in vengeful delight as her victim danced in pain, her buttocks colouring through rich pink to an angry red to purple. Only when Elune's breathing had become deep and regular and her squeals and gasps turned to broken groans did Thomazina stop, throwing down the now ragged kelp whip.

Elune's bottom was a mess, blotchy purple, the muscles squeezing to make her bottom close and open. As Thomazina watched the anemone squeezed from the small girl's vagina, falling to the rock with a squashy sound. Thomazina picked it up and tossed it into a pool, then slapped the inside of Elune's thighs to make her further part her legs. Her vagina was scarlet, her anus, vulva, sex lips and the inner tuck of her bottom inflamed with rash, the muscles twitching with pain.

'You are done,' she said. 'Perhaps that will teach you to play your dirty little tricks.'

'And I suppose you are all excited now,' Elune retorted. 'I suppose you can't help but sit your big bottom on my face and make me lick you. Can you, you beast?'

Thomazina said nothing, but pulled Elune down by the hair, laying her on a bed of thick kelp fronds. Elune went with the pressure, her thighs coming up and apart as she lay back. Thomazina stepped close, released Elune's hair, cocked a leg over her body and sank into a squat. Elune sighed, a sound muffled by the full cheeks of Thomazina's bottom as they were settled over her face. As a sharp little tongue began to lick her, soothing her own anemone rash, Thomazina sighed, let her knees slide apart in the slippery kelp and took a big breast in each hand.

Elune had begun to touch herself, her hands stroking her inflamed sex, touching the rash deliberately. Thomazina watched, thinking how funny and how rude her friend had looked during the beating, dancing in pain with the anemone's tentacles hanging from her vagina. She laughed, smiling happily as Elune's tongue slipped into her own vagina. Her breasts felt huge in her hands, the nipples stiff and prominent, enormous in contrast to those of the tiny girl whose face she sat on. Letting her hands slip lower, she felt the roundness of her stomach, the soft bulge of flesh at her mound and thighs. Elune's tongue was working wonders, teasing the length of Thomazina's sex, flicking over the sensitive skin from clitoris to anus and back, burrowing into one hole or the other, tasting her, and all the while lazily masturbating.

In no time she was coming, rubbing her full bottom into Elune's face as she bounced her big breasts in her hands, revelling in their size and weight. Elune's tongue was in her bottom hole, deep up, then forward again, flicking at her clitoris, kissing it and suddenly sucking it in between small, firm lips. Thomazina came, crying out to the grey sky and wet rocks, wave after wave of ecstasy running through her as she felt herself and thought of small, slim buttocks bouncing to the smack of a whip.

Elune kept licking, rubbing harder at herself as Thomazina came in her face. Her thighs were wide, her sex spread, the angry, scarlet flesh swollen as she rubbed. Her tongue went up Thomazina's bottom, deep in, the pointed tip wriggling in the hot rectal flesh. Her back arched, and as she came her bladder erupted, pee spraying out in a long, golden arc to splash on the rocks and weed, dying, flaring again, once more to die to a trickle of yellow liquid on hot, angry flesh.

Thomazina climbed off, sitting down in the cool kelp and letting her breath out. Sitting on Elune's face to come had been easy enough, but holding her pose while Elune took her own pleasure was far more tiring. Her sex still stung, but even with her orgasm a fresh experience she knew it would be worth it. Elune rose, grinning impishly, and sat her bottom down in a pool with a look of mock indignation for Thomazina.

'You have made me very sore, Thomazina,' she chided. 'Still, I'm certain I deserved it. Did you like my peeing trick? I learned it on Inishmaan.'

'It's nice and dirty. Is it just for show?'

'No, it feels lovely. You must try.'

'I shall. Now, you must have clothes, which I shall buy for you. What name are you going by?'

'The Celtic, in Ireland. Here I shall be Linnet.'

'I am Tammy again – Thomazina seems to be thought long. Would a little more chest not be a good idea?'

'I like my shape, and besides, if your old man thinks I'm a child he will send me away with a big ice cream while he spanks your great fat bottom.'

Joe stared from his window, watching the brighter weather move slowly in from the west. Since the previous evening he had been burning with frustration and jealousy. Ever since his encounter with Tammy he had been searching for her, failing until, walking back along the front, he had seen her, with a tall black man and another girl. The man's arms had been around both girls and all three had been laughing with excitement. As he had watched from the shadows he had seen the black guy squeeze Tammy's bottom, an intimate act which she had greeted with a happy, drunken giggle.

He had followed, and seen the three go into the back of the Royal, their reason for using the late-night door all too obvious. He had been thinking of Tammy as his, and seeing her with another man had left him feeling rejected and angry, also frustrated as he thought of her in the black guy's arms. That alone was bad enough, but the fact that there had been another girl with them made it unbearable, and it had proved impossible to get the image of the three of them having sex out of his mind.

All morning he had stayed in his room, alternating between anger and self-pity and listening to the patter of rain on the windows. Now it was stopping, and his overriding emotion was a hot resentment directed at the entire female sex, for what he saw as fickleness, callousness and a general failure to appreciate his qualities. The resentment mixed with lust, giving him an urgent need to spy on girls, which he knew would go some way to soothing his feelings.

He had always found that he got the most pleasure from watching girls who didn't want to be seen. Girls on the front in bikinis were good, but they weren't hiding anything. The posh girls on St David's were better, as he felt they would resent him watching them far more than the Tawmouth girls and there was a better chance of

81

catching some topless, even nude. Lonelier places could prove better still and his favourite was Aldon Head, with its sloping rock ledges, hard to access and quite private, save to anybody on the cliff top equipped with powerful binoculars.

More often than not there would be nobody there, but it could be pretty well guaranteed that anybody who troubled to walk over a mile and then scramble over the rocks had some reason to seek privacy. More than once he had caught girls sunbathing nude, watching them strip and oil their bodies, with his cock hardening in his pants. Once there had even been a couple, kissing and then masturbating each other on the hot, bare rock before a brief and frantic coupling.

Now he felt the need to see something rude, also to get the thrill of feeling he was intruding on the girls' privacy. There was a need to be alone as well, which he fought down as it made him feel weak, yet Aldon Head was clearly the place to go. As he had done on previous occasions, he went to the river ferry, sitting nearby with a can of cold cola to see if any pretty girls intended to cross the Taw, particularly those with towels and beach bags. The air was fresh from the rain, the wind light, weather he considered ideal, hot yet not so sultry that the walk would be an undue effort. Sure enough, the cluster of passengers awaiting the ferry included three girls who he felt would be worth watching stripped down. Two were clearly friends, one fake blonde, one brown-haired, both quite petite and slender, both with large canvas beach bags slung over their shoulders, chattering happily and quite unaware of his gaze. The third was more tempting still, a natural blonde with her hair cut in a neat bob, her figure compact, perhaps a little bottom heavy, dressed in a demure white summer dress and sandals. She lacked Tammy's glorious curves, but made up for them with a natural innocence of manner which Joe found irresistible, especially as the thin material of her dress hinted at braless breasts. Here, he was sure, was a girl for whom the idea of being peeped at in her bathing suit would be genuinely shocking.

82

He joined the ferry, taking care not to pay any attention whatever to the girls as they crossed the Taw estuary. On the far side he disembarked last, watching carefully to see what the girls would do. Sure enough, the two friends made for the tunnel that led on to Ness Beach, but unfortunately the natural blonde took the footpath up to Aldon Hill. Joe spent a while pretending to watch birds on the mud flats, then started up Aldon Hill, intending to follow the blonde and, if she did nothing interesting, then to peer down at the other two from the cliff top.

Climbing the hill made him think of Tammy and her promise to be at the solstice party, at first with anger and then with hope. She would be there after all, and perhaps the other girl had been the black guy's girlfriend and not Tammy. In any case she would be there, and she would probably be drunk, even high, so he had to have a fair chance of getting her out of her pants.

Reaching the top of the hill, he found the blonde girl seated on the grass, sketching the great barrow that occupied the summit. He ignored her, walking on to the cliff edge and into the concealment of a thick stand of broom and gorse. When certain he could no longer be seen, he dropped low, working back until he could see her. She was as before, her sketchpad resting on her knees, her full concentration on her drawing. Her position left a fair bit of leg showing, even some thigh, and he watched for a while, hoping a shift in pose would provide a flash of her panties. Her age he estimated at twenty-two or twenty-three, her figure in the well-worth-a-peep category, her face better still, delicate and fine, innocent and sweet. Unfortunately, she showed no inclination to do anything other than sketch, nor to move into a more revealing position, and presently he grew bored.

Moving to the cliff edge, he peered cautiously down. Ness Beach was below, stretching from the river mouth to below him in a gentle curve of red sand. At the far end, a family were using the sheltered bay created by Ness Head, while a lone and elderly man sat on a rock, smoking a pipe. The man he had seen before, always in the same place, and wondered if he wasn't up to the same thing. The two girls were nowhere in sight, which meant they had gone further, a fact that gave him a thrill of expectation.

Making his way to the headland, he peered down, careful not to risk making his head a silhouette against the sky. Sure enough, they were there, clambering up the steep side of a rock ledge. They reached the top and glanced around, evidently checking that they were unobserved. One spoke, and despite the distance and the rustle of the wind Joe caught what he was sure was a mention of privacy. He grinned to himself, imagining their conversation. One, perhaps the brunette, would be wondering if they were safe and expressing her distaste for being watched while she sunbathed. The blonde would reply, agreeing that there was nothing worse than having some dirty little Peeping Tom getting off over the sight of their bodies but pointing out that nobody had followed them and that the old man would be unable to manage the scramble needed to reach their hideaway. Neither would think to look up, both imagining their precious bodies safe from lecherous male attention.

The blonde bent, pulling a large beach towel from a bag and spreading it on the rock. Her companion followed suit, and to Joe's utter delight they began to undress. He watched, the binoculars shaking in one hand, the other squeezing his rapidly stiffening cock through his trousers. The blonde peeled up her top, revealing what he took to be a pink bra until he realised in disappointment that it was a bikini top. Her jeans followed, pushed down over a neat little bottom, again clad in bright-pink material.

The brunette had been unbuttoning her blouse, but now shrugged it off, revealing a neat white bra over pert breasts. She reached back, and his heartbeat rose as she put her fingers to the catch, tugged and the bra fell away, leaving her breasts bare and pink to the sun, two round little handfuls of well-formed girl meat. Joe steadied his binoculars, watching as she put her hands to her jeans, unzipped, pushed and down they came, taking her panties with them in a tangle of pale-blue cotton. Kicking them from her feet along with her shoes, she stood nude, only to pull a pair of bikini pants from her bag and slip them on.

Despite a flush of disappointment he kept watching, hoping they might grow bolder. Both lay on their towels, face down, the blonde removing her bikini as if she was on a crowded beach, slipped off under her front so that even her friend would see nothing, never mind him. Neither troubled to oil, again to his disappointment, and when the brunette pulled a pink covered book from her bag and began to read this sharpened to frustration.

Joe reasoned that they were unlikely to do anything interesting, at least not for some time, and decided to take another peak at the intellectual-looking blonde by the barrow. He moved back from the cliff top, keeping low among the bushes, then stopping abruptly at a sound. A movement caught his eye, white, presumably the girl's dress, now among the bushes. Slipping into the concealment of a thick, low clump of gorse, he peered through the spiky stems.

She was there, no more than twenty yards away and looking in the opposite direction. There was something in her hand, a piece of white tissue, moulded nervously in her fingers as she looked around herself. She was biting her lip and making little treading motions with her feet, and Joe found his grin spreading wide.

As if suddenly reaching a decision, she ducked down, tugging her dress up over shapely legs and a teardrop-shaped bottom encased in white cotton panties. He swallowed, his hand going to his crotch as she braced her feet and stuck it out, the twin cheeks of her rear stretching out her panties, her pussy a sweet bulge between her thighs. She reached back, taking the waistband of her panties and pushing, exposing her bottom, the full cheeks flared, her bumhole a tiny dimple of pink flesh, her pussy lips pouting out towards him in a puff of golden hair. Taking a grip on her panty crotch, she tugged them forward, clear of her sex, and let go.

Joe watched, his cock stiff, his mouth wide. Pale yellow pee gushed from her sex, a thick stream, so strong he could hear the pattering sound as it splashed on the ground. She was clearly embarrassed by what she was doing, glancing nervously around as her pee ran from her pussy, her dress and panties clutched tight in her hands. This made the sight all the better for Joe, as did the rude way her anal area had relaxed and pouted back to let the urine flow freely.

There was plenty, gushing out until Joe thought he would come, only to die to a trickle and stop, leaving the last few drips hanging from her thick pussy hair. She wiggled, shaking off the drops and making her lovely bottom quiver in a delightful way, then dabbed the tissue quickly to herself. Joe shook his head, thoroughly pleased with himself. He had to come, and began to tug at himself through his trousers, hoping to make it before she fully covered herself and indifferent to the mess.

He was frantic, expecting a quick covering of her bum and a hasty retreat. Instead she stayed still, squatting with her bottom stuck out, apparently listening. He kept wanking, sure the lovely view in front of him could last only so long. Her face was side on for a moment, and he saw that she was biting her lip and that her eyes were full of nervous excitement. Moving quickly, she shuffled forward, away from her pee pool, and knelt. With his mouth hanging wide, he watched as her hand found her pussy. Bare bottom stuck out, bumhole showing, fingers working in the wet flesh of her pussy, she began to masturbate.

Joe watched enthralled, wishing he had the guts to just rush forward and stuff his straining erection up her ready hole. He knew he wouldn't, but quickly unzipped himself and pulled it free, jerking at it as he watched her frig. Her head was back, her pretty hair jumping to her movements. With two sudden motions she jerked her dress up, over her breasts, then off, leaving her in nothing but panties and shoes. Once more she began to masturbate, now frantic, going down on all fours to leave Joe with what he considered the perfect view of a woman, crawling, from the rear, everything showing with her sex on offer and her tits swinging from her chest. She was supporting herself with

86

one hand, frigging with the other. He could hear her breathing, then her moans, and with a long, sharp cry of pleasure she came, only for her ecstasy to break to sobs and then snivels as she collapsed into the grass.

He was still staring, immobile, his eyes fixed to the lips of her sex, where they peeped out between her thighs, his hand sticky with the come that had erupted from his cock at the same moment she had climaxed. He gave no thought to her sudden change from ecstasy to misery, nor to why she had felt the need to masturbate among the bushes, reflecting only that the whole event bore out his conviction that the innocent-looking ones were often the most dirty.

Lily dressed hurriedly, burning with shame and embarrassment for what she had done. Yet it had been impossible not to, despite her best efforts. She had been made to suck off a policeman, a man she had never met before, and she had taken his cock in her mouth and let him come over her face. Worse still, Ed had stripped her and fucked her in front of him, then added his own sperm to the mess. As the final indignity, she had come in front of them, actually masturbated herself to orgasm in front of two men who had deliberately degraded her.

It was impossible to get out of her mind, and despite her best efforts to work she had found herself replaying the scene over and over, being groped, being told she had to suck, taking the stranger's cock in her mouth, tasting it, feeling it swell, having her jeans and pants taken down, having her top pulled up, being entered by Ed. All of it was too much for her, even being felt up, never mind taking two men's come in her face.

She had done her best to push the awful thoughts away and to deny that it excited her, going up to sketch and photograph the Wythman barrow. A letter had arrived that morning, from the university, stating that a team from Exeter would be reopening the barrow immediately after the annual New Age festival. She was also invited to join the team, news that had thrilled her enough to push her terrible erotic thoughts away, at least for a while. She had determined to make a detailed record of the event, sure that turning her mind to her work would push away the horrid, ecstatic memory.

It had, briefly, only to steal up on her after she had found herself desperate to pee. The shame and worry of taking down her knickers in the open had brought it all back and she had given in, cursing her own weakness even as she began to masturbate. She had thought of being made to do it by Ed, of his ordering her to show her bottom and pee while the horrid Jeff Perkins watched. She knew that he'd have made her strip, at least to her knickers, and with that thought had peeled her dress off, imagining them watching, gloating over her nudity and her burning red cheeks, readying their cocks for her body as she performed the most intimate of acts in full view.

She had sunk to the ground with the thought of being taken fore and aft, Ed in her vagina, Jeff in her mouth, both laughing over her degradation as they used her, pumping into her body, their cocks erupting inside her. She had come at that, imagining the policeman's sperm erupting in her face and remembering how it had felt for real, then collapsing in a sobbing heap on the ground, feeling thoroughly abused even though she had come under her own fingers with no coercion whatever.

Now, decent once more, with her body shivering over the memory of her own behaviour, she walked back to where she had left her bag. Nobody had seen her, she was certain, yet a dirty little voice in the back of her head was wishing they had, and taken full advantage of her, taking her from behind as she knelt in a puddle of her own pee.

With her mouth set in an angry frown she went back to her sketching, yet once more found it impossible to rid her mind of thoughts of Ed, albeit no longer sexual. At a pure, intellectual level she was desperate to be rid of him. She hated his right-wing views, his self-righteous morality, preaching supposedly Christian morals while happily abusing her. He saw her as his property, which she hated, yet which she found hard to deny. He was compelling, as hard, stern men had always been to her. She had lost her virginity to one of the worst bullies at her school, on her back in a pile of mouldering grass cuttings behind the sports pavilion. He had been as unpleasant as Ed, yet their relationship had lasted until she went to university. It had been much the same there, with one boyfriend from the town and another from the rugby club, both of whom had treated her as their private sex toy. Now it was Ed, and she felt a horrible certainty that she would be unable to turn him away.

With her main sketch finished and annotated, she climbed the barrow, looking out to sea. The sun was bright, the last clouds low on the eastern horizon. St David's Island appeared close, almost as if she could step on to it. The tide had turned and was beginning to run, the powerful currents tearing the water to white foam among the jumble of stacks to the west of the main island. Watching, she felt an urge to be there, her body whirled and washed in the cool, pure water, pulled away from Ed by an elemental force far beyond his coarse, bullying power. She turned with a sigh, feeling helpless and weak. Sitting among the grass, she began to sketch the scene.

The quiet and beauty of the place began to work on her, Ed retreating to an irritating niggle at the back of her mind. After a while a spotty-faced youth who had passed her earlier walked back the way he had come, not even turning a glance in her direction. For a while she managed a genuine feeling of peace, only to be disturbed again as a head appeared above the edge of the barrow.

Lily immediately recognised Nich, his striking red hair and intense expression unmistakable. She smiled, pleased to have somebody who shared her interest in the barrow, albeit from a strange, occult perspective. He was also the antithesis of Ed in many ways, which made the idea of associating immensely appealing.

'I'm sorry to disturb you,' he greeted her. 'You are drawing the barrow?'

'The view,' Lily answered, 'and the barrow. It's to be opened, so I thought I'd make a record . . .'

'Opened?' Nich demanded. 'Are you sure?'

'Absolutely,' Lily answered. 'A letter came this morning from my university. A team from Exeter's coming over.'

'Is this for public viewing?'

'No, it's a research dig, but I have permission to help.'

'Might I be there?' Nich went on urgently. 'I've made a great deal of research into the matter – possibly I could be of some help.'

'I can certainly speak to Professor Cobb,' Lily said. 'I can see no reason for him to refuse, not if you have a specific interest.'

'I do,' he assured her, 'I do. It's a fascinating site, unique.'

'There's a similar barrow in Brittany.'

'Empty, a shell set up for tourists, abandoned for thousands of years. When is this to happen?'

'The day after this party. The council wouldn't grant permission beforehand. You see, the Reverend Wilmot's dig left a shored-up passage running through the centre. They didn't want any of these New Age types getting in. Sorry, I didn't mean . . .'

'No, no, a sensible choice. I'm not offended. Have you read Wilmot's notes? They're in the local museum.'

'Yes, of course. Really he was just an amateur. I think he was more interested in artefacts than pure research.'

'As one would expect. Ha! Imagine his outrage if someone had desecrated his church!'

'Well it's not really the same . . .'

'Why not? Both are temples, and if he feels that the shrine of his god should be free from desecration, then he should extend the same courtesy to Sigodin-Yth.'

'Sigodin-Yth?'

'The Wythman deity. You may have read the name in the copy of Laverack your boyfriend stole from me. On which subject, if it is in his house, he has clearly not registered it as an official customs seizure. Would it be at all possible that I might have it back?'

'Well I'm not sure . . .'

'Lily – I may call you Lily? Whatever our differences of view, as one serious student to another, I beg you to return it. It is rare, irreplaceable even.'

'Yes, but Ed –'

'Officer Gardner, I suspect, took it from motives of simple malice. He has probably forgotten its existence.'

'Well, yes, I'm sure you're right . . .'

'You will return it, then? I would be immensely grateful.'

'I suppose so.'

'Thank you, Lily, thank you. Perhaps now, if we have time to drop in at his house before his work finishes?'

Five

Violet frowned as she looked around her. The street was crowded, men pouring from the gates of the docks across the road, most in small groups or pairs, a few single. The masts of the two china-clay ships in port could be seen, rising above the dockside structures. Greyish white dust covered the ground, the roofs, those few trees she could see. It was a scene very different from the part of Tawmouth she knew, which was bright and merry, very much for the tourist trade. Knowing that the division had existed since Tawmouth became a popular spa town nearly two hundred years before did nothing to reduce the contrast, leaving her feeling out of place but also with a sense of adventure.

She and Yasmin had begun their search by visiting Kieran Sullivan, the tattooist on the pier, a young man they knew, very much into pagan symbolism and Celtic art. He had known of no other tattooist in Tawmouth, but had pointed out that if some old guy operated in the dock area there was no reason he should have. They had walked to the docks, a matter of no more than a half-mile but completely unfamiliar territory.

Plenty of people were looking at them and she was beginning to wish that she had worn a longer skirt and rather less jewellery, while she was sure her brilliant purple hair stood out like a beacon. Yasmin seemed unconcerned and had stopped a docker to ask about the existence of tattoo parlours. Violet waited, watching as the man shrugged and then pointed along the road. Yasmin thanked him and walked back.

'He says he's not sure but he thinks there's a bloke somewhere called Exhibition Road who does it part-time. Could be our man.'

'Could be,' Violet agreed.

'Tammy's not more than twenty, she looks less,' Yasmin went on. 'She can't have been much more than a kid when it was done, it's so faded.'

'So she goes to some dodgy backstreet place,' Violet answered. 'I had my Ianthe done in a place in Walthamstow, no questions asked. I was fifteen.'

'I didn't get any until I was eighteen, the Celtic bands on my arms. That was the week after I left home.'

'Neat. So where's this Exhibition Road?'

'This way.'

They set off, walking behind the docks until the end, where the quay ended to leave them beside the mud flats of the estuary. A terrace of once smart Victorian villas faced the water, with smaller roads leading between them up the hill. The third proved to be Exhibition Road, a twin line of two-storey houses set behind tiny front gardens, perfectly straight and ending against an iron fence. Walking up it, they gave each house a careful inspection, looking for anything that might advertise the presence of a tattooist. By the end they were looking down over the estuary, with Aldon Hill beyond and the shape of the Wythman clearly visible against the skyline. The fence proved to be the edge of the railway cutting. Violet gave a last glance to either side, expecting disappointment but finding a small printed sign in an upper window of one of the end houses advertising tattoos.

'Here we are,' she announced. 'This has got to be the place.'

Yasmin nodded and they walked to the door, knocked and stood back. For a moment nothing happened, and Violet was stepping back to leave when the door swung open, revealing an elderly man, quite bald, his bright-blue eyes looking quizzically at the two of them.

'Is it you who does the tattoos?' Violet asked.

He nodded, showing no great surprise, and ushered them in. They followed, catching the smell of dust and age as they crossed the threshold. Brown paint and worn, faded carpets reminded Violet of her grandmother's house, but without the ever-present air of respectability.

'What can I do for you?' the old man asked. 'Here, come in, sit down. No sense in rushing.'

'Thank you,' Violet answered, accepting the ancient armchair to which he was gesturing. 'We saw a really neat tattoo, and we were wondering if you had done it?'

'More likely the young fellow on the pier,' he answered. 'I don't do much now, and most of it's pretty traditional: anchors and hearts and so on, not the sort of thing young girls like you would want, I shouldn't imagine.'

'I'm sure it was you,' Yasmin answered. 'My friend said it was done by a retired sailor, living behind the docks.'

'That sounds like me,' he answered. 'I was a navy man in the war, then merchant marine. I've been retired twelve years now. Who's your friend?'

'Tammy, young girl, long black hair.'

'Nobody like that. All mine are dockers or lads from the china-clay works, someone off the ships now and then. No young women.'

'It would have been a while ago, but you'd remember her. She's about my height, very curvy, unusual eyes, dark green.'

'Curvier than you? Well, I'd remember that, but no, sorry. What was the tattoo?'

'An octopus, in green, with red eyes and the arms twisting together. It's really detailed, with the suckers and everything. It's on her bum. Surely you remember?'

'An octopus? On a young girl's bottom? Why, certainly I'd remember. I wish I had, but I'm sorry, it must have been someone else.'

'Who else is there? Say five or six years ago at least.'

'Nobody, not then, not now.'

'Oh, well, never mind. What about it, Violet? Up for it?'

'I'm not sure. My Ianthe really hurt.'

'Where is it?' he asked.

'On my tummy.'

'The stomach's one of the worst. The face is worst of all, and anywhere over bone. A bottom shouldn't be bad, if that's where you want it.'

'You don't mind?'

'A man of my age, putting a tattoo on a pretty girl like you? On your bottom? No, I don't mind.'

'OK, then, but I want mine purple, as near my hair colour as you can get, and the eyes yellow.'

'No time like the present. I work upstairs.'

Violet rose, feeling slightly uneasy about showing her bum to the old man but telling herself not to be silly. Yasmin was smiling and clearly found the idea amusing. Obviously he was going to get a kick out of doing it, but he didn't seem creepy the way some older men did, while she knew that backing out would leave her feeling ineffectual.

'I've not ever done an octopus,' the man was saying, 'so you'll have to draw the fellow. Still, I was reckoned quite an artist, in my time, so I reckon I can do it. What's your name, by the bye? I'm John Pardue, or Jan as we say around here.'

'Violet,' Violet answered. 'Pleased to meet you.'

'Yasmin,' Yasmin added.

'Pretty names,' he answered. 'My granddaughter is a Jasmine, over Newton Abbot way. Now, here we are.'

He had pushed open a door, revealing a studio, cluttered with furniture, equipment and paper, most of which showed tattoo designs. Violet could smell the ink, her trepidation growing as she remembered the pain of her belly tattoo.

'Most of mine just sit in the chair,' Jan was saying. 'I suppose you'd better go on the bed. Now don't worry, you've no cause to over an old boy like me. Now, I need that drawing.'

Violet sat on the bed, watching as he passed Yasmin paper, a pen and a well-worn set of children's colours. She began to draw, outlining the bulbous mass of the octopus and the writing tentacles, tucked together in much the same intertwined pattern as the Celtic scrollwork on her arms.

'Are you sure the pattern was like that?' she asked.

'Certain,' Yasmin answered. 'It was one of the things I noticed. I thought Kieran might have done it.'

She finished, handing the paper to Jan, who quickly sketched out a more professional version and handed it over for approval. Violet took one look and knew she had to have it. Nich would be fascinated, she was sure, and also think it highly appropriate after she had dreamed of the god. She nodded, smiling, as she passed the paper back to Jan.

'Best get ready, then,' he said as he turned to his equipment. 'Where on your behind do you want it?'

'Left cheek,' Yasmin answered. 'Right on the chubby bit.'

'Tricky,' he answered. 'Hard to get at. You'll have to excuse me, miss, don't think I'm trying to touch you up or anything.'

'I shan't,' Violet promised, turning to hide an instinctive blush, but more from Yasmin than from Jan.

She twisted, laying herself out on the bed, face down. Reaching back, she twitched up her skirt, her face flushing hot despite herself as she showed her tight purple panties to the old man. Taking them by the edge, she pulled the material into the cleft of her bottom, baring one cheek.

'Pants down, if you wouldn't mind,' Jan said. 'Wouldn't do to have them slip and hit the needle.'

'No, you're right,' Violet admitted.

Raising her tummy, she reached to push her panties down, well clear of her bum. With the whole of her bottom bare her sense of exposure increased sharply, made worse by the certainty that a puff of pussy hair and a hint of her sex lips would be showing from the rear between her slim thighs. He would also be able to smell her pussy, and she found herself hoping he had the decency to keep his fingers to himself as she laid her head on her hands and tried to relax. Not that he could exactly avoid touching her anyway.

'That's the way, don't tense up or he'll spoil,' Jan remarked.

He began his work, preparing her bottom, rubbing the tuck of her cheek with the cloth, an action that made the soft flesh move and that she felt was certain to give him an accidental peep of her bottom hole. She sighed, chagrined at exposing herself so intimately to an old man, but determined to go through with it. The buzz of the needle started and she braced, gritting her teeth but forcing herself to keep her bottom relaxed. His hand touched her cheek, firm but gentle, then came the sudden stab of the needle.

Violet winced, her mouth coming open at the sudden sting, a sensation she remembered from before and which she had always compared to catching herself on barbed wire when playing as a child. Gritting her teeth in an effort to lessen the pain, she struggled not to pull away, allowing him to draw a slow curve over the skin of her bottom. It stopped suddenly, leaving her feeling dizzy and a little sick, then started again and Jan began to hum softly to himself as he worked. The pain was as before, making her wonder how anybody could ever put up with it for the sake of vanity, until she realised that it had begun to dull and knew that her endorphins had started to run.

The dizziness lasted, changing to a hazy feeling as the outline of the octopus was slowly tattooed on to her naked bumcheek. She began to relax, the embarrassment of having her panties down in front of him fading to be replaced by a sense of amusement, much like the odd occasions she had flashed her chest to people quite incapable of doing anything about it. Her thoughts turned to Nich, of how pleased he would be and how good it would feel to have sex with him, kneeling so that he could admire her tattoo while he was in her.

She felt every detail, each arm, each sucker, yet it finished long before she had expected it to, leaving her with an odd sense of disappointment. Looking back, she found Jan changing the needle, Yasmin admiring her bottom.

'Purple, you say?' Jan queried. 'With yellow eyes?'

'Yes.'

'Maybe some highlights?'

'Go for it.'

Once more she settled her chin on her hands, wincing again when the bar of needles first bit into her flesh, but quickly coming to terms with it. Without doubt the filling in was less painful than the outline, really no more than a rough tickling, like having fingernails drawn hard over her skin. Indeed, what with the feel of lying there with her panties down and the flow of her endorphins, it was becoming pleasantly naughty. With the pain dulled, the buzz of the tattooing tool was also beginning to get to her, the vibrations reaching her pussy. With a touch of embarrassment she wondered if her excitement showed, and was suddenly thankful for the presence of Yasmin.

She imagined the old boy realising, sneakily preparing his cock and then mounting her unexpectedly, pushing his penis into her from behind, his belly slapping on her bottom as he thrust into her, fucking her, taking quick advantage of her ready hole. The thought sent a shiver through her. With her bare bum in his hands he would surely be excited, and it would be so easy. Tell her to lie still while he made a needle change, cock out, up on the bed, on top of her, her legs pushed apart and he would be in, up the wet tube of her pussy as she squeaked in alarm and surprise but took it, letting the poor old boy have his fun with her in payment for her tatt. She would masturbate afterwards – she'd have to – right in front of him and Yasmin, legs apart, pussy wide, rubbing herself in an open display of pleasure. He would get hard again, despite his age, and roll her legs up, holding her by the ankles and fucking her on her back, in and out as she felt her breasts . . .

Violet came, her dirty thoughts mixing with the buzz of the tattooing tool to bring her to an orgasm quickly stifled into the bed. Jan gave a knowing chuckle and she found herself blushing hot, but he said nothing. A pause came as he switched to the yellow ink, after which it was quickly over. Rising from the bed, she thanked him, still blushing in embarrassment. He casually began to put his things away, giving no sign that he had noticed or been affected. Feeling oddly resentful, Violet went to her bag.

'How much is that, then?' she asked, wondering if he was too old to care or even if he preferred men.

'Twenty,' he answered, 'unless you two are the sort who'd like to give a lonely old man a thrill.'

Violet felt shock, a stab of anger at the dirty suggestion, only to fight it down. The reaction came from her upbringing, she knew, and suddenly she found herself smiling. So he was not so immune to her charms after all. She glanced at Yasmin, who made a face and shrugged.

'You can look,' she said quickly. 'Come on, Yasmin, you too.'

She went to the bed, her heart fluttering with a lovely naughty feeling as she bent, flicked up her skirt and pushed her knickers down, showing her bare bottom and her tattoo. Yasmin shook her head in mock disapproval, but with a quick motion pulled her top up, spilling two large, dark breasts out of her bra. Jan smiled, sat down on a chair and quite calmly took out his cock.

It was quick, his eyes feasting on the two half-naked girls as his hand jerked at his penis. Given his age, Violet expected him to take his time, but it seemed only a moment before he groaned, thanked them and walked from the room, still holding his cock. Five minutes later they were leaving the house, giggling over what they had done. Still feeling cheeky, Violet pulled her skirt up and adjusted her knickers, giving Yasmin a view of her tattoo in full sunlight.

'Neat,' Yasmin said. 'Nich'll love it. So, do you reckon Jan was the guy who gave Tammy hers?'

'Must be,' Violet answered. 'He obviously doesn't remember, either that or he's hiding something. Either way, it doesn't tell us much.'

'With luck we can find her before the party,' Yasmin went on. 'She said she often goes on the beach.'

'We'll try tomorrow. I feel good for that, you know, the tattoo, not posing for him, although that was all right. I'm not scared of dreaming again any more either. In fact, let's get Nich and suggest we sleep on the Wythman. That way I'm sure to dream again.'

'But it was a nightmare – you said you could barely handle it.'

'It was, until I called on Sigodin-Yth. After that it was scary. Imagine it, I was helpless, desperate, about to be raped and there was nothing I could do about it. He came and they ran, and all the fear and anguish I felt was transferred to them. They ran, they couldn't even look at him.'

'Did you see him?'

'No, I woke up, but I will, I'm sure I will. Perhaps I just need to be closer.'

Lily found herself unable to still the trembling of her fingers as she sipped her coffee. She had parted with Nich's paper, driven both by his insistence and a sense that it really was the just thing to do. Yet there was no doubt at all that Ed would be angry if he found out. Fortunately, he had shown no interest in it whatever and hopefully would accept her excuse that she had thrown it away if the question ever arose.

He had told her to wait for him at his house, which she had obeyed, as always. Now, with the clock moving slowly towards the time he came off duty, she found her sense of trepidation growing, and not only from the possible consequences of his finding out about the paper. After the previous night it was entirely possible that he would go drinking with his friends after work, and if he did it seemed entirely possible that he would bring back one or more, and in turn that he was quite capable of making her perform for them.

Worse still, she knew she would do it. Whether it was striptease, or cocksucking, even being sent to bed to let them have her one after another, she knew she would be unable to resist. She also knew she would finish by coming under her own fingers, but the knowledge only added to her shame and fear. In response she had sat herself by the front-room window, sipping coffee and watching the road, dreading what she might see and praying for it at the same time.

When Ed finally came into view he was alone. Relief flooded through her, tempered by disappointment, which in turn brought shame for her own dirty feelings. He was in his uniform, stern and smart despite having his jacket thrown casually over his shoulder, a look she found impossible not to appreciate. As he reached the gate she rose to greet him at the door.

'Hi, babe,' he greeted her, kissing her and slapping her bottom as he came in. 'What have you got for your man, then?'

'Got?' Lily asked.

'Food,' he went on, 'grub, tucker. Don't tell me my tea's not done.'

'Well, no,' Lily managed. 'Sorry, I didn't know you wanted any. I thought we'd be going out.'

'Hey, don't get greedy on me, babe. I'm not the sort of guy you can piss around. Do that again and you get a slap. For now I'll forgive you, seeing as I'm in a good mood, just so long as you get on with it right now. Get us a beer.'

Despite a determination to tell him what he could do with his food, Lily found herself stammering out an apology and scampering for the fridge. He went into the front room, settling himself into an armchair as she hurried in with the beer. In the kitchen she found frozen steaks, peas and instant mash, which she hastily began to put together. As she did so Ed talked, gloating over how he had stopped a group of kids coming off the French ferry and found both cannabis and ecstasy. The incident had put him in a good mood, to her relief, although his threat to hit her had left her feeling more vulnerable than ever.

'What have you been up to then, babe?' he called. 'Been working like a good girl or wanking over the fun we had with Jeff like the dirty bitch you are?'

'I've been up to the Wythman,' she answered, ignoring his crude comment. 'The barrow on Aldon Hill —'

'Not in that dress, I hope,' he interrupted.

'Yes, why?'

'Because your tits show through it, you silly cow. Christ, do you want to go flashing to half the town?'

'Sorry, Ed, I didn't think. Anyway, Professor Cobb's team from Exeter are going to open it and I've been invited to join them. It's great.'

'Great for you, digging around in some mouldy old hole,' he answered, 'and I'm paying for it, that's what gets me. Great, I call it, all the tax I pay and what does it get spent on? Some stuck-up old git digging a load of old ruins. Nice work if you can get it, eh?'

'It's very important work,' Lily answered in defence.

'Sure,' Ed answered, laughing, 'very important, digging a hole so we can learn what sort of dump our ancestors lived in. Yeah, I can see that's going to make a big difference. Now my work, that's important, stopping the country getting flooded with drugs and porn, and Jeff's work, that's important. You don't know you're born.'

Lily made no response, unable to agree and sure that anything she would say otherwise would just trigger one of his right-wing lectures. He seemed to take her silence as an admission of defeat and she went back to cooking, all the while wishing she had the courage to throw the lot in his face and run for the door. She laid the table as the food cooked, only for him to demand it on a tray while he watched the television, then to criticise her for undercooking the steak. Both times she apologised, then cleared and washed up, returning to find him slumped in his chair, drinking his third beer.

'Be a doll and nip upstairs,' he ordered as she was about to sit down. 'You'll find a pile of mags by the window. At the bottom there's some weird shit showing a girl with an octopus. Get it, would you? I promised Jeff a look and I'll forget if I don't stick it by the door now.'

Lily's stomach had wound itself into a tight knot at his words, and for a moment she considered going upstairs and pretending she couldn't find it, yet she knew such an action would only make it worse in the end. The only way out was to claim she had thrown it away.

'I . . . I'm afraid I threw it away,' she stammered. 'I was tidying up.'

He turned, slowly, looking her in the face, his expression stern.

'Look,' he said, 'I don't ask much in a woman, but one thing I do ask is respect, and respect means not going through my stuff, right?'

'I'm sorry, Ed,' Lily managed. 'I only –'

'You only nothing,' he cut in, 'and you will be sorry if you don't get your act together. Now get it out and brush it off.'

'It . . . it's not here. I threw it out.'

'Why?'

'It's a horrid thing, I didn't like it. I couldn't stand it in the house.'

'It's mine, you stupid bitch, not yours, mine.'

'I'm sorry, Ed.'

'Like I said, you will be. Now fetch another beer while I decide what to do with you.'

Lily obeyed, shivering inside as she wondered what was going to happen. Ed's anger was false, she was sure of it, or he would simply have hit her. Besides which, after three beers he was bound to be thinking of bed, and doubtless he was going to use the magazine as an excuse to punish her in some way. As she walked back to him she passed the front door and hesitated. All that was needed was to take the handle, twist and run. She would be safe from whatever degradation he was planning, safe from all the humiliation he had inflicted on her, yet she found herself walking past, into the living room, where he took the beer can from her hand without a word.

She sat, watching him drink beer and wondering why she was so easily put in the thrall of domineering men. It made no sense, at least no logical sense, yet her sex already felt warm and sensitive and for all her reluctance to admit it the answer was obvious. Ed took his time, apparently watching the television, although she was sure he was thinking of what he could do to get the most out of her. Finally he swallowed the last of his beer and turned to her.

'Right,' he drawled, 'this is what you get, and you'll do as you're told or you're out. No buts, no "please, Ed", no "sorry, Ed" – just do as you're told or get out my house. I'm going to fuck your sweet little arse.'

Lily nodded, the knot in her stomach tightening to a cold, hard ball.

'Upstairs first,' he went on, 'and grease your hole. There's some cream stuff in the medicine cupboard that'll do. Shower first, then into your nightie and knickers – I like that look.'

Lily ran from the room, scared and trembling, her bottom cheeks clutching of their own accord. She was to be sodomised, something she not only felt was unspeakably dirty, but which she was sure would be painful. Yet Ed had told her it was going to happen, and that it would happen as a punishment for her, and she knew he was right. In the bedroom she found herself fumbling with her clothes, her eyes already heavy with unshed tears as she thought of having a cock pushed up her virgin bottom hole – Ed's cock, the man who made her feel so protected, so wanted and so utterly used.

Her dress came off quickly, her panties following, kicked away with her shoes to leave her nude. She folded them carefully and took her nightie from her overnight bag, an old-fashioned one, knee-length cotton with thick lace at the hem, also a fresh pair of panties. These she laid out on the bed before skipping into the bathroom and turning on Ed's shower. The water quickly ran hot, refreshing her but doing nothing to ease her rising sense of panic. She was aroused, too, and knew it, but that didn't stop her wanting to burst from the house and just run and run, naked or not.

Stepping from the shower, she wrapped herself in a towel and opened the bathroom cabinet. There were several tubes and pots, each of which she looked at, despite the horror of having to select a cream for the purpose of greasing her anal ring for sodomy. Choosing something as neutral as possible, she unscrewed the lid and put her finger into it, drawing out a thick spiral of cool white cream. Quickly she replaced the pot, closed her eyes tight and stuck out her bottom, her face squeezing into a look of misery and disgust as she delved between her bottom cheeks, dabbed her anus and briefly allowed her finger to slip inside.

It felt good, there was no denying it. With a little despairing groan she allowed her finger to slide deeper, into the hot cavity of her rectum, all the while imagining how Ed's cock was going to feel in a hole that felt stretched with just her finger in it. Telling herself that it was to make the experience less painful, she began to work her finger in and out, making her anus loose and wet until a second finger fitted, then a third, leaving the ring stretched taut around them. Her bottom was pushed well out, her mouth wide, her eyes tight shut, her mind full of the utter degradation that sodomy represented. 'Buggered' was a commoner word, used to describe something spoiled by misuse, made useless, just like a girl who'd had a cock up her bottom . . .

'Well, well,' Ed's voice cut in, 'you are a filthy little tart, aren't you, Lily? I said grease your arse, not fist it. Now come on, in your nightie and on the bed.'

Lily pulled her fingers out, blushing furiously. She washed her hands with quick, nervous motions, then fled the bathroom, reaching the bedroom to the sound of Ed turning on the shower. She pulled on her nightie, also her panties, despite the certainty that they would soon be coming down again. Ed liked exposing her, she knew, and liked her half-dressed during sex, which she in turn found more humiliating than total nudity. A glance in his mirror showed her as a demure young woman, neat blonde hair, breasts and hips no more than hinted at beneath her long nightie, very far indeed from the sort of slatternly image she would have imagined for a girl about to be sodomised. Red would have been better, suspenders, crotchless panties and peephole bra; dirty, lewd clothes for a dirty, lewd act.

Feeling frightened yet resigned to her fate, she lay down on the bed, bottom up, feeling the sticky sensation of the cream between her cheeks as she moved. In the bathroom Ed was whistling, then the noise of the shower stopped. She listened as he went into the spare room, sick with expectancy and wondering what he was doing. Something opened, then slammed, and he came in, naked, holding the skipping rope he had used to tie her to the bed before.

'Not tied up too!' she begged. 'I'll be willing, I promise!'

'I know,' he answered, 'but I like you tied. That way I cut out your dirty little habits. You come when I'm in you, unless I say otherwise.'

She held out her wrists in resignation, crossing them as he had ordered the previous time. He made quick work of her, lashing her wrists and tying the rope off on the bedstead.

'Arse high,' he ordered, 'like before.'

Lily obeyed, coming up on to her knees to leave her bottom the highest part of her body, her knees open and her cheeks spread beneath the taut white cotton of her panties.

'Nice,' Ed drawled, 'now let's have it all out.'

She shut her eyes as he crawled on to the bed behind her. His hands went to her nightie, lifting it high over her bottom and up on to her back, pushed to the level of her neck to leave her breasts swinging bare against the bed cover. She braced herself for her panties to be taken down, only to feel his body against hers, his crotch pressed to her bottom. He leaned forward, his bare cock pressing between her buttocks as he took a breast in each hand and began to rub himself against the seat of her panties, enjoying her body without the least concern for her dignity. She moaned at the feeling, tugging at her bonds to reassure herself that she really was helpless, that what was about to happen to her was out of her hands, no longer her choice and no longer her fault.

'You do have a great arse, babe,' he said as he finally drew back. 'Not bad little titties, either, though if you're going to be with me you're going to need some silicon. I'm going to love fucking your arse anyway, but it would be great to have a big, firm pair to feel while I'm up you.'

Lily answered with a sob.

'Let's get it stripped, then,' Ed drawled. 'Here we go, down they come.'

He had taken hold of her panties and now peeled them slowly off her bottom, down to her thighs, past her knees and off, to her surprise, until he once more leaned forward and she found them balled in his hand, all too obviously offered for her mouth.

'Pop them in, babe,' he instructed. 'We can't have you disturbing the neighbours with your squealing, can we now?'

Lily gaped wide, knowing better than to try to refuse. Her panties were pushed into her mouth, the dry cotton irritating her, the taste of her own sex strong in her head. She began to chew, wetting them in an effort to reduce her discomfort.

'That's the way to fuck a girl's arse,' Ed was saying as he drew back. 'Tie her up and gag her with her own panties. That way she can't struggle or squeal when it goes up. Fuck, that arse of yours has got me randy.'

Lily looked back to find him tugging at a nearly hard cock, the fat purple head already fully out of the prepuce. It was thick, and the idea that it was about to be pushed past her anus and up her rectum gave her a fresh wave of panic, making her tug against her bonds, in a futile and half-hearted effort at escape. He gave a chuckle and began to wank faster, until his cock was a rigid bar of flesh, the head glossy with pressure. He moved forward and the awful sight of his ready erection disappeared behind her leg, only to prod against her thigh. She shut her eyes, burying her face in the pillow, only for his cock to touch her vagina and slip inside with embarrassing ease.

'Soaking as ever, that's my Lily,' he said. 'Oh, but you're a good fuck – maybe I should spare your little arsehole after all.'

Lily nodded frantically. Ed responded with a derisive laugh.

'Not so easy, babe,' he said. 'You make me laugh, you college girls. You think you're so fucking clever and you fall for a simple one like that. No, babe, it's going up your arse, count on it, but not until I've had a good fuck at your tight little cunt hole.'

107

He took her hips and began to move inside her, slowly, then faster, until she had begun to pant through her nose. Again she thought he would come, sparing her the threatened ordeal, only for him to stop suddenly and pull his erection from her body.

'That's it, nice and wet,' he drawled. 'I could have greased you with your own cunt juice. Right babe, there's a knack to this. You've got to push out your arsehole, like when you're having a shit, and push on to me, so you take my cock up yourself.'

Lily said nothing. She could feel the tears starting to well in her eyes, the crudity of his words making it worse. His hands took her buttocks, spreading them. She felt her anus stretched, and for a moment she considered resistance, clamping her ring and hoping he would decide she was too tight and abandon the attempt to sodomise her in favour of her vagina. Yet she was sure he would realise, and be cross with her for disobeying him, so with her face screwed up in utter misery and the first heavy tears rolling from her eyes she let her anus relax. His cock touched her, the head feeling round and soft against her hole, pushing at her, filling her with a sensation of absolute surrender the joy of which was impossible to deny, yet which came mixed with deep self-disgust.

'That's my girl,' Ed groaned, 'do it just like you're trying to get a turd out. Oh, yeah, you're good, oh, yes.'

The head of his cock was in her hole, provoking a twinge of pain which made her cry out. He ignored it, pushing, and with a feeling of overwhelming disgust Lily found herself pushing back as the bulk of his penis was forced slowly into her rectum. It was slow, going in bit by bit, filling her, bloating her back passage out as she gasped and sobbed into the bed. The coverlet beneath her was wet with tears, her teeth were gritted, her hands clutching together in her bonds. Yet her nipples were hard, her sex puffy and swollen, her rising need to come undeniable.

At last it was all in and the pushes stopped as Ed's balls came to rest against the mouth of her empty vagina. Lily could picture how she looked in her head, her anal ring stretched taut around his penis, her virgin anus virgin no more, but stuffed with cock, sodomised, buggered, used in a way nature had never intended. The fat, heavy feel of his turgid cock lying in her rectum made her feel as if she was desperate for the lavatory, adding a fresh obscenity to her degradation. She was sobbing, trying to hate what was being done to her and failing. Ed was right. She was a slut, a tart, a dirty bitch fit for nothing better than satisfying men, enjoying a cock up her bottom despite everything she had been taught.

Ed began to move inside her. She felt her ring pulled out, then in again, faster, and suddenly everything had been pushed from her mind but the feel of having a fat penis moving in her rectum. She began to gasp, panting through her nose as she struggled for air, each push knocking the breath out of her body. His balls were slapping her vulva, his pubic hair touching her clitoris, tickling, and she realised that in no time at all she would come, disgracing herself utterly by having an orgasm while being sodomised.

He was grunting as he buggered her. His hands were on her bottom, his thumbs spreading her cheeks to show her anus. She knew he would be watching his cock go in and out and it was impossible to get the image of her stuffed bottom hole out of her head. Her breathing became frantic. The panties dropped from her mouth, wet with saliva. She began to mewl, to moan, her mouth and eyes wide as her body was slammed over and over into the bed. He was getting faster, grunting more loudly. Her anus was burning, strained and sore around his cock, her rectum full of a delicious, disgusting squashy feeling as he rammed himself into her gut again and again. Hair touched her clit with each push, then the meat of his balls, and her buggery reached an urgent, frantic peak and she was coming, screaming into the bed, her tortured bottom hole clamping over and over on his cock, agony mixed with ecstasy as he came and she found herself milking his sperm into her rectum with her own contractions.

She was crying as she climaxed, physical ecstasy blending with an overwhelming sense of having done something so dirty that she could never forgive herself, never again think of herself as anything other than a wanton little tart, also Ed's property, to do with as he pleased. He had stopped and begun to pull back. It hurt as he withdrew, providing a feeling that added a final obscene touch to the whole dirty experience.

Lily winced as it pulled free. Her anus stung, a hot, sharp feeling, like a cut, blended with a dull, bruising ache, a pain she felt thoroughly suitable for a girl who had allowed herself to be buggered, let alone one who had come while the invading penis was in her rectum. Yet she had done it, and as her protesting sphincter closed slowly it was impossible not to feel a touch of disappointment that the experience was over. Not that she could move, with her hands still lashed to the bedstead. Ed was still firmly in control of her, and all she could do was wait, holding her blatant, vulgar position as the warm sperm trickled from her anus and down over her sex.

'Good,' Ed gasped, 'real good. There's nothing like fucking a nice, fat arse.'

'Could you untie me now, please?' Lily asked.

'Sure,' he answered, 'once I've washed my prick.'

She was left, Ed washing without hurry before returning and at last untying her hands. Her arms were stiff, and as she went to take her turn in the bathroom she found herself forced to hobble by the bruising pain between her bottom cheeks. Ed laughed at the sight, and the thought of how buggery despoiled a woman came back to her. She washed carefully, soothing her burning hole with cream. Back in the bedroom Ed was under the covers, his back towards her.

'That was good,' he sighed as she climbed in beside him. 'No, that was great. You know something? If you're a really lucky girl I might even decide to marry you.'

Lily could find no answer.

Violet watched. Nich, cross-legged and naked except for a black cloak, was chanting, his eyes closed, his face a deep red in the dark flames of the fire that danced and spat between them. Strongly scented smoke curled up, bringing a blend of exotic smells derived from aromatic powders: cloves, cinnamon and others she did not recognise. Around them the night was utterly black, their world contracted to a tiny circle of red-lit grass on the summit of the Wythman. Yasmin sat opposite, as naked as she was herself, her large eyes fixed on Nich.

Reaching out, she took his penis, lifting its flaccid weight from his thigh. He gave no response, continuing to chant gently in what she took to be Gaelic. He had told her what to do, the details of a ritual designed in the hope of mimicking the rites once practised in the same place, ardent and erotic, respectful yet frenzied. As she began to stroke at his cock she felt it move in her hand. Yasmin leaned forward, closing her hand over Violet's, the two of them pulling at him, helping him to erection, each with her other hand deep in the V of her thighs, kneading pussies that, at least for Violet, needed very little help.

The smoke was making her head swirl, and her excitement was rising fast, desire for her vagina to be filled, to come, and afterwards to dream. Nich was growing hard, his cock thick and rubbery in her grip, then firmer, fully erect as Yasmin shifted her grip to take a share of bare penis. He lay back, still chanting, his cock rearing from his body. Violet shared a glance with her friend, then cocked one leg across him, put his erection to her vagina and slid on to it, sighing in bliss as she was filled. She began to ride, bouncing on him with the heat of the fire on her bottom and her breasts in her hands.

It was ecstasy, both physical and spiritual, the feel of his cock and her own body mingling with the more detached pleasure of where she was and why she was doing it. Placing one hand on her pussy, she began to rub, moaning out her pleasure to the sky as it rose, her clitoris bumping under her fingers, her nipples stiff, Nich's erection firm inside her. She had been told to be quick, but it was impossible not to take it slowly, revelling in the feeling of what she was doing as she teased herself towards her peak, stroking, rising to let him slip free and then enter her once more, his shaft held to her hole by Yasmin's hand. At last, when he himself had begun to groan, she gave in, rubbing hard, thinking of her nudity, her body bare to the night sky and full of penis, her bottom marked with the symbol that marked her for the god, for Sigodin-Yth . . .

She came, gasping and panting as the orgasm went through her, making her arch her back and throw her head up as her vagina clamped tight on Nich's erection, contracting over and over until she at last stopped rubbing at herself and slumped down, only to remember what she was supposed to be doing and quickly climb off. Yasmin took her place, and despite her agreement to the act Violet felt a pang of jealously as her friend lowered herself on to his erection. Yasmin turned a look, a happy, friendly grin, which Violet returned, watching her friend's back and bottom as she began to ride Nich. Like her, Yasmin took her time, taking full advantage of the firm erection inside her before letting herself go and coming with a series of urgent grunts.

As Yasmin dismounted, Nich stopped chanting. Violet leaned quickly forward, taking Nich's erection in her mouth. He tasted of girl as well as man, her own and Yasmin's juices thick on his shaft as she sucked. He moaned, a sound of release after holding back so long, and as his hand moved to stroke her hair he came, full in her mouth. She swallowed, doing her best to take it all in, gulping the salty come down as his penis jerked between her lips. Even when he had finished she continued sucking, cleaning his cock and swallowing every last drop of sperm until at last he began to go limp.

'You will dream,' he said softly and pulled himself forward to tip the remaining powder on to the fire.

Violet nodded and lay down beside him as he stretched out on the grass. His arm came out, cradling her head. She let her breath out in a sigh, wondering how she would manage to sleep with so strong a feeling of expectation, only to find herself already drifting as a fresh waft of aromatic smoke blew over her.

* * *

The columns of the cathedral rose above Lily's head, impossibly high, into absolute blackness. Her dress had been turned up, the elaborate pink skirts and petticoats pinned on to her back to leave her bottom bare for all to see. A stamp on one cheek marked her as used, another as the property of Ed Gardner, filling her with shame and helplessness as she walked up the aisle, alone, drawn on and unable to pull away. Line upon line of people stood to either side, faceless people in suits and frocks. She could feel their smug superiority and contempt, hear the little whispers, half amused, half disdainful. Ahead of her Ed stood before an altar, Sergeant Perkins beside him, both in uniform, with them another, a priest, tall in black robes, his face set in an expression of benign condescension. Her anus hurt, and every one of them knew exactly what had been done to her.

She wanted to run, yet her feet drew her on, her will crushed by the overwhelming pressure to conform, to marry Ed, to obey Ed, to cook for him and clean for him, to go down on her knees to him, to worship him. She would wear dresses and housecoats. She would avoid speaking to other men and accept just punishment if she did. She would do as she was told, stripping for him, stripping for his drunken friends, obedient, placid, kept.

The priest's smile grew broader as she reached Ed's side, the smile of a patient father figure, of a dog trainer watching a recalcitrant bitch come to heel. She hung her head, unable to meet his gaze, feeling small and helpless, a tiny thing caught in the wants and needs of bigger, more important people.

Music, of which she had scarcely been aware, now stopped, leaving a heavy silence. The priest raised his chin, preparing to speak, only to stop abruptly at the sound of a high-pitched snigger. Lily looked up to find a girl climbing on to the font, naked and tiny, her face a fine oval with large, mobile features and great green eyes. Despite her size she pulled herself up with ease, sinking into a squat over the basin, the pink of her vagina clearly visible in a puff of black hair. Her imp face twitched into a smile and

113

a stream of gold erupted from her vulva, splashing into the font with a tinkling sound quickly lost beneath the outraged cries of the congregation.

Ed moved, striding forward to catch the girl, only for her to leap away, laughing and spraying him with urine as she went. He cursed, snatching up a heavy candle and advancing on her as she backed, her face twitching with merriment, her strange eyes locked on his. Beyond her, high windows of stained glass stretched up into blackness, blocking her retreat as Ed swung the candlestick in quick, menacing jerks. Lily called out, begging Ed not to hurt the tiny girl, her voice ringing loud in the silence. The girl laughed, flipped backwards, jumping away and flaunting her naked buttocks at Ed in a gesture of defiance and insolence. Ed cursed again and above him the great windows exploded in a shower of coloured glass, a vast tentacle smashing through, uncurling, reaching for Ed . . .

Lily woke, panting for breath, her skin prickling with cold sweat. Ed lay beside her, deeply asleep. She reached out, wanting comfort and the reassurance of his arms, only to pull back, certain that if woken in the early hours of the morning with work the next day he would provide neither.

Violet stood above Aldon cliffs, as before. As before, the sea stretched away, blue and twinkling with reflected sunlight. St David's was visible, and the stacks, with a sailing ship running in towards Tawmouth harbour. She turned, knowing what she expected to see, frightened yet also defiant. Sure enough, the priest and workmen stood as before, around the open mouth of the Wythman, only now staring at her pop-eyed.

Looking down, she saw that she was nude, her Ianthe tattoo clear on her belly, her amethysts sparkling in the sun. Smiling, she turned, bent, displaying her naked bottom, the rear of her sex and the fresh, purple tattoo on the buttock, her octopus. The priest hissed in anger, calling her a whore and a witch. The workmen stiffened, their faces growing stern, yet also lewd. She danced closer and he called out a command, ordering her taken and beaten.

Violet laughed in his face, raising her hands and calling on the god.

The priest's face went puce, the men came forward, the largest already loosening his belt. Behind them the mouth of the barrow remained empty. She stopped, uncertain, calling again, then moving back as eager hands clutched for her. Again she called, trying to run, her muscles sluggish, refusing to allow her escape. Hands caught at her, she tripped, sprawling on the grass. Her hair was taken, her ankles gripped, her legs jerked apart. The belt came down on her buttocks, the priest echoing her scream with a call for harder, more savage blows. She called out again as the belt struck once more, her plea now filled with urgency and fear.

The open barrow was before her, visible through the legs of the man holding her hair. His hand was fumbling at his fly, struggling to release his penis for her rape. Something moved, something green and glistening in the barrow mouth, a great head, two huge eyes staring out, a knot of tentacles writhing from where the mouth should have been . . .

Violet screamed, the priest cried out in terror, the man at her head started to shake her like a doll and she was awake, with Nich's hand on her shoulder and Yasmin bending over her in the dull red light of the fire.

Six

Mr Hobbers let his breath out, wondering for the hundredth time if there wasn't some mistake in his logic. Since meeting Thomazina he had been filled with a fascination that simply would not go away, also regret. The fascination came from the knowledge that somewhere not too far from Tawmouth there existed a farmhouse where young girls were regularly spanked on their bare bottoms. The regret came from his failure to push Thomazina's innocence and sexual acquiescence to the point where she would have ended up across his knee with her magnificent bottom a ball of burning red flesh.

She would have let him, he was sure of it. Her acceptance that girls needed to be punished, her understanding of men's sexual needs, the simple innocence of her character, her respectful attitude to her elders, all would have combined to make her do as she was told. She had been nude in his shop, the most desirable girl he had ever met, not just nude either, but nude with his cock in her hand, even her mouth, yet he had failed to take advantage of the situation to get her across his knee. It was unbearable, and he was determined to discover where she lived, not only to find her again but also her apparently equally delectable little sisters.

He had guessed her age at nineteen or twenty, which made Emily and Jane likely to be perhaps eighteen and sixteen. That meant their names would appear in the records for the early 1980s, and Thomazina's local knowledge had been too good for her to come from anywhere except the Tawmouth district. Also, her innocence and the details she had revealed about life on her farm suggested a very old-fashioned family indeed, not least the fact that the girls accepted bare-bottom spankings as quite normal.

Working on what he knew, he had decided that the farm would almost certainly be on the long spit of high land across the estuary. This was largely agricultural, and mostly National Trust land, with few houses. The only village, Abbotscombe, was tiny, while he could identify only seven working farms. None were Thomazina's, nor those to the north of Tawmouth, leaving him wondering where he could have gone wrong.

Now, standing in All Souls' Church in Abbotscombe, he had finished a conversation with the vicar that had proved no more enlightening than any of his earlier research. The vicar was old, and had held his living since 1967, yet he had never performed any service whatever for three girls named Thomazina, Emily and Jane.

Leaving the church, he turned into the graveyard, reading the stones as he wondered if he should investigate records further afield. Looking at local gravestones always gave him a quiet satisfaction, with so many of the past inhabitants having reached impressive ages. Abbotscombe was no exception, with many octogenarians and some even having reached ninety. Carved in hard slate, the inscriptions read clearly, even those from the eighteenth century, and his thoughts moved away from Thomazina, then came abruptly back as he saw the same name on a stone.

It was not a headstone, but a small slate plaque at the foot of a bigger grave, dedicated to the memory of a Thomazina Keeley, who had died on 21 June 1853, aged seventeen. A lower line revealed that she had disappeared one night without trace and expressed the trust that she was in heaven. His mouth curved up into a sad smile as he read the inscription over, thinking of the distress of the young girl's parents, who were presumably the occupants of the main grave. Sure enough, one of the twin headstones recorded a Mary Keeley, born in 1818, dying in 1894, aged seventy-five. The other recorded a Thomas Keeley, a farmer, born in 1813, dying in 1885, aged seventy-two. Both had lived long lives, if not exceptional ones, certainly less than the woman beneath the next grave, an Emily Draycott, who had made ninety-six, still less another a little way behind, Jane Pardue, who had died in 1943, aged one hundred and four.

He stopped and stepped back, then read both stones again. Emily had been born a Keeley, so had Jane, in 1840. For an instant a cold knot of horror formed in his stomach, only to dissipate as he realised he was being foolish. The answer was clear. The girl was a local, but a fake, probably a thief, using a dead person's name to hide her identity. The explanation went with the coin, which was in far too perfect condition to have spent several hundred years among the mud and stones of Tawmouth harbour. Doubtless she had stolen it from some private collection and added the details of her supposed little sisters and the spankings as a somewhat macabre joke. Probably she had worked it all out in advance, getting wet, asking to undress, everything, just to make sure she got full value for her coin. It made sense, her discovery of his spanking magazine just making her job easier, while her being unable to read had clearly been a pretence.

It had been a trick, yet he had the coin, and would be able to sell it the next time he went to a fair in London, so he felt less than cheated. Then there had been the pleasure of her body, which had meant a lot to him even if she might have considered her actions trivial. Still, the situation raised interesting opportunities, as if he could only find her, then the little brat would be in no position to refuse the spanking she so badly needed and which he so badly needed to give her.

He would research the disappearance of the real Thomazina, and if he could find her he would confront her with his knowledge. Then he would be able to demand that she submit to a thorough spanking without feeling the least guilt for what he was doing. It would, indeed, be justice.

* * *

118

' "Closed Thursday", it says,' Elune stated, giving a petulant kick at the door of Mr Hobbers's shop. 'Why don't you learn to read?'

'I will, one day,' Thomazina answered.

Elune answered with a derisive snort.

'So,' she said, 'no more money and I don't even get to watch you spanked.'

'He ought to be in,' Thomazina insisted, looking up to the windows above the shop. 'He lives up there.'

'He's probably staring at the girls on the beach,' Elune answered, 'or gone flashing, or chasing nymphs in the woods.'

'I don't think he's like that,' Thomazina replied. 'He just likes to spank girls' bottoms.'

'They're all like that,' Elune said firmly, 'or else they'd like to be if only they dared. It's only natural. Men chase, girls run, and if we please, we let them catch us. True, there are girls like you who don't run much, but you'd get caught anyway, with your great wobbling bottom and ridiculously large breasts, so why bother?'

'Do you want to be punished again, Elune? Remember how the sea anemone hurt?'

'You wouldn't dare, not here. I'd pretend to be eleven and say you were my wicked stepmother. They'd arrest you, and lock you up, and feed you porridge crusts with sperm on top . . .'

'Oh, nonsense!'

'That's what they made Aileve do, last time. She told me. A big fat policeman made her suck his penis and he spunked up all over her breakfast, then made her eat it.'

'I know, but that was last time. Besides, I could hold your ear and take you somewhere private. Anyway, we'll have to get you some clothes. Even on you that bikini looks rude. People are starting to stare.'

Elune responded with a pirouette, causing an elderly woman to throw Thomazina a dirty look and make an unheard remark as she passed. While the blue bikini covered Elune's tiny body, they had had to knot it at the sides of the pants and behind her back, creating a look that had passed on the beach but was drawing attention in the town. Taking Elune by the arm, Thomazina pulled her quickly towards a clothing shop and inside. The assistant turned, smiling benignly as they entered.

'Good afternoon,' Thomazina began. 'My sister has had her clothes stolen on the beach. We'd like to buy something.'

'Stolen?' the woman answered. 'Whoever would do a thing like that? Have you told the police?'

'No, no,' Thomazina answered. 'We really don't want a fuss or anything. Have you a frock in her size? And some drawers.'

'Well I really think you ought to report it,' the woman went on. 'I mean, it just won't do, will it? What's your name, dear?'

'Linnet,' Elune answered.

'What a sweet name. Well now, how about this?'

She held up a dress, loose cotton in canary yellow with a lacy fringe. Elune made a face.

'That will do nicely,' Thomazina said quickly, 'and a pack of girls' drawers.'

The assistant moved towards the desk, brushing close to Thomazina and wrinkling her nose. Realising that she probably smelled too strongly of the sea, she decided on buying something for herself. A display of jeans stood at the end of the shop and she made for them, pulling Elune behind her.

'We'll get a pair each,' she said, 'and tops, and new undies for me. I think I'll get blue, they seem popular.'

'Excuse me,' the assistant called, and Thomazina turned to find her making hurriedly for the door.

Before Thomazina could protest, the assistant had returned, along with a policeman.

'Sergeant Perkins,' she said, introducing him to them. 'I really couldn't let such an incident pass. This young girl has had her clothes stolen, Sergeant, on the beach.'

'Oh, yes?' Perkins answered. 'When was this?'

'About an hour ago,' Thomazina answered, 'but we really don't want any fuss. We just came in to buy some new clothes.'

Perkins scratched his chin, his eyes flickering over Thomazina's chest. His lust was obvious, and as she struggled for the best way to escape his attention she wondered if simple bribery was not the answer.

'Did you see anybody?' he asked.

'No,' Thomazina answered, echoed by Elune.

'No idea who it might've been, then?'

'No,' Thomazina repeated.

'And what exactly was stolen?'

'Little pink panties, a tiny crop top and cut-down jeans, nice tight ones that leave most of my bum showing to tease the boys.'

Elune had answered quickly, leaving the assistant staring at her and the sergeant with a puzzled frown.

'She's joking,' Thomazina said quickly and threw Elune a warning look.

'I had my clothes pinched, big deal,' Elune went on. 'It was probably just some pervert who wants to jerk off in my panties anyway. Let him have his kicks, I don't care.'

'Exactly how old are you?' Perkins demanded.

'Why, do you want a wank too? Don't worry, I'm old enough. I've got no panties, but I'll do you with my sister's bikini pants. A fiver?'

'Elune . . . Linnet, be quiet!' Thomazina snapped. 'She's sixteen, officer.'

'Come on, officer, nothing like a good panty wank,' Elune persisted. 'A tenner and I'll suck you first. Twenty, you can do it in my mouth, all the way, or you can spunk in my face!'

'Why you dirty little –' the assistant cut in.

She grabbed for Elune, who danced to the side, laughing.

'I'm sorry, I'm sorry,' Thomazina stammered. 'She's –'

'Just calm down,' Perkins ordered. 'All of you, just calm down.'

'Yes,' Thomazina agreed, only to see Elune grab the dress and panties from the desk and dart for the door.

Perkins followed, also the assistant, calling out in anger. Thomazina ran, pushing past the assistant in the doorway and turning away from where the sergeant was already in pursuit of Elune.

Sergeant Perkins reached for his radio as he ran, only to hesitate at the thought of how his colleagues would react to an assistance call for the pursuit of a sixteen-year-old shoplifter, and a girl at that. Postponing the decision, he put his full effort into the chase, sure that he would eventually catch her. She was well ahead, laughing and dodging among the crowds, the yellow dress fluttering from her hand to mark her like a flag. Her laughter was annoying him, yet her obvious lack of experience brought satisfaction. She would be caught, and then she wouldn't be laughing any more.

He saw her jump to one side, into the mouth of an alley, and his set lips turned up to a brief smile. The alley led to the first part of the old docks, nothing more, a dead end serving a cluster of warehouses and an old boatyard. He followed, sure where she would go, and slowed to a walk as he saw her ahead, scrambling over the gates that shut off the boatyard.

She was trapped, and he came after at a walk, climbed the gate and hesitated, wondering if she intended to hide and double back while he searched for her. Doing his best to seem casual, he walked to the door of the great shed in which the boats had been made, expecting her to dart from cover at any moment. Instead he saw her as he entered the huge, empty building. She was perched on one of the massive iron moorings beside a ramp, her legs crossed, her hands folded over one knee.

'None of your friends with you, then, officer?' she asked, her tone as impudent as ever.

'I don't need backup for a scamp like you,' he answered, closing the door.

He pushed an oil drum against it, closing off her escape unless she chose to jump down on to the mud. If she did she was caught anyway. At under five foot tall she would hardly be able to make her escape through the thick harbour mud.

'Good idea,' she said as the drum grated into position. 'Best to be sure we're not disturbed.'

'What do you mean?' he demanded, walking towards her.

'Well it wouldn't do to be caught while I'm giving you your wank, would it?' she answered. 'I mean, what would the inspector say?'

'Don't try it, love,' he sneered. 'Unless you want attempting to bribe a police officer on your charge sheet.'

'Come, come,' she answered. 'I'll do anything you like, for free, a nice wank with my bikini pants, a suck, or even a special show while you do it in your hand. I know some very rude tricks.'

'I'll bet you do.'

'How about it then? I can put on a pair of these silly little panties and show you what I do for my boyfriend in Ireland. You'd love it. Come on, a big, strong boy like you needs plenty of good, dirty sex.'

'That's enough of that. Now are you going to come easily?'

'I bet you will, once your cock's in my mouth. I bet you've got a big one. I like them big, to really fill my little cunt. You can do me from behind if you like.'

'I'm really not that sort of copper, love.'

'Oh, but you are, you all are. Do you know Officer Weekes? Big, fat man, huge cock.'

'No.'

'He was a dirty one. He arrested my friend and made her eat her breakfast with his spunk all over it. He did it in front of her, too, and made her suck him hard.'

'Yeah, sure.'

'It happened.'

She shrugged as she said it, a gesture of such indifference to his opinion that he wondered if she was telling the truth. The way she was talking was getting to him, her lewd offers made all the more tempting by his jealousy of Ed Gardner.

'Come on,' she wheedled. 'I'm good, and I'm dirty. I'll do things you only dream about, anything, just name it.'

He paused, thinking that it would be easy to take her up on her offer, then arrest her anyway. It would be her word against his, and she wouldn't be the first female prisoner who had claimed sexual assault by an arresting male officer. She would never be believed, just so long as he left no trace on her or in her.

'You sure you're sixteen?' he asked.

In answer she spread her legs and casually pulled aside her bikini crotch, revealing a thick, dark growth of pubic hair and a well-developed sex. A second motion lifted her bikini top, displaying breasts of tiny proportions but fully formed. She was mature, that much was obvious. He nodded, his cock twitching as she shrugged off her bikini top completely.

The boathouse doors shut off the view of the harbour. The oil drum held the door closed behind him. They would not be disturbed, and the offer was suddenly just too tempting. She smiled, perhaps reading the expression on his face. He nodded and she rose, took two graceful paces towards him and squeezed his crotch, kneading his cock through his uniform trousers with every appearance of genuine enjoyment.

'I'm going to like this,' she sighed. 'You're lovely and big. Come on, get him out, I want a suck.'

She pushed, guiding him down on to the mooring bollard even as his zip slid smoothly open. Her hand burrowed inside his trousers and his cock was out, stiffening in her tiny hand as she stroked and teased. Her touch was gently, incredibly feminine, and he wondered how he could have thought her inexperienced for an instant, never mind immature. What she was doing to his genitals was the act of an expert, someone who had spent a lot of time learning how to give men pleasure.

'Lovely,' she sighed, 'that would fill me right up. Shall I sit on you?'

'No . . .' he began, but she had already risen and turned.

At the sight of her tiny, rounded bottom his resolve went. She was perfect, two fleshy cheeks divided by a deep cleft, the bikini hiding little, then nothing as she took it down. For a moment he had a view of her tight, puckered bottom hole and the hairy rear of her sex. She sat, pressing

124

his cock between her bottom cheeks to fold it in hot flesh and wiggling, squirming her buttocks on to his penis. He moaned and began to move his cock, sliding it in her crease. It took all his resolve not to lift her and put her on his erection, but he held back, leaving her to giggle and squirm, rubbing her bottom into his lap until his cock felt fit to burst.

'That's nice,' she sighed, 'but there's no hurry. Shall I show you what my boyfriend likes?'

'What?' he demanded.

'You'll see,' she laughed, and rose, bending forward to retrieve the pack of knickers and presenting him with a full view of her naked rear.

He watched as she pushed off her bikini pants and pulled out a pair of panties. They were tiny, and tight even on her as she pulled them up and over her bottom, making sure he got a good view of the material pulled taut across her little cheeks. He swallowed and took his cock in his hand. She looked glorious in panties, a perfect little nymph, sweet and innocent.

'Watch,' she ordered and bent at the waist, taking hold of her knees with her tiny bottom stuck out right towards him.

Her legs were braced apart, her hands on her knees, giving a plain view of her panty crotch, bulging with the swell of her sex. Both lips were plainly visible, the material caught between them and rising to cover her bottom in a display somehow ruder than when she had been showing it all. She looked back, her huge green eyes bright with excitement, her mouth curved into a playful smile.

For a moment he wondered what she was doing, only to see her mouth set briefly. He heard the hiss and saw the wet patch appear on her immaculate panties, his mouth dropping wide as he realised she was peeing herself for him. It was gushing out, forming a little yellow fountain over her panty crotch and dribbling from the sides to run down her thighs. Some soaked into her knickers, drawing them tight against her sex and bumcheeks. More splashed on the ground, forming a rapidly growing puddle.

'Is that pretty?' she asked, for all the world like a girl asking him to admire a new dress.

He nodded dumbly, his hand moving instinctively up and down on his cock as he watched. The rear of her panties was transparent with pee, showing her hair and the details of her bum. She was smiling, a mischievous, taunting smile, as if daring him to pull down her wet panties and plunge his cock between her pee-sodden sex lips, up her hole, fucking her with her piddle running down over his balls and her wet buttocks squelching against his front.

It stopped, leaving her panties dripping. She was standing in her own puddle, grinning back at him, watching his rock-hard cock as he nursed it. Reaching back, she took hold of her panties, hooking a thumb into either side and pulling, then peeling them slowly down, once more exposing her bare bottom and leaving damp marks where the wet cotton had been on her bum. Her pussy came on show, wet and dribbling into her panties as they were taken to her thighs and left, stretched taut and sodden, the pee still dripping from the crotch.

'Now I shall suck your lovely cock and swallow your spunk,' she said, 'and you can think of what you saw, and my wet panties, still pulled down, just for you while I suck your cock and kneel in my pee-pee.'

He nodded dumbly, pushing his erection out as she went down, kneeling. She took it, looking up with her lovely eyes as she licked the head, treating his penis like a lollipop. He groaned at the sight, then again, more deeply as she suddenly took his cock in and began to suck with greedy, urgent motions. Almost immediately he felt himself start to come, overwhelmed by the feel of her mouth and the thoughts of what he had seen. It was perfect, her little mouth working on his erection, his mind full of the sight of her panties filling with pee, her bare bottom, her wet cunt . . .

The jerk came totally unexpectedly, a violent wrench at his ankles delivered at the exact instant he reached the point of no return. He felt himself go backwards but could

126

do nothing, his erection spraying sperm in an arch as he went over. His cry of alarm blended with her high-pitched crow of laughter as the edge of the dock struck his back, he toppled and an instant later landed in the harbour mud.

Winded and gasping, he pulled himself up, anger rising in a sudden burst. The mud was deep, and slippery, foul-smelling bubbles rising to the surface as he struggled to stand. She was laughing, a hysterical, almost demented sound, and he cursed, yelling after her. The response was a yet wilder laugh and the scrape of the oil drum, then the door slamming.

Jeff Perkins clambered to his feet, turning to find himself below the level of the docks gates and looking out across the harbour, directly at two men in a fishing boat. Both were staring, one grinning, one open-mouthed. He looked down, hastily returning his mud-smeared and still erect penis to his fly. With as much dignity as he could muster he waded to a ladder and pulled himself up, reaching for his radio only to stop and decide that as far as his colleagues were concerned she had simply lost him in the summer crowds.

Mr Hobbers walked slowly along the passage, following the librarian between high stacks, both intent on the details and dates presented at the end of each. The smell of dust and general antiquity reminded him of his own shop, while the tall cardboard binders on the shelves looked as if they had been untouched since being placed there.

'I thought so,' the librarian announced, 'right at the end, *Tawmouth Journal*, from '47, when it started, up to '83. Let's see, hang on, some of the '53s are out. Which month did you want?'

'June.'

'Typical, that's the one. Come back upstairs – somebody must have it in the reading room.'

Mr Hobbers followed the librarian back the way they had come, waited briefly while she consulted his colleague and was shown into the reading room, where he was pointed towards one of the alcoves. A young man was there, his black clothes, jewellery and bright red hair in a ponytail suggesting he was one of the pagans who had been flocking to the town every summer for the past few years. Spread before him was a yellowing newspaper, evidently the June edition.

Thinking at first to wait politely until the man had finished, Hobbers found it impossible not to be curious. If such a person was reading the 1853 *Journal*, then it almost had to be for a reason related to his own, making him wonder if the man might not know more of the girl who called herself Thomazina. The man appeared studious, serious, but in no way aggressive, and Hobbers decided that he should open a conversation, from which he could easily keep out improper elements such as his purchase of the stolen coin and any mention of sex. Slipping into the chair opposite the man, he gave a polite smile.

'Excuse me,' he remarked in a whisper when the man failed to respond. 'I'm sorry to trouble you, but are you seeking the details of the disappearance of a Thomazina Keeley?'

Violet lay on the beach, face down, the feel of her fresh tattoo keeping its presence in her mind. Yasmin was beside her, their efforts to find Tammy having quickly given way to hunger, then, after a meal in a café, to a desire to sunbathe. Nich, she knew, was in the library searching for records of odd events in Tawmouth over past years and also for a photograph of the Reverend Clerebold Wilmot.

Yasmin and she had taken turns to oil each other's back, leaving her pleasantly relaxed and just faintly aroused, if too sleepy to want to do anything about it. As on the first occasion, her dream had scared her, but once again the fear had faded with the morning. Nich had had more trouble than ever at hiding his delight, and had been in a manic mood all day, now certain that her dreams related to the barrow god. She had agreed, her doubts gone in the face of fact and the thrill of being called. The result was that they had not slept, but spent the night talking and making love, until in the morning she was exhausted. Nich had barely seemed tired.

Thinking pleasant thoughts of the sex they had enjoyed and what was doubtless to come, she began to drift, only to hear his voice calling out. Raising her head, she found him striding along the front. She returned his wave, waiting until he had thrown himself down on the sand beside them before speaking.

'Did you learn anything?' she asked.

'Yes,' Nich answered, 'perhaps more than I sought.'

'How come?'

'First,' he said, 'the man in your dreams is Wilmot, tall, red-faced, white muttonchop whiskers, it must be him.'

'I wouldn't call my man tall,' Violet answered, 'and his whiskers were grey.'

'I'm sure they were, in 1853,' Nich went on. 'The picture I found was of him in his old age, 1879. It is him, Violet, you are called, no mistake.'

At his words her sense of excitement rose again, along with a touch of fear.

'What else?' she asked.

'Something puzzling, perhaps disturbing,' he replied. 'I was lucky to discover it, because while I was reading about the opening of the barrow a man came in after the same paper. He's called Hobbers, he owns an antique shop, and he wanted to know about a girl called Thomazina Keeley. Some girl had used her name apparently, when trying to sell him stolen goods. He had seen her gravemarker in Abbotscombe churchyard. She disappeared in 1853, June the twenty-first 1853, to be exact.'

'Solstice night,' Yasmin put in.

'Solstice night, when the barrow was open,' Nich went on, 'after developing a habit of sleepwalking over three weeks. Wilmot began his excavations at the Wythman on May the thirtieth.'

'Shit!' Violet answered as her mild fear rose to a sharp pang.

'The farm where she lived is only a half-mile from the barrow,' Nich continued. 'She is supposed to have walked over Aldon Cliff, although no body was ever found.'

'Oh, shit,' Violet repeated. 'What have we done?'

'Nothing, necessarily,' Nich answered, 'but we must be careful. I'll keep an eye on you, don't worry.'

'So you reckon she was called down into the barrow?' Yasmin asked. 'That's creepy.'

'They'd have found her,' Nich pointed out. 'Everything I've read points to fertility rituals. There's nothing about sacrifice or death. Women are called and become priestesses, that's all. Besides, no bones were found during the excavation, although Wilmot wasn't as thorough as he might have been. Also, it's the only case I could find and I cross-checked on their computer. There are plenty of cases of women having odd dreams, though. And one other thing I came across when searching for references to the Wythman: a group used to go up there in the fifties, rock-and-roll types. They got busted on solstice night 1957. Among the people arrested, for drugs and what are described as "lewd acts", was a girl who claimed to have been called to the barrow in dreams, Rosemary Evans. No one got hurt then.'

'It didn't last until sunrise,' Violet answered.

Thomazina watched the water, her face set in a petulant frown. Aldon Head reared above her, three hundred feet of sheer red rock, cut at its base into gentle ledges following the plain of the strata, one of which she sat on. To her right a great sea cave opened into the cliff, her ledge narrowing as it entered the mouth. The opening was huge, angled to the rock plain, reaching nearly a third the height of the cliff. Thomazina paid no attention to the magnificence of the scenery, watching the water until at last the telltale swirl she had been expecting came and Elune's head and shoulders appeared above the surface. The small girl was grinning, her wide mouth curved up between round cheeks, her eyes glittering with delight. She pulled herself on to the ledge, stood and stretched, her naked body dripping water on to the sunlit rock.

'Don't you ever learn?' Thomazina demanded.

'Don't be sour,' Elune replied. 'It was fun.'

'We might have been caught!'

'You got away. I got away.'

'Yes, but –'

'I tricked the big ugly policeman into letting me suck him, then threw him into a dock! It was so funny! He went right in the mud!'

'Elune! Now he'll be furious! We daren't go back to town!'

'So what? I hate your towns. They smell, and everyone's so big and clumsy.'

'I like them!'

'Just so you can fuck and suck with all the boys.'

'No, not just that. I like ice cream and sweets and fried fish and . . . and lots of things. I wanted my tattoo refreshed. You always spoil it, Elune!'

'An ice-cream van stops on the Ness, near where they play that funny game with the little white balls and the sticks.'

'Golf.'

'I'm sorry, Thomazina. I'll get you a limpet, one of the big white ones.'

'I hate limpets.'

'No, you don't, you're just sulky. I'll lick you, then. You can pee in my face. Will that make you feel better?'

'No.'

'Sit on my face, do it in my mouth. I'll hate that.'

'No, you won't.'

'Punish me, then, any way you like, but stop sulking.'

'Any way?'

'Any way.'

'Oh, all right. I'll ask Juliana's advice.'

'Juliana!'

'She's inside. She was just finishing changing when I got here.'

'Oh, no, you bitch!'

'Don't call me names, Elune.'

'I'm sorry, Thomazina, I'm sorry. Couldn't you just give me a spanking? Maybe with a snakelocks in me? That hurt.'

131

'I know it did. No, Juliana's better, she always knows what to do with you.'

'She's . . .'

Elune stopped, glancing towards the cave mouth. Thomazina followed her gaze, finding another girl emerging from the shadows, a slender, black-haired girl of her own height. She was naked, her body glistening with fluid, her skin marked with several large, red circles, two of which covered her well-grown breasts. Her expression was blissful at first, the look of someone who had been through an exquisite experience, but changed as she saw them, becoming warm and friendly, yet with a hint of the malign.

'Juliana!' Elune exclaimed. 'It's been so long!'

'It has,' the girl replied, 'and Thomazina tells me you haven't changed.'

'It was a joke, just fun.'

'You never could resist policemen.'

'No, they're so pompous, so self-important, like the fascists. You understand, don't you?'

'Of course, but now Thomazina can't take me into town and help me buy pretty things.'

'She has some money, and she knows a place we can sell coins and things, at the best price, just in return for a spanked bottom. It's a shop, with an old man. He's easy to get round, isn't he, Thomazina?'

Thomazina just smiled, enjoying Elune's rising panic.

'You've spoiled my fun in the town,' Juliana said calmly, 'so it is only fair I have my fun with you, is it not?'

'I suppose so,' Elune answered sulkily, 'but not Pietro's cross or your horrid cunt wedges. I really couldn't bear it.'

'I shall do as I please,' Juliana answered, 'but we have no time to make wedges and I'm sure they're not for sale in Tawmouth, so you are lucky. Now what shall we do with you instead?'

'We're not really private,' Thomazina put in. 'There's a Peeping Tom and an old man who comes to watch the girls. Either might be up by the temple, others too.'

'Do we care?' Juliana answered, glancing up to where a few bushes could be seen at the cliff edge high above.

'Going bare is one thing, torture another,' Thomazina said.

'Seeing a pretty little girl tortured?' Juliana replied. 'I would think they'd love to watch. Still, you probably know best. Hmm, I have it. Do they still throw the refuse down at Daccombe Bay?'

Elune lay prone, her body half submerged in the pool, her limbs spread-eagled, each firmly tied to a weight far too heavy to shift. She could see little, only a broken, fuzzy image through the wet hair that sprawled across her face. The smell of the sea was strong in her nose, mixed with tar, earth and ripe, rotten scents.

They had taken her to Daccombe Bay, Thomazina uncertain, Juliana gloating over what they were going to do. It was as she remembered it, a tiny cove beneath a high, funnel-shaped cliff, once a public tip, now given over to illegal use but still providing everything Juliana's malignant and fertile brain could desire. First a suitable site had been chosen, a shallow pool out of sight of the cliff top. She had been staked out, her wrists tied to a mess of twisted concrete and iron, her ankles spread wide and tied to rocks. They had taken turns to urinate on her, splashing her body and face to leave her soiled and panting. Juliana had then put a hand to her sex, teasing her to orgasm and talking of painful and degrading punishments until at last Elune's will had snapped. She had come, sucking at a strand of her pee-sodden hair to the sound of Juliana's laughter and Thomazina's nervous giggling.

They had left her, but she could still hear them, discussing the next stage of her punishment as they searched among the refuse for things to use. She could do nothing, only think of her ecstasy and what it had driven her to while she waited for more and worse. Her breasts were clear of the water, as was her pubic mound; everything lower was submerged, with her vagina full from where Juliana had opened the hole with a finger.

'Perfect!' Juliana declared. 'How many are there?'

'Five, I think,' Thomazina answered, 'no, six.'

'Good, I will start. You fetch some crabs.'

Elune listened as Juliana approached, her body stiffening automatically as something clattered to the rock near her head. A new smell joined the others; a sweeter, richer decay.

'We have a treat.' Juliana's voice came from beyond the can. 'A fine treat, just for you, my pretty one.'

'What?' Elune demanded.

Juliana just laughed, although Elune was already thinking of crabs, her flesh shivering and jerking at the prospect. Something soft touched her belly, smeared on to her skin, and the sweet, rotten smell became stronger. A wet, squelching noise came to her and something cold, hard and round touched between her breasts, then something else, as cold, but soft, running between them. A shiver went through her as Juliana's hands found her breasts, smearing some sticky, lumpy substance over them, tweaking her nipples, then moving up to her neck. The smell was getting stronger, stronger, rich and heady, and as Juliana's hand slapped a lump on to her pubic mound she recognised the smell of meat.

'Bitch!' she managed. 'Wicked, evil, bitch!'

Again Juliana's only response was a light laugh, and Elune felt a finger burrow into her vagina, then another. She was opened, her hole stuffed with the mess, Juliana pushing it in until Elune's vagina felt utterly bloated. Some squeezed out as Juliana let go, a feeling yet more obscene. As more of it was smeared over her vulva she found herself sighing and arching her back, unable to deny her pleasure in the awful punishment as her tormentor's fingers found her clitoris. Juliana giggled and began to rub, making Elune squirm and wriggle her hips for more, only for the touch to stop as abruptly as it had begun.

'Not yet, little one,' Juliana chided. 'Come, come, you wouldn't be happy unless it was done properly. We must allow the full indulgence of your senses.'

As she spoke Juliana had taken the hair on Elune's face and pushed it aside, leaving her blinking in the suddenly bright sunlight. Thomazina was visible, down the shore, turning over a rock. Juliana was to her side, squatting, her sex open, swollen and wet to reveal her excitement. Beside her stood six cans, each showing a picture of a large and contented dog, his head lowered over a bowl of brownish chunks and meat jelly.

'Dog food,' Juliana said happily. 'Here, have some.'

Elune shied away, then opened her mouth at the sudden look of warning on her tormentor's face. Juliana smiled and stuck a finger into a can. Elune stared at it, gaping, then closed her mouth on Juliana's finger, her senses filling with the taste. She swallowed, her face screwed up at the slimy texture as it went down. Juliana's own expression was of glee, of utter, unrestrained delight in Elune's degradation.

Once more Juliana's hand found Elune's sex, massaging her, fingers slipping into her filthy vagina, then lower, to penetrate her anus and give the tiny hole and her bottom crease a share of slimy filth. Elune moaned, feeling her bottom hole pop open and squeeze on Juliana's finger. In response the digit moved inside her rectum, making her writhe and gasp in pleasure, only to have it stop abruptly.

'I have seven,' Thomazina's voice came suddenly. 'One's an edible.'

'Give him her cunt,' Juliana ordered. 'We'll spare her face, but not those darling little titties.'

Elune's body tensed further, her skin already squirming in anticipation. Something heavy came to rest on her pubic mound, then scuttled quickly down, its legs tickling her skin as it took refuge between her thighs. A claw touched her bottom, gently, testing for the taste of the meat. She moaned, shaking her head.

'Hold them until they get the flavour,' Juliana commanded. 'Give me that big green one.'

Again something touched her, on her breasts, first the cool smoothness of the crab's underside, then the claws, waving in its efforts to escape, scratching her skin. She squealed, her pained response drawing a hiss of pleasure from Juliana. The crab relaxed, tasting, its mouthparts starting to work, in the meat but touching her skin. A claw

135

closed on her flesh and she cried out again, her back arching.

The crab at her sex had begun to feed, his big claws grating over the skin of her bottom crease and sex lips as he scraped up the food. Another was placed on her free breast, more on her stomach, each scuttling across her flesh until the abundant food made it overcome its fear. She was writhing, shaking her head from side to side, her senses swamped by the smell and the pain of claws on her naked flesh.

Juliana moaned and Elune saw she had begun to masturbate. Thomazina giggled, nervous, but plainly aroused, and Juliana gave soft thanks for some intimate caress. Elune tried to watch, to enjoy her friends taking their ecstasy over her tortured body, only for a claw to fasten hard on to a nipple and everything but her own pain to vanish in a long scream.

Another claw caught in her belly button, legs skittering across her tummy. Mouthparts touched her other nipple, testing her flesh for taste. The big crab pinched her sex lips, pulling them open, his mouthparts touching her inner flesh, feeding on the same smeared dog food that plastered her body and filled her mouth with its horrid taste. Part of him touched her clit and her mouth came open, her tongue pushing out. Claws gripped tight to both nipples, tighter on her sex, stretching her, cutting into her. Mouthparts touched her clitoris, provoking agonising tickling as the big crab fed on the meat, then pure, unbearable ecstasy as he began to feed on her.

She screamed as she came, a scream pushed out with all the force of her lungs. Her head was shaking, her hair scattering drops of water and pee over the rocks, her body arched and taut in blended agony and bliss as she screamed and cursed and thrashed in her bonds, calling Juliana a bitch over and over until at last the crabs were pulled from her body to leave her mumbling broken thank-yous through her mouthful of dog food.

Slumped down in the pool, she was gasping for breath, soiled and exhausted, her body sore and throbbing. The girls were looking down at her, Thomazina with excitement but concern, Juliana with pure, beaming delight, still squatting, her fingers sunk between her thighs, wet with juice.

It was Thomazina who moved, rising to walk behind Juliana, cock a leg across Elune's head and sink down. Elune sighed, poking her tongue out an instant before Thomazina's full, soft bottom settled in her face. Thomazina wiggled and Elune began to lick, first her friend's anus, then her sex. With a tongue lapping at the bud of her clitoris, Thomazina came quickly, crying out her ecstasy to the empty sky.

Thomazina rose, to be replaced by Juliana, who took the same treatment of Elune's tongue on anus and vulva before reaching a second orgasm. With that the punishment was declared over, Juliana's mocking tone making it quite clear that Elune's need for correction had been no more than an excuse to indulge herself. Elune was untied and washed in the sea, her body kissed and held before they found a sheltered area of rock on which she could recover.

'Does that satisfy?' Elune asked Thomazina as her friend sat down.

'Oh, I think so,' Thomazina answered, 'but behave yourself, please.'

'I shall try, but it is hard when you tempt me with such cruel pleasures. How can I resist?'

'Try, for his sake,' Juliana answered. 'You say you have seen nothing of Aileve?'

'No, neither of us.'

'She was with me briefly, but came up. She had a restaurant, just beyond the Seven Sisters, with a great bear of a man, all hair and muscle. She would feed me by night and we would play on the beach, but he began to think she was seeing someone so I had to leave.'

'A pity. We had hoped you would come together. Tell Elune what happened after we parted.'

'I got to Rome, but it had changed and it only made me sad. I went down, and to the islands west of Africa, where I danced for money and had sex with ever so many men.

They are dull, though, and become frightened at the least suggestion of pain . . .'

Thomazina laughed, to which Juliana grinned.

'They are soft, Juliana, sweet,' Elune stated, 'and you are cruel.'

'Not so cruel, Elune. Do you remember what the soldiers did to me at Exeter, when I wouldn't follow the Christian creed? I was staked out on the midden. Nobody would help me. They just laughed at me when I begged for mercy, telling me I only had to accept their religion and they would let me go. I refused, told them to do their worst. Thirty or more must have had me before I fainted, but when I woke I asked for more. They said they would bury me in dung and scraps, let me suffocate unless I swore faith. That was cruel.'

'What happened?' Thomazina asked.

'He came,' she answered.

Seven

'A crazy, fucking bitch!' Jeff Perkins declared and took a swallow of his lager.

'You've got to laugh, though,' Ed answered. 'Anyway, you'll get her. How many girls answering to that description can there be?'

'One,' Perkins answered. 'Yeah, I'll get her, then we'll see what's so fucking funny.'

'So it's a gang, you reckon?'

'Yeah, two, maybe more, young girls putting on the innocent act. I've seen it before, shoplifting, stealing, picking pockets, and all the time they look like butter wouldn't melt in their mouths. There'll be loads of incidents, you'll see, once it comes out. For now we could only find one other, this old bloke, Mr Hobbers, runs the antique shop opposite. He says a girl tried to sell him an old coin, obviously stolen. She's the one with the knockers, can't be two alike.'

'So what're you going to do?'

'They'll be back. Cocky little bitches always are, until they get caught.'

'Good. Anyway, I've got news for you. I'm going to marry Lily.'

'Jesus, that's a bit quick, isn't it? I mean, no offence, but . . .'

'None taken, Jeff, none taken. She's a gem, too good to miss. I been out with dirty bitches and I've been out with girls who'll do what they're told without having to be slapped. Lily's both.'

'Nice. Well, congratulations and all that.'

'Cheers. Still, after the other night I'm sure you'll agree, she's too hot to miss.'

'Dead right, best little cocksucker I've met in years. Shame you're so keen on her, really: I could've done with a bit more of that, eh?'

'Very funny, Jeff. Seriously, though, you never know your luck. You know me, I'm not one to leave my mates out in the cold, and as long as it's understood that I'm in charge, who knows, there might be more. She'll do as I tell her, that's for sure, and she loved it last time.'

'Yeah, Christ, that's not a night I'll forget in a hurry.'

'There's better. I fucked her up the arse last night.'

'What, up the shitter?'

'Yeah, right up. She made a fuss, but I wasn't taking any of it. I made her kneel and fucked her first, then put it up her arse, all the way, until my balls were banging her cunt.'

'Nice.'

'You bet it was nice. Of course she did her normal bit, crying and that, but she came off while I was up her, so I know it's all bollocks.'

'Typical woman. No, no, no, and all the time they're desperate.'

'You're right, Jeff, always the way. I told her I'd marry her afterwards. I've never seen a girl so grateful.'

'You're a lucky man, Ed.'

'No luck in it, Jeff. Treat them rough and they'll eat out of your hand. Another pint?'

Mr Hobbers sat at his desk, the local telephone directories spread around him, mingled with spanking magazines, the pictures of naked bottoms and kicking legs glossy in the feeble light of a single bulb. Since being visited by Sergeant Perkins he had been more determined than ever to track down the girl who had called herself Thomazina. She was a thief, and she was not alone, that he now knew; yet he had given the minimum of information to the sergeant, knowing that he personally could put it to far better use.

It seemed impossible that she could wriggle out of accepting a spanking, just so long as he found her. So many of the stories in his magazines told the same tale, of a girl caught shoplifting and given the choice of arrest or a good old-fashioned spanking. Invariably they chose the spanking, and down came their knickers, across the shopkeeper's lap, bare bottoms raised as just punishments were dished out. Despite his enjoyment of the stories, they had always been spoiled by a niggling doubt as to their plausibility. His limited experience told him that most girls lacked the reasoning ability to weigh a simple spanking against the consequences of arrest. More likely they would react by instinct, angrily refusing the spanking and counting a police record a lesser price to pay than the surrender of their dignity.

In Thomazina's case it would be different, he was sure of it. For one thing, she was somewhat simple; for another, she was used to being spanked at home and so the idea would not bring the outrage it did to most modern girls. Also, she had already had sexual contact with him and seemed not to mind, showing a sense of gratitude he considered extraordinary in a girl, vanity and selfishness being more usual traits. She could be coerced, he was sure of it, maybe made to accept a punishment for her thefts and for selling him the coin, maybe talked into accepting her spanking in gratitude for his not telling the police all he knew. Failing that, there was simple blackmail.

The problem was finding her. His researches had been interesting, fascinating even, but they had given him little clue as to her real identity. One thing alone stood out. The original Thomazina had been a dreamer – considered somewhat fey and unworldly by her contemporaries, even her sisters. It seemed entirely possible that to a young, rebellious girl she might be seen as a role model. Yet it seemed unlikely that any young girl would have heard of Thomazina Keeley. After all, teenage tearaways and thieves were not normally historians, nor likely to be reading gravestones in an obscure village churchyard. Clearly the girl had seen the graves, and the most likely explanation seemed to be that she was a descendent of a Keeley, probably one of the sisters.

With nothing else to go on he had begun to search for Keeleys, Pardues and Draycotts. No Keeleys lived closer than Exeter. Draycott was common in Newton Abbot but there were none in Tawmouth. A single Pardue was listed in Tawmouth, John Pardue of Exhibition Road. Other avenues existed, married names of female descendants in particular, yet somehow John Pardue had the right feel. Exhibition Road he knew, a terrace running up from the docks to the railway cutting, one of the poorest streets in the town. The environment seemed perfect to have produced his little thief, a thief he now felt confident would shortly be too sore to sit down.

Lily sat at her desk, her mind fully concentrated on the sheet of paper in front of her. On it, the Reverend Wilmot's diagram of the Wythman was taking shape, each detail carefully annotated as she went. She had spent the day working, trying to push the memories of how Ed had used her from her mind, also her overriding compulsion for sex. This she was certain came from her need for Ed, a piece of self-awareness that filled her with shame and disgust, yet about which she could do nothing. She had masturbated four times already, returning to lie stripped on her bed however hard she tried to turn her mind to work.

Her only crumb of comfort against the way she was being drawn in to Ed were her dreams, yet the strange connection of sex and the gigantic octopus they produced filled her with confusion and guilt. Guilt also came from the certain knowledge that to escape Ed she would also have to renounce the religion she had been brought up in, leaving her more bewildered than ever. Now, dressed in culottes and a loose shirt, she had once more turned to work, forcing herself to concentrate despite a growing need to once more bring herself to orgasm.

The tone of the bell broke into her thoughts. She rose, walking quickly to the window, hoping to see kids running away or some drunkard who had pressed the wrong bell. It was neither, but, as she had feared, it was Ed, and worse, the police sergeant, Perkins, was with him.

'Come on, babe, let your lover in,' Ed called, his slurred voice showing only too clearly that he was drunk.

Lily hesitated, willing herself to tell him to go away and come back when he was sober. His expression, already aggressive, turned to annoyance and she found herself hastily pulling on a dressing gown as she ran for the stairs. He pushed in, kissing her and squeezing her bottom before demanding beers. In the flat he threw himself into one armchair, Perkins taking the other. Lily hurried to get the beer, then to dress, apologising for her appearance and keen to reduce the vulnerability she felt in her dressing gown.

'Don't bother, babe, we like you like that,' Ed called out. 'Come in here and give me a kiss.'

Lily obeyed, certain of what was going to happen but powerless to prevent it. He pulled her close, his breath tasting of beer and cigarettes as he kissed her. His hand closed on her bottom, kneading a cheek in full view of Perkins, an act that sent the blood rushing to her face despite what Ed had made her do before. At last he released her, sending her stumbling with a heavy slap to her bottom as she rose.

'In fact,' he drawled, 'I know what I fancy. I fancy a bit of topless service. What do you say, Jeff?'

'Nice,' Jeff answered, his eyes already fixed to where Lily's dressing gown had fallen open to reveal the lacy front of her culottes.

'Got your sexy French knicks on, eh, love?' Ed remarked. 'That's great, topless in tarty French knickers, just the job.'

'Nice,' Jeff repeated.

'Come on, Lil, get them off,' Ed ordered. 'Mustn't keep our guest waiting, must we?'

Lily turned to him, her self-esteem dropping yet another notch at the misuse of her name. She was Lily, she had always been Lily, a pretty name she had always loved and which she felt suited her. To be called Lil was awful, a vulgar name, making her think of cigarette stubs and overdone make-up. Yet she knew it was pointless to protest, even if she had been able to find the courage to do so.

Her hands had already gone to her dressing-gown cord. She tugged it open and it fell wide. She eased the shoulders down and it dropped to the floor. She took the hem of her shirt and pulled it high and off. She was topless, bare but for her culottes, her breasts showing, also a fair bit of bottom cheek, making her nothing more than a topless waitress, fit only to serve ogling men – and she was not even a *paid* waitress.

'That's my girl,' Ed drawled. 'Fuck me, but you're a turn-on, you horny little bitch. Right, get some more beers, and fix yourself something while you're at it, why not?'

Lily walked quickly into the kitchen, acutely aware of their eyes on her rear view. Bending to the fridge was worse, knowing how much of her bottom showed and the way the culottes pulled tight against her sex. It would get worse, she was sure of it: probably she would be made to suck and swallow; certainly it would not be long before she was made to surrender her final garment.

She knew she would do it, obeying every dirty command Ed chose to give and at the end coming in helpless abandon unless she was stopped. In ways the shame of knowing how she would respond was worse than that of being nude, even of being made a sex object for them. After placing the beers on top of the fridge, she poured herself a glass of white wine, then hurriedly stepped back out of sight of the living room and upended the bottle over her mouth. She held it as long as she could, cold, sharp Muscadet flowing down her throat, then stopped, finding she had drunk close to half the bottle.

'Come on!' Ed called. 'We ain't got all day, or are you after a slap?'

'I reckon she is,' Perkins laughed. 'On her big arse!'

Ed laughed in response, Lily colouring furiously as she gathered up the drinks.

'On your knees, crawl out with them!' Ed crowed. 'Come on, get down, show some respect, you little tart!'

Lily dropped quickly, crawling out into the living room on her knees and holding the drinks out to the men. Ed squeezed her bottom, his fingers slipping briefly under her culottes and between her thighs.

'She's fucking soaking, the dirty bitch!' he called. 'She loves this stuff, the rougher the better.'

'Take your belt to her arse, Ed, teach her what happens to whores,' Perkins answered. 'Come on, I love to see a whipped arse.'

'All right, I will,' Ed answered. 'Come on, Lil, arse up, let's see it.'

Lily looked at him, unable to speak, trying to plead with her eyes. He merely clicked his fingers and pointed to the floor at his feet, then began to undo his belt. She bent, trembling, raising her bottom and feeling the culottes pull up between her cheeks, leaving them bare but for a puff of lace sticking out between.

'Fucking gorgeous, what an arse!' Perkins drawled. 'Whack her, Ed, make her squeak.'

'Dead right,' Ed answered and Lily heard the slither of leather on cotton as he drew his belt free of his trousers.

She tensed, gritting her teeth and screwing her eyes up. It came, the whistle of the belt through the air and the crack as it hit her bottom, the explosion of pain and the sound of her own cry. Again he did it, and again, laughing as he beat her, beer sloshing from his full can and splashing on her naked back and in her hair. Perkins watched, squeezing his cock, then laughing and slapping his thigh in merriment as she began to lose control.

Her feet were drumming on the carpet, her squeals and protests sounded distant in her ears. The pain was dreadful, her bottom bouncing to the smacks, the sound of leather on flesh blending with the men's laughter. Her mind had gone, all attempts at dignity abandoned in a desperate effort to dull the pain, kicking and squealing, thrashing and writhing as she collapsed to the carpet, in a flurry of tears and beating fists.

It stopped, as abruptly as it had started, leaving her to reach back and clutch her burning bottom, her teeth

145

gritted in pain as she squeezed her cheeks. Tears of shame and misery were running down her face, made worse by the hot throbbing of her bottom and the swollen, aroused feeling in her sex. She knew what the beating had done: other men had done it before, provoking a sexual reaction by smacking her buttocks and leaving her on heat, just as she now was.

'Oh, that does look funny!' Perkins laughed. 'It's ages since I saw a woman get a good whacking, but it always makes me laugh. Here, Lil, show us your arse, full on.'

'Do it,' Ed ordered.

Lily turned and lifted her bottom, presenting it to Perkins, who gave an amused grunt.

'Wet patch, I knew it,' he said. 'They love a good whacking, bitches, always turns them on.'

'Turn around, slut,' Ed demanded.

Lily hastened to obey, wheeling to give him the same rude display of reddened buttocks and wet panty crotch.

'Jesus, that's a horny sight,' he breathed. 'Cunt time, Lil, and you can give Jeff a suck.'

She nodded, numbly accepting her fate. Expecting her culottes pulled down, she lifted her bottom and spread her thighs, then went up on her arms, opening her mouth for the policeman.

'You're too fucking eager, you know that?' Ed grated. 'Maybe I should fuck you up the arse again, just to teach you what happens to sluts.'

'Yeah, do it,' Jeff agreed. 'Right up her shitter.'

'I'm going to,' Ed answered, 'and, just to show what a good sport I am, you can have your go when I'm finished.'

'No, not that, please,' Lily begged. 'That's special, just for you.'

'No, babe, you don't get it, do you? You're my girl, you're going to be my wife. Sure your body's special, and don't get your pretty head in a muddle. I'll be the one who fucks you, me and me only, for the rest of your life. Still, you're mine and I'm a generous guy. I like to share with my friends.'

'But not that,' she said, begging. 'Not up my bottom.'

'Hey, hey, babe, now come on. Whose are you?'

'Yours,' Lily answered faintly.

'I can't hear you, speak up.'

'Yours,' she repeated.

'Right, mine, so you do as I say.'

'But I'm still sore!'

'You'll soon get over that. Come on, you little bitch, you know you love it. Now drop them and show us that sweet little arsehole.'

Lily stood, slowly. She felt a surge of utter misery as her hands went to the waistband of her culottes. Ed was staring at her, his hand down his fly, obviously feeling his cock. Perkins was staring too, his little piglike eyes feasting on her bare breasts.

'Turn around, show us what you've got,' Ed urged. 'Jesus, Jeff, she's hot, but she's a slow learner. Come on, babe, do it like the strippers do, nice and slow with your bum stuck out so we can see your cunt when they come down.'

Lily turned obediently, her eyes welling with tears as she pushed out her bottom. Steeling herself, she began to take down her culottes, feeling every inch of her exposure as the silk slid down over her bottom. Ed grunted, Perkins smacked his lips, and then it was bare, her chubby bottom on show to the two men. She knew it was true, her sex lips showed from behind, pouting out in a nest of golden curls, her most intimate secrets bare, naked for the attention of two drunken, lecherous men. She let out a sob, no longer able to hold back, but continued to lower her culottes, all the way to her ankles and off.

'Nice,' Ed drawled. 'Stay like that, babe. Ain't she got the sweetest little cunt, Jeff?'

Perkins grunted agreement. Lily stayed still, her face burning with blushes as she held her rude pose and watched the men back between her legs. Ed had taken his cock out and was tugging at it, a casual, dirty gesture in response to her show. Perkins was only marginally less obscene, his trousers open to reveal grey underpants with his erect cock a solid bar beneath the material.

147

'Pull them open,' Ed ordered, 'let's see your arsehole.'

Lily reached back and spread her buttocks, stretching her anus for their inspection. She was shivering, near to panic, thinking of how she must look, standing nude with her bottom stuck out and her cheeks held wide, her bumhole a dirty brown wrinkle between them, pulsing in her expectation. Perkins pulled out his cock, peeling the foreskin up and then down, his eyes never leaving her bottom.

'Now grease your hole,' Ed drawled. 'Grease it while we watch.'

'What with?' she asked.

'How the fuck would I know?' Ed answered. 'Whatever you normally use when you grease your arsehole, you little wanker!'

'Make it something tasty!' Perkins laughed. 'Ed might want to stick his cock in your mouth while I'm having my turn!'

Both men burst into drunken laughter as Lily ran for the kitchen.

Juliana took a last bite of skate and tossed the crushed remains of the cartilage into the bin at the foot of a lamp-post. She looked up, watching the brightly lit window from which such interesting sounds were coming. The street was empty, the last stragglers heading home from the pubs already passed, the fish-and-chip shop in the act of closing. Twice men had assumed she was a prostitute, despite the baggy, sea-stained black clothes that hung loose on her slight body. Both had hurriedly changed their minds when they saw her eyes.

She had come in response to a sympathy, buying the skate as much to kill time as from any need to eat. Now, with the last people gone from the street she had begun to concentrate. The noises coming from the room suggested cruelty, and she had heard the smacking sounds and the heartless male laughter mingled with feminine cries and guessed that a girl was being beaten. That there was pleasure in it she had no doubt, and she wanted to see.

Bracing her legs around the post, she gripped it and began to pull herself up, rising quickly to the level of the window. She could sense the sympathy, now strong, and half expected to see Aileve, perhaps indulging herself with a pair of drunken dockers. Instead there was a young blonde woman, naked, on her knees with a full, pear-shaped bottom pushed out towards the window. A man was visible, sprawled in a chair, beer can in one hand, erect penis in the other. Another was nearer, against the window, only his head showing above the back of an armchair.

Juliana smiled, sensing the girl's fear and excitement. She was beautiful, also timid, yet what she was doing suggested a delicious streak of lewdness. In her hand was a jar, the lid off, the girl's fingers delving in, scooping out thick, dark honey. Juliana licked her lips, thinking of the sweet, rich taste, then again as the girl reached quickly back and smeared herself between her ripe bottom cheeks. A finger disappeared into the tight anus, then withdrew, sticky with honey, only to be plunged back and joined by another.

The men were talking, making lewd remarks as the girl fingered her bottom, remarks that had made her face a furious red with blushes. Equally red was her bottom, the heavy, parted cheeks showing dark bruises from her beating, the whole full peach flushed red from punishment. Again Juliana licked her lips, thinking of the thrill of beating such a beautiful girl and the taste of sweet honey licked from between another woman's thighs.

The girl now had three fingers inside herself, her anus a ring of strained pink flesh, a tiny, black hole visible at the centre. The honey was running down over her sex, thick and golden as it caught in her hair and dripped from her clitoris. Juliana let her own fingers slip on to her crotch, kneading her sex lips as she wound her limbs firmly around the post. In the room the man was coming forward, poking his cock at the girl's face. She seemed hesitant, but took it, her cheeks sucking in as her mouth was filled. The other man barked a sharp command and the girl's fingers pulled free of her bottom hole, leaving it gaping wide, a black orifice into her body with golden honey running from the open hole.

Juliana pushed her hand into her trousers, finding her bare sex beneath. Clinging hard, she watched as the second man knelt, blocking her view of the blonde girl's bottom. He grunted and she saw her muscles jump, and at the thought of his cock being forced into her honey-filled rectum she came, teeth gritted in the effort of keeping her hold at the moment of orgasm.

Lily knelt, her mouth pursed around Jeff Perkins's cock, her bottom high, the hole stuffed with Ed's own penis as he sodomised her. It stung, as before, the sharp pain mixed with a dull, bruising ache. Yet the pleasure was too great to deny, the breathless ecstasy of having a penis moving in her rectum, the dirty submission of sucking another man's cock as she was buggered, even the awful shame of being naked and used in both ends while they watched. Ed had his hands on her buttocks, spreading them with his thumbs as he buggered her. Perkins was holding her head, fucking her mouth and mumbling obscenities as she sucked on his cock. It was too good, and she knew her resolve would soon break, that she would reach back and masturbate shamelessly in front of them, at least if the slapping of Ed's balls on her empty vulva didn't get her there first.

'She's so tight!' Ed grunted. 'You're going to love this, Jeff. Come on, Lil, you little whore, suck him and think where his cock's going, right up your dirty little arse!'

'I've got to do it, Ed, or I'm going to come,' Perkins grunted. 'Come on, let me plug her shitter. You can make her suck while I'm doing it.'

'Hang on,' Ed gasped.

'Come on, Ed, you've got to do it,' Perkins growled. 'Make the little bitch suck! In her mouth, Ed, when it's been up her arse!'

Ed stopped, suddenly, and Lily felt a horrible certainty. He was going to do it, he was really going to do it. Perkins had her hair, holding his erection in her mouth, making it

150

impossible to voice her protests. Ed was pulling out, her ring everting, stinging as his erection left her bottom hole. It came free and she farted, then winced with new shame as both men laughed.

Perkins let go of her head, moved to one side, his cock slipping free, glossy with her saliva. Ed approached, his erection nudging her arm. She turned, looking up, begging with her eyes but unable to speak, unable to refuse the filthy act to which she was about to be subjected. He merely grinned and pushed it at her face, the taut red skin glistening with honey and mucus. She swallowed, trying to stop herself but knowing she was going to do it, to suck an erection that had just been up her bottom, a turgid, dirty penis, wet with her own slime.

Her head came forward, her body responding to what her mind could not accept. She gaped, gingerly, reluctantly, struggling with her boiling emotions, only for Ed to lose patience, grab her hair and push his filthy erection deep into her mouth. Lily managed a muffled gasp and she was sucking, her eyes closed as she tasted herself and him, also the honey, swallowing over and over, incredulous that she could be so filthy.

'She loves it, cocksucking little tart,' Ed grunted. 'Oh, that is good. Come on, Jeff, put it up her arse.'

Hands took Lily's buttocks, spreading the cheeks. Her anus stung, but she knew it was wet and loose and that he would soon be in her, not her lover but a man her lover had allowed to use her. The round, firm tip of his cock nudged her bottom hole, pushing, slipping in the slimy mess that was oozing out of it. Again he pushed, holding his cock to the hole. There was a stab of pain and her ring gave, several inches of his erection rammed home in her gut to make her gasp and gag on the penis in her mouth. Ed gave a pleased grunt and pushed his cock deeper, into her throat. Perkins pushed at the same time, forcing the rest of his cock into her rectum until his balls met her vacant, sopping vulva.

They began to use her, rocking back and forth, their cocks sliding in her, mouth and rectum, both places she

151

had been taught never, ever to allow a man to put his penis. Her mind was swimming with utter, total humiliation, yet less came from what she was doing than from not wanting it to stop. The policeman's balls were slapping her vulva as he buggered her, the same obscene sensation that had brought her to orgasm the first time. Now she needed it again, and reached back, grabbing his scrotum and pressing it to her sex.

'Jesus!' Perkins gasped. 'The little whore's rubbing herself on my nuts.'

'Dirty bitch,' Ed managed and came in Lily's mouth.

She felt it happen, his sperm erupting down her throat as he wedged his penis deep into her gullet. He groaned as she began to choke, then again as her muscles began desperate, spasmodic contractions on the head of his penis. He moaned deeply, ignoring her attempts to pull back, only to suddenly reverse, pull his erection from her mouth and deposit a last blob of come on the tip of her nose.

'Nice,' Perkins grunted, then gasped as she once more began to rub his balls on her sex.

Ed had slumped back, pulling Lily's head into his crotch. She began to lick his balls, then took them into her mouth, sucking them and rolling them over her tongue. His cock was deflating but she didn't care, she was coming, coming with the policeman's cock hard in her rectum, the rough skin of his scrotum bumping over her clitoris and two balls that tasted of Ed, of honey and of her own juice in her mouth.

Her anal ring clamped on Perkins's cock again, and it began to pulse, along with the mouth of her vagina. The orgasm exploded in her head, the whole, filthy experience running over and over, stripping, sucking, being buggered and most of all, best of all, sucking Ed's cock when he had had it up her bottom. For one long moment it was perfect, even the hard, slamming of Perkins's gut against her buttocks as he started to come. Then it went, her mind filling with shame and guilt even as the policeman gave a final, heavy grunt and shot the full mass of his sperm into her rectum.

Lily slumped down, sobbing, indifferent to the pain as the policeman pulled his cock from her anus. The hole was left gaping, a burning inflamed mess, running sperm and honey and her own fluids. She let it come, feeling the hot slime ooze down over her sex and into her pubic hair. Soiled and spent, she no longer cared that she was making an open, obscene display of her buggered bottom, nor that her mouth was full of sperm.

'One up the dirt box, eh, Lil?' Ed drawled. 'Nothing like it.'

'Thanks, Ed, that was great,' Perkins added. 'She's one hot bit of fluff, your Lil.'

'I'd better wash,' Lily said, stung by Perkins's open and total disregard for her as a person but unable to find words with which to answer him.

'See if there's any more beer in the fridge first, babe,' Ed said.

Lily had risen, and changed direction at his words, going quickly into the kitchen and retrieving the last of the four-packs of lager Ed had ordered her to stock up with. In the living room the men had gone back to their chairs, their limp cocks still hanging from their flies.

'That's for later,' Ed joked, seeing the direction of her glance. 'If you're a good girl you might even get your cunt fucked while you suck Jeff again.'

Lily said nothing, handing over the beers and walking to the bathroom. She washed slowly, thinking of what she had done. Shame and guilt burned in her head, yet it was impossible to deny the pleasure she had taken and how good her climax had felt. She also felt more protected than ever, totally Ed's property, although a weak, angry voice in the back of her mind was telling her that she was pathetic, that any woman with the least courage would rebel.

Having showered, she applied soothing cream to her bottom, shutting her eyes in bliss as she rubbed it into the bruised cheeks. The belting had hurt, yet again she could not deny the excitement of it, nor the sense that it was no more than she deserved. Her anus came last, the sore, bruised little ring creamed and a finger slid into the hot interior of her bottom. It was impossible to forget that two men's cocks had just been where her finger was, and as she slid it in and out she wondered if they would bugger her again during the night.

She finished with powder and brushed her hair, reasoning that if she was to be used she might as well look pretty. Ed may even compliment her, although he was more likely to demand that she put her mouth straight to his cock. With her face set in a wry grimace for what she expected to happen to her, she returned to the living room. Both men were unconscious, slumped in their chairs, a beer can still gripped in Ed's nerveless fingers.

Violet lay still, her head cradled in the crook of Nich's arm. He had done his best to calm her fears, but without much success. The timing of Thomazina Keeley's disappearance and the opening of the barrow was beyond mere coincidence, she was certain. What had been a playful game had become a terrifying reality, and she was scared to let herself sleep for fear of what sleep might bring. Yet she was tired, not fully recovered from the previous night, while the two bottles of heavy red wine she had shared with Nich and Yasmin were making her drowsy. Her mind kept slipping to the space on top of the Wythman, the warm, dark night, the scent of incense and summer grass . . .

Once more she was on the cliff top, looking out over the sparkling sea. She was not nude, but wearing the short, loose top in which she had gone to bed. It was black, the front emblazoned with occult symbols in silver and gold. It was also short, leaving her bare below the waist and acutely conscious of her naked bottom and pubic mound. She turned, knowing exactly what to expect. Sure enough, the Reverend Wilmot stood before the open Wythman, his workmen gathered around him, all staring. She stepped forward, unable to hold herself.

'A witch, I knew it!' Wilmot hissed. 'A wanton also: see how she flaunts herself!'

She found her mouth opening, meaning to apologise, then shut it, confused, unable to control her mind or her body.

'Take her, beat her!' Wilmot yelled and the workmen moved forward.

She was taken, bent down, her face pressed to the earth, her naked buttocks thrust high. Her top was pulled up, exposing her breasts. Her knees were kicked apart, spreading her sex. Hands took her, holding her firmly in position. Wilmot began to read from his bible as the biggest of the workmen came behind her, his spade clutched in one huge, red hand. Her bottom jerked as the spade smacked down, but there was no pain, only the shame of being beaten and the fear of what would happen once her buttocks were red and her sex wet.

Ten hard smacks were delivered to the tune of her cries and the priest's droning voice, leaving her blubbering on the ground, soaked with tears and begging for mercy. Wilmot merely nodded and turned his back, walking towards the sea. The biggest workman put his hands to his belt, and only then did she think to call on the god.

She yelled, but cocks were springing out of flies on every side, huge red cocks, as large and coarse as the workmen themselves, each erect and ready for her body, for her rape. Violet screamed, begging the god, babbling apology for her fear, for her lack of faith. Her head came up, her eyes fixing to the dark mouth that led into the ground, tears streaming from her eyes as big, dirty thumbs took her buttocks and prised them apart. A huge, round cock head bumped her pussy and something green moved in the blackness.

The men screamed and vanished. She was dropped, sprawling on the ground, grovelling in a position of absolute abasement as Sigodin-Yth climbed from the earth. No muscle in her body would respond, her stare held immobile as the god came, manlike, with Nich's body, lean and muscular, the head a grotesque contrast, a fat, green octopus, great green eyes staring ahead, tentacles writhing towards her. He was erect too, a huge penis projecting from his groin, the same pale green as the body, like a man's cock, but with eight wriggling tentacles projecting from around the bulbous head.

155

He took her, his tentacles enfolding her head, his hands gripping her arms. She looked up, into his face, watching the tentacles spread to reveal a wet, thick-lipped mouth. Relief warred in her brain with revulsion, yet her body would not obey her and she let herself be drawn forward, her mouth opening of its own accord to kiss the blubbery octopus mouth.

Tentacles took her, folding around her breasts, the suckers pulling out her nipples to erection. More took her bottom, opening the cheeks, probing at her anus, parting the lips of her vagina. The kiss stopped and her head was being pushed down, towards the grotesque, tentacle-ringed cock. She gaped, unable to stop herself, tasting fish as the fat head pushed past her lips and in, the tentacles writhing in her mouth as she sucked on his penis. Her body was being pulled, held firm by her legs and buttocks, drawn forward and into the mound, his tentacles enfolding her as she sucked on him, bending her body until his knees met hers and pushed them wide.

She went back, the penis slipping from her mouth, her thighs opening to the god as he mounted her, his tentacles writhing across her body and head. His cock found her hole, the ring of tentacles moving on her flesh, squirming in her vulva, penetrating her anus, sucking at her clitoris. His mouth found hers, her head smothered in between all eight tentacles, his cock now in her, the cock-tentacles still spread wide over her sex. She could feel his suckers as they began to kiss, all over her body, wrapping her, holding her completely enclosed. His flesh was pulsing, the penis swelling in her vagina, the tentacle in her bottom expanding to bloat out her rectum. Her breasts were being sucked, her belly and neck tickled, her clitoris teased and she was coming, squirming in his embrace, fucked by a god, spread high and wide with his body engulfing her and her in turn engulfing him, thrashing, screaming in ecstasy unlike anything she had ever known . . .

Violet woke screaming, her thighs clamped on her hand, the bedclothes wrapped tight around her body and soaked in her sweat. Her sex was sopping and she knew she had really come, reaching orgasm despite the terror and revulsion that had blended with the rapture of her dream. Nich was awake, leaning up on one elbow, his eyes shining green in the dim light.

'He came for me,' she managed. 'Sigodin-Yth, he came for me and he had me, in the Wythman, and he had your body, your eyes.'

Lily woke, shivering. It had been the same as before, only more vivid, more detailed. She had been in the cathedral, walking up the aisle to become Ed's bride. Once more the tiny, impish woman had brought shock and outrage, desecrated the font by urinating in it, her sex spread for all to see with the pee gushing from the middle. Again the great tentacles had smashed through the high, stained-glass windows.

This time they had not taken Ed, but her, wrapping around her in an embrace of immense power yet extraordinary delicacy. She had been lifted high, taken from her fate, and, as she had left, a wonderful feeling of security had come over her, stronger by far than the sense of protection she gained from Ed, or had experienced with any other man. Surrender had been easy, the simplest thing to do, and she had felt neither fear nor horror as she was carried away from his side.

She had woken, but she had known what was going to happen. The arms would have pulled her in, gently opened her thighs, spreading her sex. She would have been entered, willingly, offering herself as her wedding clothes were stripped away, then accepting penetration and in doing so breaking her ties to Ed and giving herself utterly to the god.

It was a god, she was sure of that, the same god whose image was carved beneath the Wythman, the pre-Celtic god Nich Mordaunt had spoken of, the eightman, Sigodin-Yth. In the back of her head the voice of logic was telling her not to be absurd, that no such entity existed, yet to accept the voice brought only discomfort and sorrow.

Lying awake, it was impossible not to let her mind wander, thinking of how octopus mated. She would be

taken by eight strong arms, folded in, entered, filled with
cool, firm tentacle, the fat sperm arm writhing inside her,
swelling out her vagina, the suckers fixed to her body,
tugging at her skin, pulling her nipples to erection, teasing
her clitoris towards orgasm . . .

She stopped, shaking herself. Her hand had gone to her
sex, feeling the soft mound beneath her culottes, the other
tugging the old shirt she wore up over her belly, towards
her breasts. She had been about to masturbate, over an
octopus, an inconceivably dirty thing to do, worse by far
than fantasies of being controlled and humiliated by Ed. It
was the way her mind had been going, though, as usual
finding paths beyond the control of her will. Any strong-
willed woman would have rejected the dirty thoughts, put
them from her mind with a touch of self-admonition. Not
her, she was too weak, too weak even to resist her own
darker urges, yet sometimes being weak wasn't so very
bad.

With a despairing groan Lily let her hand slip back to
her crotch, sliding into her knickers to find her sex wet and
swollen with need. She closed her eyes, shook her head in
a final, hopeless effort to break free and began to stroke
herself, gently massaging her pussy and a nipple as she let
her mind drift.

She was on the beach across the river mouth where few
people went, under the towering cliffs cut into Aldon Hill.
The day was hot, the sun sparkling from the rock pools on
the shelves and ledges below Aldon Head. She was alone,
and nude, having stripped for the naughty pleasure of
feeling the air on her bare skin, the tingling rudeness of
having what she was supposed to keep hidden on show, her
breasts, her bottom, the tangle of pale hair that hid her sex.

As she so often did, she was looking for animals in the
pools, only this time she would discover more than she
expected. The octopus would be in one of the biggest
pools. He would be a monster, pulled up from the deep by
a storm, his skin the red of the sandstone he sought to
camouflage himself against. She would be intrigued, wading into the big pool to get a better look at him, going

158

slowly, gaining his confidence until he emerged into the open, his great pale eyes looking into hers. He would touch her, his tentacles sliding over the bare skin of her legs, as gentle as her own caresses, as strong as ropes.

His touch would tickle, making her giggle and shiver, making her want more, and in more intimate places. She'd try to resist, but her resistance would snap, as it usually did, and she would find herself slipping down into the water, sitting her bare bottom down on the smooth-worn rock and spreading her thighs. He would move into her, his arms coiling around her thighs, holding her, taking her under her bottom and around her back. All eight would grip her, gently but firmly, never hurting her but rendering her completely helpless. He would explore, as he would a female of his own kind, caressing her skin, stroking her belly and breasts, squeezing the cheeks of her bottom, touching the nape of her neck.

She would be helpless, totally under his control as his sperm arm began to trace a path down her front, towards her sex. Her breathing would become quicker as the tentacle slithered down her belly and into her pubic hair. She would be rebelling in her mind, calling herself a slut and a tart, yet lost in the horrid pleasure of his grip, unable and unwilling to stop it. The sperm arm would touch her sex, squirming against her clitoris, finding her vagina and filling her, squeezing inside as she cried out in her ecstasy and dismay. Her vagina would swell out as he pushed more and more tentacle inside, stretching her, filling her beyond anything any man could ever be capable of. All the while his firm, cold flesh would be pressing to her gaping vulva, to her clitoris, teasing her, tormenting her until at last she came, screaming out her lust . . .

Lily came with a choking sob, misery and bliss blending in an orgasm far beyond those she had taken over Ed and the way he used her for sex. She let it come, rubbing at herself with her back arched and her mouth wide, riding wave after wave of pleasure until she could take no more and was forced to lift her fingers from her sodden vulva. Sobbing, shaking, with tears running from her eyes, she collapsed back on to the bed, utterly spent as the great wash of guilt and shame rose up inside her, just as she had known it would from the moment she put her fingers to her sex.

Eight

Joe sat in his usual place, sipping a cola and watching the river ferry. In the queue were two girls who seemed worth watching. One was the smart young blonde he had watched masturbate. It seemed entirely likely that what she had done once she might do again, and her presence had his pulse racing. The other possibility was less obviously exciting: a slight girl with jet-black hair wearing stained black jeans and a top, both baggy and shapeless on her body, except across her breasts, which were full for her figure. They would be well worth a look, he was sure, even in a bikini top, yet her real attraction was her face, which was not only beautiful but gave her an air of poise and confidence. Watching her strip would be highly appealing.

As the blonde climbed on to the ferry he followed, using his normal procedure of sitting well away from his targets and watching the sights of the estuary as they crossed. The tide was in flood, tugging them towards the harbour mouth so that the ferry beached close under Ness Head. Joe disembarked last, watching to see where the girls would go. The dark-haired girl was carrying a heavy bag, and he half expected her to turn for one of the hotels or the snack bar on the miniature golf course. Either would have been a loss, but she took the path to the beach tunnel, as did the blonde.

Joe weighed his options: following or watching from the cliff top. He would get closer on the beach, yet the cliff offered a better chance of a leisurely stare. Also, the girls were likely to be ruder if they thought they were safe, and it was hard to go unobserved on Ness Beach. He was about to turn up the hill path when he remembered how it had been with Tammy. She had seemed as distant as any of the girls he had watched, yet once he had propositioned her she had been out of her bikini as soon as they were alone. Maybe it was worth trying it on with the blonde girl, who had a meek air about her. The dark girl seemed less likely to respond as he hoped. He followed towards the tunnel, thinking of Tammy's lush curves and wondering if she would keep her promise and attend the solstice party that evening.

Lily walked slowly, seeking an excuse not to do what she was about to, but unable to find one. She wanted to masturbate, and to do it in the open, as she had done on Aldon Hill. It was a compulsion, far beyond her will to resist, a need to be bare and to be rude, to come in the open with her mind full of dirty thoughts. She had visited the far end of Ness Beach before, looking for marine animals among the rock pools, a lonely place, and the one she had chosen for her fantasy the night before. Sometimes there were people there, and there had been more as the season progressed. Yet beyond the pools a series of rock ledges thrust out into the sea, directly beneath Aldon Head. The east face of each was near vertical, a hard scramble even for somebody fit. Certainly the old man who invariably sat on a boulder and watched the girls pass would be unable to follow. The west faces were shallow slopes of red rock, worn smooth by the wind and waves, perfect sunbathing places.

She knew exactly what she was going to do, despite telling herself that it was improper and that Ed would disapprove. She would climb as many of the steep faces as she could, find a sheltered place and strip nude. With her body well oiled with sunblock, she would relax, slowly allowing her dirty thoughts to build up until at last she could wait no more and was driven to masturbate.

As she reached the mouth of the Ness tunnel she glanced back. Footsteps could be heard, echoing in the tunnel, then someone appeared, a slim, dark-haired girl who had been on the ferry with her. Her mouth set in an irritated pout, then relaxed as she told herself the girl was unlikely to take the trouble of going right out to the point. She climbed down the steps and set off along the beach. The old man was there, as always, puffing on his pipe. He greeted her with a nod and she smiled back.

At the rock pools she looked back again, finding to her annoyance that not only was the dark-haired girl still following her, but that another figure was visible, a male, skinny and underdeveloped, scarcely more than a boy. She frowned, wondering if he was the same boy she had seen up by the Wythman the day she had masturbated. A horrid thought came to her, that he may have watched her and now be following her, but she dismissed it as paranoia.

She climbed the first face, glancing back at the top. The boy had sat down on a rock and was looking out towards St David's Island through a large pair of binoculars. The girl was among the rock pools and smiled at her as she approached. Lily returned the smile, but nervously, finding something odd about the girl's face. She was pretty, beautiful even, but her eyes seemed unnaturally bright and were green.

As she moved to the next ledge she remembered the colour of Nich Mordaunt's eyes, paler than the girl's but with the same disturbing intensity. Reasoning that she might well be his sister, and telling herself not to be silly, she moved on. She had intended to cross three or four ledges, but knowing that people were coming up behind her she went further, scrambling on to the next two with ever greater difficulty. The seventh proved larger, with a great gentle slope of rock, warm in the hot sun, but angled away from the sea. It was perfect, the area by the cliff providing absolute concealment unless someone actually peered over the cliff top. That seemed unlikely. Besides, the eighth appeared unclimbable, a sheer face three times her height with no obvious footholds.

Glancing back, she saw no sign of the black-haired girl. The last climb had been difficult, some twelve feet of nearly sheer rock, surely enough to put other people off. Sure enough, neither the girl nor the boy appeared, and after a time she felt bold enough to pull off her dress. For a while she lay still, feeling the sun and the cool, light breeze on her skin, enjoying being in just her bra and panties. Gradually her sexual pleasure rose and with it her fear of being caught reduced. With a deliciously rude thrill, she reached behind her back and unclipped her bra, letting it fall from her breasts.

Being bare-chested felt wonderful, deliciously exposed, and for a while she sat still, revelling in the feel of daring to go topless and the knowledge that shortly she would be naked. Her breathing was coming fast, her sex felt ready. In the back of her head she knew that what she was doing was generally considered no more than mildly risqué, yet for her it was more, much more, especially when she fully intended to follow her nude sunbathing with masturbation.

Obeying a sudden impulse, she lifted her bottom and pushed down her panties, sliding them the length of her legs and off, tossing them aside, casually, as she imagined a stripper might do. She was near naked and it felt great, her shoes only emphasising her nudity. The feel of being bare was exquisite, with even her sex showing, open to the warm air as she deliberately spread her thighs wide. Ed would have been furious at her, she was sure, taking the view that she was his property and should be demure and reserved unless it was for his pleasure. She smiled, thinking of him at work, imagining her in her flat or out shopping, buying the steak he had ordered her to cook for supper. Instead she was out on the rocks, stark naked, her body nude to the air.

She spread her towel, smiling all the while, and began to oil herself, applying generous amounts of sunblock to her fair skin. It was cool, and felt good, her body extra-sensitive as she caressed herself, wondering why she was feeling so wonderfully rude but enjoying it far too much to worry or even feel more than a twinge of the guilt that always plagued her. Her breasts were in her hands, smooth and oily, the nipples stiff and excited. She played with them, squeezing them and lifting them, wishing they were bigger but thoroughly happy with the way they responded to her touch.

With her body oiled she lay down, determined to take it slowly. Her towel was at the top of the ledge, allowing her to see the next one and so cover herself if anybody did come. She set her legs apart, deliberately showing off her sex, and closed her eyes, her mind drifting pleasantly to the sound of seagulls and the gentle wash of the waves. Without really knowing what she was doing, she reached down, her hands stealing to her vulva, her fingers stroking, spreading her sex lips, finding her clitoris and beginning to tease.

She knew she was masturbating, that she was out in the open, that she might be caught. None of it mattered, providing only an exciting edge to her rude behaviour, while she was certain that Ed's fury would know no limits if he found out. The belting she had been given the night before had been for fun, though her bottom was marked with bruises and even now ached as she moved her cheeks against the towel. If Ed knew she liked to masturbate outdoors she would get worse, far worse, but Ed never needed to know. It would be her secret, her special thing, proving that however much he might rule her body he would never possess her mind.

Lily cocked her legs open, too excited to care as she spread her vulva to the sky. Her back arched up, pushing her sex out, her fingers now rubbing firmly at the taut bud beneath them. Ed would never know, nor would he know what she thought about, the strange, obscene fantasies she had been having since reading Nich Mordaunt's book, fantasies of tentacles and suckers, of eight strong, pliant arms to hold her body, of sex with octopus.

She cried out, imagining how it would be, a great, heavy creature pulling himself up the rock ledge. His tentacles would take her, holding her, caressing her. She would lift her arms and spread her thighs as wide as they would go, offering herself, unstinting, to his embrace, wide and free as he took her in. His sperm arm would penetrate her

165

vagina, filling it far beyond anything Ed could manage with his feeble penis. Her bottom hole would be entered, a tentacle tip squirming inside to tease the flesh of her rectum. A tentacle would go into her mouth, suckers would cup her breasts, the huge, bulbous, heavy body would be on her stomach, pressing her down as a lover should, not hurting her but holding her, keeping her.

Lily cried out as she came, writhing her fingers in the oily mush of her sex, her back held in a tight arch, her erect nipples pointed skywards, her mouth wide in ecstasy. Nor did her orgasm break to guilt and shame as it normally did, but went on, keeping her moaning and dabbing at her clitoris until at last the feelings began to subside and she lay back, moaning softly. For a while she stayed still, utterly content, only then opening her eyes to find three naked black-haired girls watching her.

Joe walked forward, feigning nonchalance. Both girls had climbed on to the rock ledges. He had waited long enough and both would be sunbathing, naked or near naked, and it was a treat he did not intend to miss. The blonde may even be masturbating, a thought that had his cock hard and made him dizzy with lust. He felt scared, yet he was determined to act, at the least to ask for sex. The blonde girl seemed timid, so timid he was sure he could squeeze a blow job out of her with a bit of pushing, maybe more. If she was masturbating, then he was sure to get more. It was all down to timing: catch her when she was coming and she would want him to join in, she had to.

His strategy was set. He would climb the ledges, casually. After all, he had as much right to be there as they did, and he could not be expected to alter his behaviour merely because they chose to take their clothes off in public. He would watch as he went, taking in whatever was on offer. The dark-haired girl would hopefully be showing her tits, maybe everything, but he had decided not to accost her. Her manner suggested he would be given short shrift.

The blonde was another matter, and his target. He would be blunt, stating his admiration for her body and suggesting sex. Hopefully she would respond as Tammy had. If not, then at least he had shown the courage to try, and hopefully would have got a good eyeful into the bargain.

He began to climb, finding each ledge empty but with his hope rising as he realised the effort the girls had gone to for privacy. The fourth face was hard, the fifth actually frightening, yet the girls were on neither of the slopes beyond. The sixth face was easier, the seventh the worst, but still the slope proved empty. Puzzled, he stopped, surveying the fifteen-foot face that cut him off from the eighth slope. Both girls had gone in front of him, he had passed neither. The cliff itself was effectively unscalable, which left the sea.

There, clearly, was the answer. They would have stripped to bikinis, thrown their clothes up on to the ledge and swum around. The sea was calm enough, and by doing so they made absolutely certain of their precious privacy. For a moment he felt anger, cheated of his prey, as, however much he liked to watch girls' bodies, he hated to show his own. Stripping and swimming around to the next slope was out of the question, besides which, he could hardly throw his binoculars on to the rock or swim with them.

He looked at the face, thinking of the beautiful bodies spread on the slope beyond, almost certainly naked in the hot sun – stark naked. The girls had probably met and were chatting. They may even rub sun-tan lotion into each other, and that could lead anywhere. The thought of watching a lesbian encounter between the girls was too much. It may be unlikely, but there had to be a chance, and it was not a chance he was about to miss.

Walking back up the slope, he noticed a smudge of oil on the dry rock, confirming his suspicions. Somebody had been there, recently. It had to have been one of the girls, and, to judge by the shape of the smear, she had been sitting on the rock, probably with her bottom bare. It would have been the blonde, he decided: she had gone first. She would have been stripped, sitting and oiling herself when the dark-haired girl caught up. They would have talked, discussing how nice it was to sunbathe nude and expressing annoyance that he was on the beach at all. The dark-haired girl would have suggested swimming round to the next ledge, pointing out that he had been fully dressed and carrying expensive binoculars. The blonde would have agreed, laughing at the thought of his frustration when he found he could not follow.

Joe set his mouth in a determined line. The cliff face was rough, jagged ledges of harder rock following the same strata lines that had caused the formation of the ledges. Higher it was smoother, unclimbable, yet he needed to go only so far. There was a ledge, some thirty feet up, with tufts of grass and a single straggling bush clinging to it. He could reach it, he was sure, and from there he would be able to look down on to their hiding place.

He pushed his binoculars on to his back and walked to the face, starting the climb before common sense could get the better of him. It was hard, the sandstone rough yet with few purchases. Twice he nearly slipped – finding himself clinging to the face with his heartbeat hammering in his ears – but at last he made it, pulling himself on to the ledge and into the shelter of the bush. Immediately his face broke into a wide grin. There were girls on the slope, not just two either, but four, three stark naked, a positive goldmine of nubile flesh, tits, bums and pussies, all on show for his pleasure. The fourth was the blonde, in her dress but with wet bra and panties clutched in one hand. Two were eating, scooping what appeared to be ice cream from a large tub. A moment later he realised that he had seen one of them before: it was Tammy.

'We are being watched,' the smallest of the girls remarked, so casually that Lily managed not to turn around.

Her first instinct on discovering that the three of them had watched her masturbate had been to run in blind, blushing panic. There had been nowhere to run to, short of jumping from the ledge, and they had immediately begun to talk, making light of what she had done, complimenting her, arguing that it was nothing unusual to want to masturbate, even saying how beautiful she had looked at orgasm. They had shown no shame, no embarrassment, no reproach, only a delight in her and the pleasure she had been taking in her own body. In the end she had given in, responding to their requests to sit and talk and share their meal.

By then she had been back in her bra and panties. They had persuaded her to join them on the next slope and she had followed their advice and thrown her dress up and then swum around, removing her underwear and putting on her dress. They had stayed nude, the smallest even teasing her for covering up. The slope was bigger even than the one she had sunbathed on, a broad expanse of gently sloping rock, cutting back into the cliff and ending not in sheer rock, but in a great sea cave. Nor did it end at the next face, but sank below the water, which disappeared into the blackness of the cave mouth.

The girl who had followed Lily along the beach, Juliana, had brought food, ice cream, honey and peaches. She had accepted a peach, her anus twitching at the sight of the honey. They had introduced themselves as they ate and she had responded, finding herself relaxing despite the way they had seen her.

'Who by?' she asked in response to Linnet's statement.

'A Peeping Tom,' Tammy answered. 'I've met him before. He's called Joe.'

'He followed me along the beach,' Juliana added.

'Him!' Lily answered. 'The dirty so-and-so! I knew he was like that. Shouldn't you dress?'

'Why?' Linnet answered.

'He's seen everything anyway,' Tammy pointed out.

'We should catch him,' Juliana went on. 'We could make him strip for us. They always hate it when you turn the tables.'

'You wouldn't!' Lily answered.

'She would,' Tammy replied, 'but you're not to hurt him, Juliana. He's not a bad sort at all, really. He bought me an ice cream.'

'Typical,' Juliana said. 'It used to be honeycomb. The men would feed me some, then smear it on their cocks so that I'd suck.'

Lily felt her blushes rising, thinking of Ed's penis, sticky sweet with honey, but hardly fresh honey. Linnet giggled, looking up at Lily's reddening face through a mask of ice-cream-sticky fingers.

'What if we take him and he tells?' Tammy asked.

'A Peeping Tom?' Juliana answered. 'He'd love it, underneath, at least. It's probably what he's thinking about right now.'

'Would you, really?' Lily asked. 'I mean, not that he doesn't deserve it, but wouldn't we be better to just report him to the police?'

'Oh, I don't mind being peeped at,' Juliana answered. 'I just want some fun with him. Tammy, he's had you, you get him to come down.'

Tammy rose, wiping her fingers on her stomach and walking down to the water. She slipped in, swimming with enviable ease as Lily wondered if she had given herself to the Peeping Tom or if Juliana was teasing. In either case, the sheer ease and confidence of the girls was wonderful, fascinating, also something she wished she could have herself. It was hard to see any of them allowing themselves to be bullied in the way Ed treated her, impossible in the case of Juliana.

'Let's watch,' Linnet suggested, rising, still with the tub of ice cream in her hand.

Lily turned. Joe had realised he'd been seen and came out of his partial concealment behind the bush. He was sitting on the ledge, looking bashful as he watched Tammy climb from the sea. She was smiling, and as she stood she cupped her breasts, holding the big globes of flesh out in obvious invitation.

'Hi, Joe!' she called. 'Why don't you come down?'

Joe hesitated, looking very unsure of himself.

'Come down,' Tammy urged. 'I'd like some fun. So would my friends.'

Juliana gave a friendly wave. Linnet turned and wriggled her bottom at him.

'What about the big black guy?' Joe asked, glancing around as if expecting half a dozen angry boyfriends to rise from the sea.

'He was just a fancy man, a one-night stand,' Tammy answered. 'You were much more fun. Come on, I've told my friends all about your lovely big cock. We'll let you put it in us, all of us.'

'Promise?' Joe answered.

'Promise,' Tammy replied.

Lily found herself smiling, astonished by the boy's lust and stupidity. He had been peeping at them, and yet he believed Tammy's offer.

'Come on, girls, swim round!' Tammy called as Joe began to climb down, her voice happy and playful, anything but menacing.

Juliana chuckled, Linnet gave a delighted giggle and both girls turned to run down the rock. Lily followed, then paused, realising that she would have to take her dress off in front of Joe if she wanted to follow the others. She stopped, deciding that all in all it was best to stay where she was.

Sitting on the edge of the face, she watched as the girls swam over, joining Tammy before Joe had reached the ground. When he did get down, the three were standing together, Tammy with her arm around Linnet, Juliana a little to the side, her hands on her hips. He looked at them and shrugged, a gesture both of uncertainty and apology.

'Come on, then, strip,' Juliana urged. 'Let's see if it's as big as Tammy says.'

Joe began to undress, obviously hating it. Lily watched, embarrassed but unable to ignore a satisfied feeling at watching a Peeping Tom given a dose of his own medicine. The girls also watched, Linnet giggling, Tammy and Juliana with quiet smiles and occasional prompting when he tried to retain first his socks and then his underpants. At this final exposure he balked.

'What's the matter, Joe?' Tammy asked, her voice at once sweet and mocking. 'Come on, *I've* seen you. Why not my friends?'

Joe stammered something unintelligible to Lily.

'Now, now, Joe,' Juliana urged. 'You've seen us, and you didn't even ask, so down they come, right now.'

Lily heard the hard tone in Juliana's voice, knowing that if the command had been directed at her she would have been struggling to get her knickers down fast enough. Not Joe, who crossed his hands over his crotch and gave a glance in the direction of the beach and safety.

'Do we have to do it for you?' Tammy asked.

'I think we do,' Juliana agreed. 'In fact, I think that's what he wants.'

'Sure it is,' Linnet added. 'What randy little boy wouldn't like to be pinned down and stripped by three fine girls? You'll love it, won't you, Joe?'

Lily found her smile growing broader despite her sense of shock. What Linnet had said was so like the way Ed talked to her, telling her what she did and did not like, what she should and should not do. A sudden picture came to her, Ed in the same position as the hapless Joe, and she giggled.

'Come on, girls,' Joe managed as they began to advance on him. 'I'll take you on one by one, down behind the rocks.'

Tammy shook her head, smiling and reaching out as if to take hold of his underpants. He put his hands to hers, backing, only for Linnet to move forward at speed, jam one tiny leg between his ankles and kick. Joe went back, his arms flailing, his underpants wrenched down as he went. Lily felt a sudden, not unpleasant shock as his cock came on view. It was longer than Ed's, if thinner, and very pale, with the head already poking out of a meaty foreskin.

Joe fell, Juliana immediately pinning him by the arms, Tammy by the legs as Linnet skipped back, laughing. He struggled, but Lily could see that it was half-hearted, and then he had surrendered completely as Juliana's mouth found his penis and gulped it in. He lay back, the expression on his face turning to ecstasy as Juliana began to suck, only to vanish as Tammy moved up and cocked a leg across his head.

Lily's mouth went wide as Joe's face disappeared beneath the fleshy white cheeks of Tammy's ample bottom. His arms beat at the ground, but only briefly, then Juliana

172

had cupped his balls and he went limp, apparently resigned to licking pussy as he was sucked. Tammy wiggled her bottom on to Joe's face, pressing her sex to his mouth. Lily saw Tammy's expression change from one of happy mischief to pleasure and knew that the helpless boy was licking.

Joe's cock was hard in Juliana's mouth. She was masturbating him, nibbling on the bloated end of his penis as she stroked his shaft, a technique Lily quickly filed in her memory. Juliana was also in a thoroughly rude position herself, kneeling with her bottom pushed out towards Lily. Every detail of her sex showed, not just pouting sex lips and the wet, pink flesh of her vulva, but the wrinkled star of her anus, dun brown between olive-skinned buttocks. Lily swallowed at the sight, imagining how similar she herself would look in so shocking a pose. It was hard to watch, with her guilt rising at being a party to such a rude scene and a scene in which the Peeping Tom had little choice. Yet it was impossible to tear her eyes away, besides which, she could feel a trickle of moisture on the inside of her thigh.

The last of the fight went out of Joe, his arms coming up to cup Tammy's bottom, feeling the big cheeks as he licked. In response she squirmed in pleasure, rubbing herself in his face. His erection was now rigid, pointing skywards in Juliana's hand as she drew back. Lily watched as he was mounted, Juliana cocking a leg over his middle, taking his cock and rubbing it to her vulva, then rising up and sliding her body down until she was seated on him, her sex filled with penis.

As Juliana began to ride Joe, Tammy moved forward. Lily gasped in delighted shock as she realised that the boy was being made to lick Tammy's bottom. Not that he seemed to mind, his hands still clutching her plump cheeks as she rode him. He was obviously lost to decency, much as she herself had been after being buggered, a knowledge that made her feel ruder still. Biting her lip, she pulled the front of her dress high and slipped a hand beneath. Her sex was wet and warm, badly in need of being touched.

Reasoning that if they were prepared to be so openly dirty it hardly mattered if she just touched herself she began to stroke her pubic mound.

Linnet had been watching, never still, jumping on her toes, her fists balled in glee. Now she skipped down to the sea, vanishing beneath the surface in one smooth motion. For a moment Lily was puzzled, only to see the dark swirl of hair, then Linnet's head. She was grinning, and holding a thick strand of kelp and what looked like a mass of purple-green jelly. Running light-footed to her friends, she knelt down, pushed her face between Juliana's bouncing bottom and the rock and kissed Joe's balls, then pressed the thing in her hand to his scrotum.

Lily then realised what the object was, a huge snakelocks anemone. Linnet was grinning maniacally, her face close to Juliana's bottom. Joe was near orgasm, thrusting his hips up, pressing his cock into his mount's vagina. Tammy was also coming, one hand on her sex, one cradling her big breasts as he licked at her bottom hole. Juliana went forward, grinding herself on him, crying out as Linnet's lips found her bottom. The two girls came together, riding the helpless Joe and crying and laughing in their ecstasy. He was pumping frantically, his hips jerking, his cock jamming in and out of Juliana's stretched vagina, in Lily's clear view. Linnet was squeezing the anemone against his balls, but he seemed not to notice, only to jerk as the thick head of the kelp stalk was pushed to his anus. The hole was slick with Juliana's juices, and Lily saw the kelp stalk go in, Joe's protesting hole forced wide as his feet hammered frantically on the rock. It was great, she could not deny it, watching a man given the same dirty, degrading treatment as Ed had pushed her into, with a thick, hard object rammed home in the anus. Linnet was laughing, a high-pitched, manic cackle as she began to bugger the helpless Joe, her eyes locked to his gaping anus as the stem worked in and out. He had struggled, but his efforts slackened as Linnet worked the stalk inside him and abruptly every muscle in his body locked and Lily knew he had come inside Juliana. She was coming herself, quickly, not

174

wanting the others to see but with her eyes locked on the rude scene: Tammy's big bottom sitting square on Joe's face; Juliana's smaller, trimmer rear spread, anus on show, vagina filled with cock; Joe with the fat green anemone pushed to his balls and the stalk protruding obscenely from his anus . . .

As Lily came Linnet danced back, pulling the anemone away and hurling it out to sea, then turning again, all innocence. Tammy and Juliana slowly dismounted, leaving Joe to sit up, his face wet with white juice. With a look of displeasure he pulled the kelp from his anus, only for his face to break into a happy grin.

'Great,' he managed. 'Wow, just great. You girls are hot.'

'Any time,' Linnet answered happily.

'Sure,' Joe said. 'What was that thing you did to my balls?'

'Just a trick,' Linnet replied. 'It didn't really work.'

Joe looked down, his expression changing, from happy satisfaction, through surprise, to alarm and finally shock.

'Jesus, my balls!' he yelled. 'They're on fire!'

'That's your punishment!' Linnet laughed. 'The rest was just fun, even the stalk up your bum. Tell your friends that's what dirty little boys get for peeping!'

Mr Hobbers paused at the door to John Pardue's house, rehearsing his lines in his head. It was, after all, hardly practical to march in and demand to spank the man's daughter. Nor could he admit to purchasing the coin, or even to seeing it, as the parents were unlikely to know anything about her delinquent behaviour. Instead, he intended to take advantage of the family's obvious poverty, pretending to be calling at random and gaining an introduction by offering well over the odds for anything in their possession that had even the slightest antique value. If his line of reasoning proved false, then it would be easy to retire gracefully.

Peering cautiously within, he began to smile. The room was typical of Tawmouth: a smart front parlour, intended

175

for show and seldom entered. There were several pictures, country and maritime scenes, just prints, but old enough for his purposes. Better still were three model ships displayed within bottles, something that always sold well to tourists. Two he did not recognise; the third had his lips curving into a satisfied smile. She was the *Redoubtable*.

With new confidence he stepped back to the door and rang the bell. The response was slow, a man older than he had expected but not impossibly so, bald, stooped, but bright-eyed.

'I'm sorry to disturb you, sir,' Hobbers began. 'Mr Hobbers, Mr Frank Hobbers. I believe you are John Pardue.'

'Jan Pardue, that's me,' the man answered. 'How can I help you?'

'I am an antique dealer,' Hobbers went on. 'You may know my shop, in the High Street. I understand you possess a model of the *Redoubtable*.'

'I do,' Pardue answered, 'but she's not for sale.'

'That is a shame. I am prepared to make a generous offer. Perhaps two hundred pounds?'

'Sorry, can't be done. Anyhow, how did you know I had her?'

'Ah . . . A young lady told me. Your daughter? Perhaps your granddaughter?'

'I've no daughter, just three sons. Could be my granddaughter, Jasmine. She was over a while back.'

'Very likely. She came into my shop and saw a painting I have of the *Redoubtable*. I am very keen to have the model as well.'

'I dare say you are, but she's not for sale. An ancestor of mine served in her you see, under Captain Warrender, a relative, rather, James Keeley. The model came down from my great-grandmother, Jane Pardue, lived to be one hundred and four, she did. So I won't sell, you see.'

'I quite understand, although it is a shame. In the circumstances I might be prepared to offer you a discount on the picture, if you're interested.'

'Certainly I am. Still, I've been in your shop, and I doubt I can afford your fancy prices. Still, I've other models aplenty. Would you care to make an exchange?'

'Very possibly. Might I see them, if you've the time? I might well want to buy in any case.'

'I've all the time in the world if you're offering good money. Come in.'

Mr Hobbers smiled as he crossed the threshold.

Thomazina pulled herself on to the steps, feeling conspicuous in her tiny bikini. An elderly couple glanced at her as she reached the path, the woman disapproving, the man with a smile. She ignored them, glancing up and down the road, hurrying across. The throb of noise came from the docks, where china clay was pouring into a ship's hold from a storage hopper. White dust rose in the hot sun, settling to stain her bare feet as she padded quickly along the street. A little way beyond the dock gates she stopped, scanning the houses and shops, once, twice, then halting in indecision. Where the tattoo parlour had once been was a shop selling bathroom fittings. She bit her lip, once more glancing nervously along the road. Her heart jumped at a voice and she turned, expecting to see the blue uniform of the police. A man was looking at her, but not a policeman.

'You all right, love?' he asked again, peering into her face.

'I am sorry,' she stammered. 'I am a little lost. I thought there was a tattoo parlour along here. Next to a sweet shop.'

'Not next to a sweet shop, love. You must mean old Pardue. Top of Exhibition Road, on the left.'

'Exhibition Road?'

'On the right, back that way.'

She thanked him and ran, indifferent to the feel of his eyes on her wobbling, near-naked bottom. Finding Exhibition Road, she slowed. Only one person was visible, a man washing his car who gave her no more than a brief glance. At the end she quickly identified the sign offering tattoos and rang the bell, fidgeting as she waited. The door opened after what seemed an age. An elderly bald man looked out at her with a smile spreading slowly across his face.

'Mr Pardue?' she asked.

'That's me, call me Jan.'

'I was wondering if you could ink a tattoo in for me, if you have the time that is. This one. I'm Tammy, by the way.'

She turned, pushing out her bottom to show her tattoo, at which his grin grew broader still.

'Certainly I can,' he stated, beckoning her inside. 'You'll be young Yasmin's friend, then. She mentioned you. Given you don't seem to have any money in that bikini I suppose you'll be wanting to pay the same way, then.'

'I have money, although I'm afraid it's a little wet. How . . .'

Thomazina broke off. From the man's open leer it was quite obvious what he expected. She shrugged and smiled shyly, then followed him into the house. The door at the end of the passage was open, a man visible within, seated at a table with two model ships in front of him. Pardue ushered her in, offering tea.

'Oh, hello, Mr Hobbers,' Thomazina addressed the man. 'No tea, thank you, Mr Pardue, I'm rather in a hurry.'

'Hello, Jasmine,' Hobbers answered her.

'This isn't my Jasmine,' Pardue said. 'Just a customer, come for a tattoo. Would you excuse us a moment?'

Mr Hobbers nodded, throwing Thomazina a puzzled glance. She returned a smile and followed Pardue as he made for the stairs.

'Was Yasmin here then?' she asked as they entered his workroom.

'Yes. Her friend Violet wanted a tattoo the same as yours, an octopus, only in purple.'

'An octopus, like mine?'

'Exactly like yours, so she said. I've the drawing somewhere.'

'Her friend Violet had it done, you say, not Yasmin.'

'Yes, Violet. Pretty girl for all the purple hair. Had it done on her left cheek, she did, just like yours.'

'Could you tell me what she looks like?'

'Tall girl, purple hair, pierced nose, belly button too. Don't you know her?'

'Oh yes, of course,' Thomazina lied. 'There are two Violets, you see.'

'And are you anything like your friends?'

Thomazina didn't know quite what he meant. 'I suppose so.'

'Right,' Pardue answered. 'Well, then, if you'd lie on the bed and pop down your pants.'

Thomazina did as she was told, squeezing her bikini bottoms off and placing the money she had concealed down the front on the table. Pardue had shut the door and now turned back to her, his eyes travelling slowly down her body.

'How about a peep of your tits, before we start?' he asked. 'Seeing as how they'll be bare anyway, once it's done.'

With an easy shrug Thomazina took off her last garment, leaving herself nude as she lay down. Pardue's eyes followed her chest, watching her breasts squash out on the fabric of the bed. She watched him in return, smiling at his obvious enthusiasm. He gave a last, dirty grin and turned to his workbench, suddenly professional as he began to choose needles and ink. Thomazina tried to relax, remembering the pain of the needle and also the warm glow she had felt after it had been done.

'Old one, is it?' Pardue asked as his hand took hold of her bottom. 'You can't have been more than a nipper to judge from the fading.'

'Too much sunbathing,' Thomazina answered sleepily, 'but it was never very dark. I'd like it really bright green this time, and scarlet for the eyes.'

'Bad job, I'd suppose,' he went on. 'This'll be better. I'll be using some of them new inks. Bought them in London, I did, last time I went up. Hold still now.'

Thomazina winced as the tool hummed to life, forcing herself to relax, then swallowing as the needle bar bit into her bottom.

'Easy, love, it's hard to keep a grip with so much flesh. Not that I mind a bit of flesh, mark you.'

'I'm sure you don't. What did Yasmin do for you?'

'Hang on, love, we can't have that sort of talk, not while I'm working.'

Thomazina chuckled and went quiet, thinking of Yasmin's smooth, dark skin. Their sex had been pleasant, passionate and rude, making her sorry that it was not Yasmin who herself had been moved to have the tattoo. The initial pain of the tattooing needle had begun to fade, leaving a dull, warm throb that was going straight to her sex. Pardue, she was sure, would want a suck, maybe a feel of her body, but he was unlikely to give her an orgasm, at least not a truly satisfying one.

He paused, changing the needle, then returned to work on her bottom. She knew she was wet, that he would be able to smell her excitement, and that doubtless he was anticipating the pleasure of her body. At his age it was likely to take a while, and she wondered if he might be persuaded to lie on the bed and let her take her pleasure mounted on his erection. True, it would not really be a payment, not as such, but it promised the best orgasm and as a dirty old man he was unlikely to refuse such a request.

'Done,' he announced and the low buzz of the tool stopped.

'Thank you. You are very kind,' Thomazina answered. 'Now, you hinted you might like a little something for your payment.'

He nodded, his hands going straight to his fly.

'What did Yasmin do?' she asked.

'They posed,' he answered. 'Both of them, Violet with her pretty bottom stuck out for me, Yasmin showing her tits. You're nicer than either, with those great big titties and your meaty behind, so how about the same?'

'Oh, I can do better than that,' she assured him as she rose. 'I'll suck you, or you can even put your little man in me. I'm very wet.'

'I know, you've left a patch on the bed.'

Thomazina giggled and reached for his cock. It felt rubbery in her hand, heavy too, and it was already beginning to stiffen.

'We'd better be quick,' he breathed. 'That fellow Hobbers is waiting downstairs.'

'Never mind old Mr Hobbers. I want to suck you. I want to rub while you're in me.'

'You're a dirty one and no mistake.'

He finished with a grunt. Thomazina had knelt, taking his cock in her mouth. It was growing, swelling with blood. The taste of male and tattoo ink was strong in her mouth. Her tattoo was throbbing, keeping her firmly on heat and reminding her of how she was marked. Sucking eagerly, she put her hand between her thighs and began to knead, feeling the soft flesh of her sex and the wet, open centre. Pardue settled back, against the edge of the bed.

'Rub it in your tits, love,' he groaned. 'I love that.'

Thomazina complied, rising to fold his now stiff penis in the fleshy valley between her breasts. He began to push, making short jerking motions, his cock head emerging and disappearing between the fat pillows of her chest with each push. His front was rubbing her nipples, making her giggle with pleasure as he went faster, faster still and then grunted as he ejaculated, full in her face. She gasped in shock as the unexpected eruption splashed in her mouth and across her chin. He had caught one eye, shutting it, and her nose, from which a long piece of sperm was dangling. There was more on her breasts, smeared in the groove he had been fucking and spattered over their upper surfaces.

'Mr Pardue!' she exclaimed as his cock slid back from her slimy cleavage.

'Sorry, love, couldn't hold myself,' he answered.

'I wanted to come,' she protested. 'Help me come, please.'

'Sorry, love, no time for that nonsense,' he went on. 'Besides, who's paying who here?'

He chuckled and she sat back, doing her best to look angry. For a moment she considered masturbating anyway, and then she thought of Mr Hobbers.

Mr Hobbers sat stiff in his chair, his cock a rigid bar within his trousers. It had been bad enough knowing that Pardue had his hands on Tammy's naked bottom, but the giggles and groans that had followed the end of the tattooing session could mean only one thing: Tammy had paid him with sex.

Evidently she was genuinely not his granddaughter, or at least he hoped not, but the puzzle had been pushed from his mind by his overwhelming desire for her. Now, as a door slammed upstairs and he heard her giggling thank-you, his determination became stronger than ever.

'Sorry to keep you waiting, Mr Hobbers,' Pardue announced as he returned to the room. 'I'll just show the young lady out and we'll get back to business.'

'As it happens I must be going myself,' Hobbers answered quickly. 'I really had forgotten the time. The models are splendid, simply splendid. I shall take both if I may. Perhaps if I bring the picture round next week?'

'That would be fine . . .'

'Perfect, perfect. Now I must be getting along.'

He rose, offering his hand to Pardue. They shook and left the room, finding Tammy standing in the hallway, gazing at a picture, her mouth drawn down in a sad bow. For a moment the light caught the edge of her eye, and Mr Hobbers saw that the rim was heavy with tears. He felt a trace of guilt, realising her response was probably due to being made to suck Mr Pardue's penis, which he was sure was what had happened. Then she had turned and was once more all smiles.

'That's another old one,' Pardue remarked. 'Eighteen fifty, or thereabouts. The youngest is Jane Pardue, the ancestor I mentioned earlier, when she was a little girl. The others are her sisters, Emily and Thomazina.'

Hobbers looked at the picture, a sketch of three young girls in pinafores seated on a bench beside a wall. All were buxom, the eldest especially, her ripe curves obvious even in the loose dress and a picture that had never been intended as erotic. He glanced at Tammy, who gave a nervous smile, then back.

'My, you do look like little Thomazina,' Pardue remarked. 'I thought your face was familiar. You a Tawmouth girl?'

'Newton Abbot,' Thomazina answered quickly. 'Yes, she is a little like me. Perhaps we're related.'

She smiled and moved to the door, opening it to flood the hall with daylight. Again Hobbers looked at the picture, then back at Tammy. The resemblance was striking, only one feature spoiling it. Thomazina Keeley had a mass of tawny curls spilling out from under her bonnet, totally unlike Tammy's straight, jet-black hair.

'Must be going, then,' he said quickly, following Tammy to the door.

It closed behind them and he took her arm, determined not to let the chance slip away.

'I think we ought to pay a visit to my shop, don't you?' he began, steering her towards his car.

'Your shop?' she answered, in obvious shock. 'No, no, I really couldn't. Look . . .'

'Ah, but you should,' he went on. 'You see, I know everything.'

'How do you mean, Mr Hobbers?'

'And you needn't put on the little-lady act either. I know you're not simple. I know everything, about the gravestone, everything.'

'The gravestone?'

'Thomazina Keeley's gravestone, the one you took your name from for your little thieving spate.'

'I really don't know –'

'Come on, you needn't play coy with me. I've been to Abbotscombe and seen the stone. Remember the little story you told me about how you and your sisters used to be spanked? Your sisters Emily and Jane. Only they're not your sisters, are they? They were Thomazina Keeley's sisters. You're a thief, young lady, along with your little friend who stole the clothes, and I know what to do with little thieves, especially dirty little thieves.'

'No, no, Mr Hobbers, please not the police. Wasn't I nice to you?'

'Yes, you were, and if you were nice to me again we might forget the whole matter.'

'But of course! Dear Mr Hobbers, you only had to ask! I don't mind at all. I suspect you heard what I did for old Mr Pardue.'

'Well, yes . . .'

'Then I shall do the same for you, and more. Oh, you are a silly, thinking I'd mind!'

'Don't you?'

'Not at all. I understand how you feel. It must be awfully lonely. Not in your shop, though: I might be seen. I'll tell you what: I have to get up to Aldon Hill, but if you drive me around the estuary I'll do whatever you like, anything at all.'

'What you actually need is a good, firm spanking,' Hobbers answered, trying to reassert his control.

Tammy answered with a giggle. With his heart hammering in his chest, Hobbers opened the car door for her. She got in, her face set in a happy, mischievous smile. He would have preferred her to look a little more worried, perhaps contrite, sullen or miserable, the expressions the girls always wore in the spanking magazines. Still, a few hard swats on her naked bottom were bound to wipe the smile off her face.

He drove as fast as he dared, up the estuary and across the Taw on the bypass, turning on to the Abbotscombe road and then into a side lane. He knew exactly where he was going: Rocombe Woods, a shallow, tree-grown valley that led down towards the cliffs beyond Aldon Hill. He had walked there often, a favourite fantasy being to catch some young girl there and trick her into taking a smacked bottom. Now it was real, and the girl beside him was as lovely as the finest creature of his fantasies, also in thrall to him, expecting a just punishment, a punishment he intended to make the most of.

'So why pick Thomazina Keeley?' he asked as he drew the car to a halt. 'Are you a descendant of hers?'

'In a way.'

'I thought so. You've been very bad, you know, pretending to be someone else and stealing things, not to mention selling me that coin. I am going to have to punish you properly, you know, this won't be just a play-spanking.'

'Oh, dear. Well I suppose if you must.'

'I must. Now come on, a little way into the woods and we'll be quite safe. If you are related to Thomazina Keeley, you must be related to old Pardue as well. Didn't you know?'

'No, but I do look like her, don't I?'

'Yes, but then so do plenty of other well-built Devon girls.'

She didn't answer, but nodded, then gave him a look that might have been doubt, even fear. There had been a mocking quality to her conversation, as if she was unable to take her coming punishment seriously. It was an attitude he had read about, the girl due for punishment trying to make light of it, then becoming more fearful as she realised she was not going to get off.

They had reached an area of broken ground, the tangled, earth-clogged roots of a fallen tree blocking off the view of the road. A smaller tree had come down with it, providing the perfect seat, a place where he had picnicked before, often imagining how good it was for the purposes of taking an errant girl across his knee. Tammy, barefoot, had been picking her way carefully and now stopped, looking at him as he sat down, her hands crossed in her lap.

'Well then, my dear, I think it's time for your spanking,' he announced and patted his knees.

She gave the tiniest of grimaces and came forward, bending across his legs and resting her weight on her hands and feet. As she moved the tiny bikini pants pulled into her crease, displaying yet more of her generous bottom. She looked back, her big green eyes showing through a cloud of fallen hair.

'Don't be too rough, please, Mr Hobbers,' she said softly. 'My tattoo's a little sore.'

'I dare say it is,' he answered. 'Beats me why you'd want an octopus tattooed on your behind anyway, or anything else. It ruins a girl's innocence.'

'It's a private thing.'

'Just wilfulness, I suspect, when all is said and done. In any case I think it warrants a few extra slaps, if not on the actual area.'

185

'Do it, then, I don't care.'

'You will, my dear, you will. Now, let's have these silly little bikini pants down, shall we? It's not as if they cover much, anyway.'

She gave an odd sound as he took hold of her bikini pants, halfway between a sigh and a groan, expressing shame, he hoped, but possibly simple resignation. It was impossible to resist a grin as he peeled the scrap of material away from her bottom. She was truly glorious, her buttocks big and firm – meaty hemispheres, one on either side of a deep cleft. Cocking his leg up and tightening his grip on her arm, he forced her to lift it, spreading the cheeks to expose the tight dimple of her anus and the lips of her sex. She was wet, her vagina a moist oval of pink with beads of white fluid at the mouth.

He took her firmly around the waist, lifted his hand, waited one delightful moment and then brought it down hard on her bottom. She squealed and her big cheeks parted and bounced, only to bounce again to a second smack. Again she squealed and he set to work, grinning as he spanked her, his eyes feasting on her wobbling bottom, listening to her cries in delight. She began to kick, losing control of her legs, then to pant in between her squeals and grunts. Each slap had left a print on the pale skin of her bottom, a pink flush that spread quickly as he beat her, slapping and slapping to the sound of her cries. She was writhing in his grip, really kicking, obviously taken by surprise at the force of her punishment. His hand stung, but he kept on, fully aware that he might well never again have the chance to spank a girl, never mind such a beauty, and bare as well.

With her bottom a ball of glowing red she began to cry, choking sobs and then a full-blown bawling interrupted only by her squeaks of pain as each slap landed. He had found a rhythm, making her fat buttocks bounce in time to his slaps, parting to show her anus and fanny then closing, only to spread once more. Her kicking legs were wide, her fists beating on the ground, leaving her full weight on his lap, but he kept on, spanking and spanking, slapping each fat, rosy cheek until at last the stinging pain in his hand became too much and he was forced to stop.

He was panting, exhausted. His cock was pressed to her flesh, rock hard through his trousers. She made no objection, nor any attempt to get up, lying limp and beaten across his lap, just as he had always imagined a punished girl should. Her compliance seemed absolute, and he wondered if he might not push his advantage further. Already he anticipated having his cock sucked, or tossed off at the least, but it seemed more than likely that now she was beaten she may be persuaded to go further still. Besides, she had said he could do anything, even if she may not have understood the full implications of her offer.

She was sobbing and breathing hard, while a trickle of juice was running from the open hole of her fanny. Her inner thighs were wet, too, smeared with the juice that had come out during her punishment. Hobbers reached out a finger, touching her thigh, the lips of her sex, then sliding into the tight embrace of her hole. She did nothing to prevent the violation, only giving another, louder sob. Encouraged, he cocked his legs higher to keep her in place and slid a hand beneath her chest, cupping one huge breast, then the other. She whimpered, but again made no effort to stop him. A quick tug had her bikini top up, her breasts spilling bare into his hands. Again she whimpered.

'Right, my girl,' he announced, now certain she would do as she was told. 'You've had your punishment. Now it's time I had a little fun with you.'

As he let go she rose to stand, facing away and looking back over her shoulder as she rubbed her red bottom. She had been well spanked, both big cheeks glowing a rich pink, with reddened goosepimples crowning each one. If she had failed to look right before, this was no longer the case. Her face was set in an angry moue of resentment and contrition.

'So what do you want now?' she demanded. 'I suppose I'm going to have to suck your little man.'

'You are,' he answered. 'Come down on your knees and stick that bottom out so I can see.'

Her grudging expression deepened as she knelt down among the leaf mould and twigs, but she made no objection. He freed his penis, which was so stiff it hurt, a condition he could not remember experiencing since his teenage years. She came forward, her beautiful mouth opening, her big, green eyes turning up to meet his gaze, and then it was in her mouth, his penis, stuck in a pretty girl's mouth, a girl whom he had spanked and whose naked, reddened bottom was in plain view.

It would have been easy to come, so easy, jerking his cock when the pleasure became too much and spraying his come over her beautiful, sulky face. Yet it would have been a waste. He had spanked her, now he was going to fuck her. Fighting down the urge to just let her suck, he took her gently by the ears and pulled her head back, leaving his penis glistening with her saliva in the broken sunlight.

'I'm going to have you, my girl,' he managed. 'Properly. And I'll have no nonsense.'

'Shall I bend?' she asked softly.

'No,' he answered. 'I'm not a young man any more. I will lie down and you must climb on top.'

'Yes, sir,' she answered and shuffled back to let him rise.

He went down, glorying in the power he had over her and her absolute obedience. Lying back, he wished for a moment that he had the strength to take her kneeling, with her big bottom stuck high as she had offered, yet he knew he would never have managed to summon the energy to reach orgasm in so energetic a position. Tammy made no comment, but watched as he held his cock up for her to sit on.

'Turn around,' he ordered. 'I want to see that fine red bottom I've given you. And you're to do the work.'

Tammy turned and he watched, unable to take his eyes away as she lowered her huge, reddened bottom on to his crotch. The tip of his penis touched her hole and disappeared inside, followed by the length of his shaft until her buttocks settled on his legs, still spread wide to show her anus and the taut pink ring of her vagina where it engulfed his cock.

She began to move, slowly at first, then with more enthusiasm, until she was bouncing on his cock with her big breasts slapping together and her buttocks wobbling in time to her motion. He let her do it, his eyes feasting on her plump, firm young body, drinking in the way her flesh moved and the sight of his cock sliding in her vagina. She had leaned forward a little, making her anus a dark, prominent hole between her big, red cheeks, wet with sweat and her own juice. He groaned, thinking of how many pictures of spanked girls with their buttocks spread he had seen and how often he had imagined pushing his cock into the tight rosebuds of their bottom holes. It was the last trick he played in his fantasies, the dirtiest, the most satisfying, to trick a spanked girl into accepting buggery.

'Wouldn't do to give you a baby,' he grunted. 'Which is what's going to happen if you keep that up. Lift up and I'll show you a trick I bet your boyfriends don't know.'

Tammy lifted her bottom obediently, letting his cock slip free, white and slimy with her juice. He took it, rubbing the tip in the mush of her sex, bumping the head on her clitoris. Sure enough, she sighed and wiggled on to him, arching her back and taking a breast in either hand.

'Oh, Mr Hobbers, that is nice,' she said. 'Oh, do go on.'

He chuckled, changing the motion of his hand to rub from her clitoris to her vagina, then further, smearing her own lubrication on to her anus. As his cock head touched the tiny hole he expected an objection, but she gave none, continuing to moan and play with her breasts. He carried on, prepared to use threats if needed, as he was sure they would be when the time came to penetrate her undoubtedly virgin anus.

It was wet, a slimy brown ring, pink in the centre, open enough perhaps to be buggered. He went on rubbing, listening to her ever more aroused sounds, then, when she had begun to pant, he pressed his cock to her ring. She groaned, a sound of pleasure but also despair, and he found himself grinning from ear to ear as he watched the head of his penis press into her anal opening.

'Oh, no, Mr Hobbers, not that,' she gasped, but she made no move to rise.

'Sorry, my dear,' he answered, 'if you didn't want to be buggered, you shouldn't have grown such a fine, fat behind.'

He had taken her hips and pulled down as he spoke. She gave a yelp as his cock popped past the tight constriction of her anal ring. The head was inside, embedded in warm, rectal flesh, her sphincter tight on the neck.

'Relax, my dear,' he ordered. 'It's going up you, one way or another, so best to make it easy.'

Again she gave her little despairing groan, but began to lower her weight even as he felt her ring give. He watched, eyes bulging as the full, greasy pink length of his penis slid into her bottom hole, his cock in a young girl's bottom hole, a *spanked* young girl's bottom hole. Her bottom settled on his hips, her cheeks still hot from her beating. It was all the way in, her wet sex pressed to his balls, the last half-inch of his cock all that remained outside the straining ring of her anus. Once more she groaned, expressing misery, humiliation, helpless pleasure, all the emotions he would have expected in a girl with an old man's penis in her back passage.

'Ride it, nice and slow,' he ordered, 'and start feeling yourself again – I like to see that.'

She obeyed, once again starting to bounce on his cock, only this time with it firmly pushed up her ample bottom. He watched her ring move on his shaft, lost in ecstasy at the feel of the inside of her rectum rubbing on his glans. She began to masturbate, one hand to her sex, the other holding up a breast, stroking the nipple. He groaned as she began to move faster, her long black hair shaking to the rhythm of her movements, which also sent delicious little quivers through her fleshy bottom cheeks and her sides. He lay back, letting her do the work, buggering herself, feeding cock in and out of her dirty little hole until she made him come, which he knew would not be long, nor for her. Her ring began to contract and she cried out, no longer in sorrow but in pure pleasure. She was coming on his cock, her anus going into spasm on his shaft, her buttocks bouncing and wobbling, his cock rubbing in the hot, slimy tube of her rectum. He felt the jerk as he shot the full mass of his sperm into her bowels. She screamed out and rose, lifting herself clear for one instant and then jamming her gaping anus back on to his cock. Sperm erupted from around his cock, splashing his balls as she sat hard on him, and his vision went red with ecstasy, his final view that of her sperm-slick ring sliding down on his shaft.

Nine

Violet jumped down from the gangplank of the river ferry, her shoes crunching into the coarse red sand. Nich followed, taking long steps in a fastidious attempt to spare his Cuban heels. Yasmin came last, after passing out their bags.

The shore was crowded, the tiny parking area for the miniature golf course packed with vans and cars. A road crew was unloading a generator from one of these; Topher Knight stood by another, flicking through a case of discs. Yasmin waved and called, but failed to attract his attention, her voice lost in the general buzz of noise.

'Catch him later,' Violet suggested. 'Anyway, Nich's been through everything with him.'

'Right,' Yasmin answered doubtfully. 'Hey, look, that's Tammy, in the blue bikini, with that old boy.'

Violet turned to where Yasmin was pointing, finding a well-built young girl stepping from a car. A man was standing at the opposite door.

'The shame of it,' she laughed, 'brought to the party by her dad!'

'No, no,' Nich cut in, 'that's Mr Hobbers, the man who I met in the library.'

He jumped to the low wall that bordered the beach, walking quickly towards the couple. Mr Hobbers had been about to get back into his car, but paused at the sight of Nich. Violet and Yasmin followed, Tammy smiling at Yasmin, then giving a glance of unmistakable excitement towards Violet's hair.

192

'Good afternoon,' Nich greeted them, nodding formally to Mr Hobbers. 'It is Tammy, I believe.'

'Yes,' the girl answered. 'Hello, Yasmin.'

'You friends?' Hobbers asked, his manner now somewhat uneasy.

'Yes,' Yasmin answered. 'Hi, Tammy.'

'I had really better be going,' Hobbers said quickly. 'Well, then, goodbye, "Thomazina Keeley", enjoy your party.'

He ducked back into the car, quickly starting the engine and backing away.

'What got to him?' Yasmin asked.

'Oh, don't worry,' Tammy laughed. 'He thinks I'm a thief and I suppose he thinks you're my gang. He spanked me too, and maybe he thinks we might try to get even.'

'He did what?'

'He spanked me. He is funny. He is desperate to smack my bottom, but he lacks the courage to simply ask. He did in the end, but only when he thought I couldn't refuse. I put on a fine show for him.'

'The dirty old bastard!'

'Oh, it wasn't so bad. I made a fuss, but that's always the best way, then they get too excited to do it properly. Are you Violet?'

'Yes,' Violet answered, 'and this is Nich.'

'Hi,' Tammy said, nodding to Nich and then turning back to Violet. 'Is it you who had an octopus tattoo done, like mine?'

She turned as she spoke, displaying her bottom. Violet swallowed as she saw the flushed pink skin, realising that not only had the old man spanked her, but that he had done it recently. The tattoo also had a raw, recent appearance, suggesting it had only just been filled in.

'Yes, mine's purple. It's a bit scabby now, but I'll show you later. You're coming up to the Wythman, aren't you?'

'To dance?' Nich asked.

'Yes,' Tammy responded. 'So why did you get the tattoo?'

'Yasmin saw yours,' Violet answered. 'It sounded really cool, so I got one myself, from this old guy down by the docks.'

193

'I went to get mine redone. That's where I met Mr Hobbers.'

'And you let him spank you, a dirty old man like that? Why?'

'I suspect I know,' Nich put in.

Juliana stood at the highest point of the barrow, looking out to where the sun was sinking in the west. Elune was beside her, also lost in reflection, indifferent to the gathering crowds. Inside her excitement was rising, and occasionally her eyes would flick to where Lily was standing, pensive and obviously embarrassed by the cheerful throng of pagans and other partygoers.

They had spoken, and Lily had admitted to dreaming, shyly at first, giving no details, and then in greater depth as both she and Elune had admitted to the same experiences. Lily was now fascinated, and by the time they had reached the summit of Aldon Hill she had been talking openly, of the dreams, of her feelings, and of the man Edward Gardner, who ruled her. She had even been persuaded to remain at the party, and Juliana's sense of hope had risen until her throat felt tense and her stomach weak. One thing alone spoiled her pleasure: the absence of Aileve – yet in turn this increased her determination.

She turned from the glare of the sun, letting her eyes run over the gathering crowd. Most wore bright, revealing clothes, many had body jewellery, a colourful display that suggested an ease of spirit very far from the Christian rigidity. Moreover, there were many symbols on display, few of which she recognised, but which were clearly not related to the cross or fish symbol.

A voice called out her name, then Linnet's, and she saw Thomazina climbing over the stile, with others, a man and two women. As the group approached she saw the man's earrings, red enamel and eight-pointed, each point set with tiny flecks of gold. One girl was dark, the other pale, but with purple hair and amethysts set in her ears, nose and belly. Around her navel purple symbols had been tattooed, in Greek script.

194

With her pulse racing she watched them approach, then cast Thomazina a questioning look, which was answered with a smile. The other three broke off, towards where the control system for the party was being set up, Thomazina walking on alone and climbing the mound to join them.

'Who are they?' Elune demanded, Juliana echoing the question.

'She is a dreamer, the purple-haired one,' Thomazina answered, her voice bubbling over with excitement. 'She has a tattoo, like mine, but purple to suit her taste.'

'What have you told her?'

'A little. She is already intrigued; I think she is caught. Tonight, when we have danced, they will perform a ritual. The man is a heathen, a priest of some sort.'

'A pagan, Thomazina,' Elune corrected. 'What of the ritual?'

'He would not say. It is pagan, it can only do good.'

Elune nodded. Juliana looked to find the purple-haired girl. She was with the others, by the front of the mound, talking to Lily. Beyond, a group of people were approaching: a small man with a brush of greying hair, other, younger men and a woman. The woman was tall, elegant, her face a delicate oval in a frame of jet-black hair, her expression detached, almost ethereal, and familiar. She looked up, her eyes meeting Juliana's, and the last doubt vanished: it was Aileve. Juliana nudged Elune, who gave a delighted squeak. Thomazina waved, and, as the people who had been with her stopped, Aileve came forward, climbing the mound.

'Where have you been?' Elune demanded. 'We thought you lost, or worse.'

'I have been in Exeter,' Aileve answered, then bent to kiss each of them in turn, 'and for now I am Dr Alice Chaswell, a much-respected expert on medieval archaeology. Those with me are my colleagues, Professor Cobb and others. Tomorrow we open the Wythman.'

'Open the temple!'

'Indeed, and why not? Surely it is a better contrivance than our last attempt.'

'Yes, I suppose, but how did you manage this? To join the people who are going to open the temple?'

'How did I manage it?' Aileve answered. 'I arranged it. I, while you have been cunting the length of the sleeve and more, have been working for our Lord.'

'He has no understanding of such things,' Elune replied tartly. 'Also, I'm sure that the word "cunting" is neither current nor polite.'

'No, but it describes your behaviour,' Aileve went on, 'and his understanding is irrelevant: liege duty is liege duty.'

'Well I think you've done jolly well,' Thomazina broke in, 'but we've not been dallying, or at least I've not. I have permission for us to dance tonight, nude. It is sure to bring someone.'

'With the way closed?'

'Maybe. It can be opened.'

'And doubtless we will be caught again and I will be molested by fat policemen. My way is better.'

'Perhaps,' Elune admitted. 'In any case, I am happy you are with us. Tonight will now be as it should.'

'Two dream,' Juliana stated. 'A wild young girl with purple hair and jewels in her flesh. She has taken a tattoo, showing him, a replica of Thomazina's.'

'She is called Violet,' Thomazina added, 'and is already heathen. She has adopted the name Ianthe as deity. She says it is for a sea nymph.'

'Wonderful, and the other?'

'The other is shy and sweet, and she is drawn to him, without doubt. The girl beside your friends, with the pale hair.'

'Lily Tompkins?'

'Yes, Lily. She came to us this morning. You know her?'

'She is a student, studying ancient sites, and will be with us tomorrow. If she dreams she is caught, surely.'

Lily responded to Professor Cobb's introductions with a pleased smile. It was impossible not to feel privileged, with so many of those whose work she had studied talking to her as an equal. Not only Cobb, but Alice Chaswell, whose ability to find lost medieval sites was legendary, and who also, to Lily's surprise, seemed to know the girls she had met that morning.

'. . . sometime before 3000 BC,' Cobb was saying in response to a question. 'My guess is as much as five hundred years previously; Alice thinks earlier still. Possibly we will be able to obtain more accurate datings.'

'If old Wilmot has left anything to go on,' another put in.

'His excavation was fairly cursory,' Cobb replied. 'So Alice assures me. He expected a burial chamber, a typical kistvaen, and when he found nothing in the central chamber he assumed anything of value had been taken and gave up. I think we can hope for a great deal.'

'So what would these people have been like?' Lily asked, gesturing at the mound.

'We know very little,' Cobb answered. 'They left no written records and little other than their stone artefacts remain. They seem to have been polytheistic, and great temple builders, as the Wythman attests. We do know they were small, from the dimensions of their huts and what few skeletal remains have been found, also dark-haired and delicate. In fact, look at the little girl Alice is talking to, in the yellow dress. To them she would have been tall, but not atypical.'

'I know her actually,' Lily put in. 'She's a grown woman.'

'She is?' Cobb answered. 'Then she may well have more than a normal share of pre-Celtic genes. She could have walked into the settlement at Grimspound and been thought no more than an attractive stranger.'

'So they interbred with the Celts?'

'To some extent. Genetic studies of the populations in the West Country and Ireland indicate as much. Nothing is known for certain, although there is one piece of amusing speculation.'

'What's that?'

'Pure speculation, it really is, no more, but it has been suggested that the Celtic legends of pixies, fairies and so forth derive from their contact with their forerunners. It is easy to imagine. The pre-Celts were small and seem to have been peaceful agrarians. You can imagine their shock when the Celts arrived, far larger, warlike and temperamental. They would have been quickly pushed back from the more fertile land, on to Dartmoor and other high places. To the incoming Celts they would have seemed shy, elusive people, tiny and with no shared language. It is easy to see they might have been thought supernatural.'

'I see, and when they died out the legends persisted.'

'Absolutely. Again it is purest speculation, but the legends may even give a hint to their character. Pixies are portrayed as unnaturally agile and full of mischief, leading people into bogs, spoiling milk, even stealing babies. Who knows? There may be some truth behind it, although it can hardly be considered as scientific evidence.'

'It's a nice story, anyway,' Lily replied. 'Actually, Professor Cobb, I was wondering if I might ask you a favour. The man over there, with the red hair in a ponytail ... He's a Mr Mordaunt, who is a keen amateur with a special interest in the Wythman barrow. I promised I'd ask if he might join us to watch the dig.'

'Certainly,' Cobb answered. 'We could always do with an extra hand, as long as he knows his stuff and doesn't pinch anything.'

'I'm sure he'll be fine,' she answered. 'Shall I introduce you now?'

Cobb nodded and she went to Nich, who proved eager for the introduction. He was quickly accepted, exerting his full charm and knowledge on Professor Cobb and the others. Alice Chaswell rejoined the group and began to talk to Lily, comparing the map of the mound with how she herself imagined it had once looked. Somewhat in awe of the young woman's reputation, she found herself filling with girlish pride at being singled out, only for the feeling to be replaced with trepidation as Ed appeared, walking towards them. Glancing at her watch, she realised that she should have been at his house, making his tea.

'There you are,' he announced. 'I thought I'd find you up here. Aren't you going to introduce me to your colleagues?'

'Yes, of course,' Lily stammered. 'Dr Chaswell, this is Edward Gardner.'

'Her fiancé,' Ed added. 'Call me Ed. Lil said you were coming today. Digging up some old bones, eh?'

'Excavating the barrow,' Lily said hurriedly. 'It's not really bones we're after, more things like post holes. But this is Professor Cobb, Mr Mordaunt I think you've met . . .'

She went on, introducing the others. Ed scowled at Nich, who answered the look with a cold stare. Now feeling uneasy and embarrassed, she tried to return to her conversation with Alice Chaswell, only to have Ed place a proprietorial arm around her shoulder.

'You must excuse Lil and I,' he said. 'We really must be getting back to the town.'

Lily let herself be steered away, wanting to remonstrate but knowing exactly what Ed's response would be. He pulled her towards the stile, his grip tightening on her arm as they moved away from the group around the barrow.

'Ow, Ed, I'm coming,' she managed as his fingers pinched into the soft flesh of her arm.

'You bet you are,' he answered. 'Jesus, I've never seen such a bunch of dropouts and weirdos, and the eggheads are as bad. What a waste of taxpayers' money!'

'It's important research.'

'Important research? Bollocks more like. You're lucky you found me, or you'd have ended up like that. I can just see you, a right little egg bonce you'd make!'

'But that's what I want to be, an archaeologist. Like Dr Chaswell. She's brilliant.'

'No wife of mine spends half her life up to her fanny in dirt. Drop it, and I don't want to hear another word.'

'But Ed . . .'

'Do you want a slap?'

'No, Ed, I'm sorry.'

'That's more like my Lil. Now look, a woman's privileged to be with me, but to be with me she's got to know her place, and like they say, that's barefoot, pregnant and in the kitchen. Now come on.'

'What about the party? There'll be food. Why don't we stay?'

'With that bunch of weirdos? You've got to be fucking joking. No, my girl, you're coming home, making my tea, and then it's upstairs and panties off, and that way you stay. Any argument and you get a slap. I'm an easy-going guy, Lil, but I mean it: I won't take any shit. Besides, Jeff and his boys are going to raid the place and I don't want you in the cells with a load of drugged-up weirdies.'

Joe pushed up the path, his eyes fixed guiltily to the jeans-clad bottom of a woman some way in front of him. His balls hurt, and he had spent most of the day alternately bathing his scrotum in ice and rubbing in antihistamine cream. It had made little difference, and they were still swollen and sore, but he was sure what they had done to him had been more a joke than a real punishment, if only from the way they had laughed afterwards. The little one had been vicious. The others had wanted sex more than anything, he was convinced, and even though Tammy had made him lick her bottom hole it had been the most exciting sexual experience of his life.

He wanted more, and intended to seek Tammy and her friends out at the party. With luck the blonde, whom he'd heard called Lily, would put out. Maybe all three would, which would be something else, just as long as he could keep clear of the demented little one. In any case he was determined to try, and he was sure that at the least he could expect a fuck with Tammy, especially as in addition to an eight-pack of beer he had brought a sizeable chunk of black resin.

Ahead he could already hear the roar of music, indistinct through the trees, yet wild and urgent, increasing his lust and excitement. It had to be good. Just as long as he had enough courage he would get what he wanted, maybe even the jackpot: Tammy and both her friends.

Having reached the stile, he climbed over, finding the rough ground around the barrow packed with people.

Some he knew, most not, but he walked forward greeting all and sundry, pulling the first beer from his pack as he reached the top of the hill. It was getting dark, but spotlights had already been switched on, swinging to and fro across the crowd to make the multitude of heads seem to move and throw long black shadows behind them. A stroboscope flickered to life, sending the scene into a mesh of jerking, black-and-white shadow.

Joe moved towards the mound, intending to climb it and so look down on the crowd to find who he wanted. People were on the mound, and his lust swelled inside him as he recognised first Tammy and then Juliana. Others were there, too: a girl with purple hair he had seen on the beach, her Indian friend with the big breasts and fleshy bottom, and another, taller, black-haired girl, slim and elegant. He increased his pace, only to falter as the small girl came into his vision, jumping up from the far side of the mound. His balls twinged in pain but he shrugged, preferring to risk her sadistic humour than to back away. Reaching the mound, he ran quickly up the face, greeting the girls with a knowing grin.

'Hi,' he shouted. 'Beer? Something stronger?'

'We're busy just now,' the purple-haired girl answered him.

'It's my little Peeping Tom,' Juliana cut in. 'It's all right, Violet. He's the one I was telling you about.'

'Is he?' the Indian girl demanded. 'Well I want a word.'

'Sure,' Joe answered.

'Did you steal my clothes?' she demanded.

'No, honest,' he answered, taken aback. 'No, no, I swear it.'

'Sit on his head, Yasmin,' Juliana laughed. 'That'll make him tell the truth.'

'I didn't, I swear,' Joe stammered. 'Why would I want your clothes?'

'Because you're a dirty little pervert!'

'It wasn't me, I swear it. Look, I'm sorry I peeped, yeah, but they got me for that. I didn't nick your clothes. I really swear. Look, I've got some great gear here. Have some?'

'What is it?'

'Black, good stuff.'

Yasmin's look of aggression softened and she nodded towards the far side of the mound, where shadows would make what they were doing less obvious. Joe felt a fresh surge of lust and satisfaction and followed.

Violet took a draught of air, wondering why her head was swimming so strongly and why she felt so overwhelmingly dirty. She knew it came at solstice parties, but now it was stronger than ever. She wondered if the feeling was linked to her dreams, yet she was clearly not alone. All around her people were dancing with frantic energy, and in their movement there was more passion, more open erotic display than she had ever known. Several girls had stripped off their tops; a few were in just panties; one or two were naked, as were more than one man. Below her, at the foot of the mound, Yasmin had allowed the Peeping Tom, Joe, to lift her top, and he was nuzzling her breasts in between puffs of the joint they were sharing. Further off, a girl was on Topher's lap, and appeared to be stroking his crotch beneath the shelter of his turntables. Beyond, in the jerking, half-lit shadows, more than one couple could be glimpsed, locked together, buttocks bobbing between spread thighs.

Lowering herself to the ground, she turned to see the four girls, who alone seemed calm, chatting quietly or staring out into the blackness beyond the lights. Linnet's face looked unworldly, barely human, with her tiny features and her huge eyes reflecting brilliant green with each flash of the strobe. The others were gathered behind her, and as Violet watched they began to undress.

Tammy was quick, pulling her bikini top off her ample breasts and throwing it to one side. Her pants followed, pushed down and kicked away to leave her nude. Linnet had lifted her yellow dress to reveal her tiny, naked body and like Tammy she threw it carelessly to one side. Alice and Juliana finished last, peeling away jeans and tops, bras and panties until all four stood nude. Tammy signalled to Topher, and as the music changed they began to dance.

Violet watched, entranced. Each was different, each compelling in her own way. Tammy was gay, abandoned, yet rude, performing the dance of a girl who has stripped and who knows it is rude, displaying her abundant charms with the certain knowledge that men's cocks will be hardening in response. Alice was slower, shy and teasing, performing the dance of a girl unused to nudity, stripped for men's pleasure and aware of every eye feasting on her naked flesh. Juliana was sensuous, her movements sinuous, sometimes fast, sometimes slow, but judged to taunt with her body, one moment showing little, the next the most intimate details of her sex, offering and withholding. Last, there was Linnet, moving in a frenzied, erotic jerking, her limbs blurring, her buttocks and breasts quivering with motion, her body flaunted into one lewd position after another in frantic succession.

Staring, utterly unable to break away her gaze, Violet found her hands going to her dress. She began to unbutton it, feeling the front fall open, the cool air on her braless breasts. Her legs came up, the dress was pushed away, discarded on the grass. Her fingers found her waistband, gripping her panties and pushing them down and off. She stood, nude, and Tammy's hand stretched out, beckoning, welcoming her to join them. As she came forward her body began to move, her limbs taking up the rhythm, her hips swaying, her feelings of arousal rising to a crazed peak as she danced.

The girls began to touch, fingers finding Violet's body in teasing, taunting motions, stroking her flesh, touching her belly or breasts, her back or buttocks, only to dance away and turn their attention to one another. She responded, indifferent to the thousand eyes on her, eager to touch and explore. Tammy pulled her close, smothering her face in between heavy breasts. A nail touched her back, raking down her spine even as a hand caught up one of her breasts. Their bodies came together, still moving, fingers gliding over sweat-slick skin, lips kissing, long hair entwining and tickling. Violet let it happen, allowing them to draw her into the centre and to close around her. Tammy was kissing her, their tongues meeting and writhing together, wet and urgent. Juliana was to one side, Linnet to the other, both with their arms around her. A hand slid down over her pubic mound, cupping her sex, a finger sliding into the wet, open hold of her vagina. She felt hair against her bottom and pushed it out, into Alice's lap, feeling the warm bulge of the girl's pubic mound pressing between her buttocks.

She was going down, on top of Tammy, eased gently to the ground. Hands took her, turning her, gently but firmly, end to end, until her face was over the hot, musky swell of Tammy's sex. Her legs were spread, a tongue found her sex and she was licking herself, her face buried between Tammy's thighs, licking female flesh which tasted of the sea. Linnet cocked a leg across their bodies, settling her naked bottom on Violet's back and starting to squirm her open sex on to her spine. Something pressed to her bottom, a face, and she felt a tongue begin to lap at her anus, then to probe the hole. More weight settled on her back, Juliana straddling to join Linnet, both girls rubbing on Violet's back as they kissed and fondled each other.

Dimly, Violet was aware of the music, of clapping and shouts, catcalls and yells of encouragement, but only dimly, beyond the welter of eager, wet female bodies enfolding her. Tammy's legs had come up, clamping her head and crossing behind it, pulling Violet's face hard into her sex. Tammy's tongue was on her clitoris, Alice's well up her bottom. Her back was wet with juice, Linnet and Juliana now both rubbing themselves on her. Her own hands were on Tammy's bottom, groping the big cheeks and pulling them wide.

She felt her riders slip and move to either side, their hands moving in to touch her, finding her breasts, and Tammy's also. Linnet's legs closed on one of Violet's and began to rub, much as a dog might, grinding wet flesh to smooth skin. She responded, pushing out to let Linnet get better purchase. Fingers found her vagina, pushing inside and suddenly she was coming, screaming out her pleasure into Tammy's sex, her clitoris burning, her vagina and anus contracting over and over on their loads.

It went on, the orgasm rising to an unbearable peak, but nothing stopped, the girls grinding and licking and rubbing her and on her, hot vulvas spread on her skin, legs holding her tight as she came and came into Tammy's face. Her senses were going, merging into a blinding head of ecstasy as Tammy reached orgasm, clutching over and over at Violet's buttocks. Alice's tongue pushed deep, to a seemingly impossible depth in Violet's bottom hole as she too came. Linnet cried out, jamming her sodden vulva on Violet's leg and it was all too much. Smothered in Tammy's swollen sex, licked, probed and groped, she felt her vision go red and she was fainting, collapsing under a pile of writhing female bodies as Juliana finished herself off on her thigh.

Awareness returned slowly, Violet finding herself lying spread-eagled in the grass, wet with sweat and juice, both from herself and the other girls. Juliana was beside her, kneeling, still stroking her breasts in slow, easy masturbation. Tammy was lying, exhausted, but with Linnet mounted on her stomach, slowly rubbing her vulva on the firm, plump flesh. Alice was at her feet, knees wide, looking down at her with an expression of triumph and satisfaction.

Remembering what she was supposed to be doing, Violet heaved herself on to one elbow. Her body was sore, her anus and vagina wet and gaping, more than ready. Getting slowly to her feet, she braced herself, blinking as she looked out over the crowd. Few people retained their clothes, girls especially, dancing naked or in just their panties. Many were engaged in sex acts, with erect cocks in girls' hands or mouths or faces buried in damp pussies. Below her Yasmin was nude, down on her knees, Joe's cock in her vagina from behind, another boy's hard penis in her mouth. At the turntables Topher had a girl bent over, his cock resting between her slim white buttocks as he rubbed himself in her crease.

Staggering slightly, Violet raised her hands. For a moment Topher appeared to pay no attention, taking his cock and slipping it into the girl bent in front of him. As he began to fuck her he waved to Violet, reached for a switch and flicked it. The music stopped, leaving a silence that seemed absolute in contrast. Light swung in towards Violet and she found herself the focus of the beams, the crowd lost in the glare. Bracing her legs apart, she raised her chin, caught the microphone as it was tossed up to her and called out.

'People, the pagan, the free, you who have come to celebrate the rising of the summer sun, you who have come for pleasure alone. Know this, that I stand on a temple, a temple not of the Christians, not of Lah, but of an older god, a god of our own land, the abundant, the protector. People, join me in my worship, join me and behold the god, behold Sigodin-Yth!'

Her words had risen to a scream as she finished and she stepped back, raising her hands and dropping the microphone. Before her the grass moved, slowly, then faster, pushing aside as a seam opened in the soil. A mass appeared, green, then a bulbous head, great glowing eyes and a fringe of tentacles. Shouts sounded from beyond the light, and a few screams.

Nich rose, soil falling from the green of his body, great head swaying on his shoulders, the tentacles writhing as he moved. Behind Violet, Linnet's high-pitched laugh sounded in a peal of delight. He stood, green body in the full glare of the lights, his penis straining and erect from his groin. Violet went to her knees, lowering her head to kiss his feet and pushing her bottom high. He moved, two swift steps and he had mounted her, his erection sliding into her willing vagina with one smooth push. The girls were laughing, crowding close as once more the music started. Nich's cock was working inside her, pushing ever faster.

The lights swung aside and once more the strobe started, the crowd now a frenzied, jerking mass, all naked or near naked, many together on the ground. Behind her Linnet was gabbling, alternately laughing and demanding her turn. For a moment more he pushed into Violet, and when he stopped she felt no jealousy, only pride and desire. Her vagina empty, she rolled back, at his feet. He stood tall as

Linnet moved forward, climbing him and straddling his hips to lower herself on to the thick, green penis. Her head went back in ecstasy as her vagina filled, then forward, smothering her face into the tentacles. With her tiny hips grinding against his front and her bottom wiggling and jerking behind, she began to rub herself, all the while gasping and crying out words Violet could not understand.

Watching, Violet let her hand stray to her sex, stroking slowly, her eyes watching Linnet's tiny, round bottom bobbing up and down above Nich's sea-green scrotum. Her arousal was complete, a plateau of ecstasy from which she never wanted to come down. Putting a finger to her clitoris, she began to dab at the little bud, rapt in the sights and sounds of sex.

Nich went down, allowing Linnet to ride him, her face pushed in among his tentacles, her little bottom bouncing in the frantic motion of his cock. Violet expected him to come, only to see Juliana come forward and begin to dance once more, coming slowly forward towards Nich's body.

Sergeant Perkins pushed aside the screen of bracken, the tension on his face turning to shock as he took in the sight in front of him. The ground around the barrow was thronged, hundreds of figures twitching in the flashing light. Most were nude, others half nude. Many couples had gone down to the ground, some stroking, kissing and fondling, others in the throes of full sex, the movements of their copulation turned into a frenzied jerking by the lights. Jealousy welled up inside him, for the pleasure that was denied him, and blind anger. Lifting his radio to his mouth, he spoke a rapid string of words, then once more turned his attention to the party, seeking the worst of the offenders.

To one side, by the piled speakers, was the black, Topher Knight, whom he had already marked as a certainty for arrest. He was in a girl, from behind, his dark skin a stark contrast to hers, his dreadlocks shaking as he fucked her, his arrogance in mounting a white girl adding to the sergeant's anger. In his mouth a thick, white roll-up was visible, causing Perkins's lips to twitch up into a vicious smile. Others were nearby, the organisers, and again he spoke into his radio, detailing men to move in behind the stack of speakers.

His gaze moved towards the mound, picking out a spotty youth, his thin buttocks bobbing frantically between the open thighs of an Asian girl, both naked, the girl's breasts bouncing to the rhythm of their movements. Beyond was the barrow itself, those on the top hard to see. There were several girls, all naked, dancing around something on the ground. Three were slim, one full-figured, her plump bottom jiggling as if to taunt him. She turned and he realised that she was one of the shoplifters. Again his mouth twisted up into a grin.

The most full-chested of the slim girls was in the centre, her movements sensuous as she bent her knees and pushed out her pubic mound. She seemed to be over something, and as he watched a head appeared, a small head, turning to reveal the laughing elfin features of the girl who had pushed him into the dock. His teeth grated together as the small girl rose, obviously dismounting a man. Seething with jealousy and disgust, but also triumph, Perkins watched as the sensuous girl beckoned to the ground. Someone rose, a man, but green, with an octopus for a head, the tentacles waving to his movements, also a blatant erection sticking out from his groin.

'Fucking weirdos,' Perkins growled as the girl took the man by the shoulders and mounted, curling her legs around his back and rubbing her face and breasts in among his tentacles.

The green man's hands cupped the girl's buttocks, lifting her and spreading them to show the dark spot of her anus and the pink flesh where his cock was inside her. Perkins swallowed, wishing his colleagues would respond so that he could order them in. No response came, and he watched with his anger and jealousy growing by the moment as the couple fucked and the four naked girls danced around them. It was sending his cock hard in his pants, adding embarrassment to his emotions, and he felt relief when the slim girl dismounted, only for his feelings to come back, more strongly, as another danced to the centre. She was taller, and slimmer still, without the opulent breasts of her friends. With a smooth, elegant motion she came in, kissed the grotesque octopus head and then bent quickly, turning as she went, to grasp her ankles and leave her tiny, neatly rounded bottom pushed out to the man's erection. Perkins grunted in outrage, realising that the man in the mask was going to fuck all five girls, one after the other, and that, far from minding, each seemed keen to watch.

'Bastard!' he snarled under his breath. 'You wait until I get you in the cells, you fucking pervert.'

The green man entered the slim girl, taking her by the hips and easing his erection between her trim buttocks. She threw her head back at the entry and he began to fuck her, jerking so that his tentacles waved and smacked down on her naked back. The others were becoming frenzied, and touching more and more. The small girl had gone to the one with purple hair and was kissing her, on the breasts, the belly, then directly on her sex. The last two girls closed, hands going to bottoms, mouths meeting in an open kiss, and Perkins's radio crackled to life.

He put it to his ear, his tension rising as first one, then another constable signalled that they were ready. With a final instruction to secure the lights as soon as possible, he stepped clear of the bracken and put his megaphone to his mouth. The music stopped with a grinding sound and he yelled out, ordering the crowd to stay put.

Somebody screamed, another cursed and abruptly the lights went out. Once more Perkins yelled, calling for light and running forward as shouts and screams rang out on all sides. The mound was ahead, its bulk silhouetted against the sky. Figures could be seen, the grotesque octopus head, a tiny form, no bigger than a child. No light came, only the crash of equipment and a bass voice cursing the police, then laughing. Perkins swore, pushing aside a naked body, determined that whatever else happened he would catch the girl who had tricked him before.

* * *

Aileve had felt a wave of panic at the blare of Perkins's voice. Even as Nich cursed and pulled quickly from her body the memories came back, of the fat belly of Constable Weekes wobbling as he masturbated over her bowl of porridge, the taste of his cock in her mouth and of the sperm as she ate what he had done.

She ran, stumbling as the lights went, falling across a naked body, rising and stumbling on again. Shouts were sounding on all sides, screams and curses, the flash of torches cutting through the dark. Again and again she struck people, until she had lost all sense of direction. Forcing herself to stop, she ducked low, fighting her panic. The moon was visible, a brilliant crescent. Using the flashes of the torch beams to find her way, she ran forward, crouching, down the slope and to the right, towards Aldon Head. Somebody bumped her and she felt naked flesh, hard and muscular. She grabbed for him, finding his arm, then a hand, which he took.

They moved together, down among the bracken and gorse, the sharp points scratching her body as she went. The noise moved behind her, the flickering of the torches away, and slowly her heartbeat began to return to normal. Still she pressed on, following her companion's lead, her eyes gradually adapting to the moonlight until she saw the pale reflected gleam on the surface of the sea, far below, beyond the cliff edge.

'Shit!' her companion swore suddenly. 'We've come the wrong way. Who are you, anyway?'

'Alice, and you?'

'Topher. You're Alice Chaswell, the scientist who's going to open the barrow?'

'Yes.'

'You are one hot lady. You were on the mound, with Tammy, yeah? Nice moves.'

'Thank you. Do you think they will search here?'

'Maybe, maybe not. Bastards, eh?'

'How true.'

Lights flared and Aileve flattened herself into the grass. Topher cursed and his arm came around her back, pressing her down and hugging her to his body. She watched, trembling as the spotlights were turned on to the mound and set to full width, bathing the area in brilliant white. Police were swarming over the grass, dealing with those partygoers too dazed or drunk to try to escape. They were in blackness, the scent of his body strong and male in her nostrils, his arm firm and protective about her shoulders. He had been in a girl when the raid began, a slim, white girl, much like her, bending for him as she accepted his cock from behind. Nich had been in her at the time, the same way, the way she liked best, with hard, male flesh pushing against the softness of her bottom.

'Get on me,' she said softly. 'Take me like you took your girlfriend.'

'Here? Now?' he answered.

'Yes, now, before they take us, if they do. Cover me, protect me.'

He gave a grunt, maybe scepticism, maybe defiance to the police, then moved one heavy leg across her body. The other followed and he was on her, his cock thick and firm against her bottom, then between her buttocks as he moved. Aileve sighed and pushed herself up, feeling the firm meat slip deeper into her crease. He began to rut, his cock growing as it rubbed in her crease until its full length was jammed between her pert buttocks.

'Lift it up,' he whispered and his weight rose from her body.

She obeyed, raising her bottom as his erection probed between her legs. His hand came down, guiding it, and then it had found the mouth of her vagina and was sliding inside, filling her as his weight once more settled on her bottom. He began to hump, pushing into her with little, sharp grunts, his front slapping on her bottom with each thrust. She was moaning, and squirming her bottom into him, with her pleasure once more rising to fill her head, as it had while she danced and made love, to Violet and to Nich.

Pushing up, she forced a hand in under her belly, finding her sex. His balls were rubbing between her thighs, then slapping on her hand as she opened her legs and he came down between them. She began to masturbate, alternately clutching at his big, rough scrotum and rubbing at her clitoris. He kept moving, making her head swim with pleasure until she began to feel the rise of her approaching climax.

'In, right in,' she begged. 'Push it in.'

'You are one hot lady,' he gasped and pushed the full length of his erection into her.

The firm, hardness of his belly was pressed to her bottom, his cock filling her to the hilt. Grabbing his balls, she began to rub them, squeezing the big sac on to her vulva, and moving its contents over her clitoris. He grunted, pushing yet harder into her, and she began to rub faster, finding her rhythm, one big testicle bumping her clitoris, over and over, her mouth opening, her nipples tingling against the grass, and she was coming, biting the ground and panting, pushing her bottom up on to the intruding penis, over and over as he once more began to move inside her.

She was still coming, riding her orgasm and rubbing herself as he grunted, jerked his cock from inside her and came over her. She felt his sperm splash between her buttocks and into the mouth of her vagina, then the firm rod of his penis as he pushed it into her crease and finished himself off, rubbing it between her buttocks in his own sperm. Aileve relaxed, letting him finish at leisure.

He rolled off and she lifted her eyes again, finding the mound much as before, brightly lit, but with fewer people visible. These were scattered into groups, and seated, each with a police officer standing over them. Some were dressed, more clutching ill-matched clothes to their bodies. The beams of police torches could be seen to the side, searching the slope that led down towards the estuary.

'They'll wait on the roads,' Topher remarked. 'It's only the organisers they want, and anyone who was dealing. Too much hassle to nick everybody just for stripping off, I reckon. They'll take the clothes, though, just 'cause they're mean bastards.'

'There's a way down,' Aileve answered, 'to the west and through Rocombe Woods, down to the sea. At high tide you can jump.'

'Jump? How far?'

'Thirty feet.'

'Right. Well maybe, but we'll still be naked, and wet. Anyhow, they know me and they know I was there. You go for it, if you're crazy enough. I'll stay here, and the longer they take searching for me, the better.'

Aileve moved to kiss him, then rose into a crouch and left, moving through the black shadows of the gorse.

Perkins flashed his torch along the line of a hedge. She was in there, he was sure, crouching among the foliage, doubtless scratched and bruised after her flight across the fields. By luck he had seen her leave, another policeman's torch catching her as she ran north, down the slope of Aldon Hill towards Abbotscombe. He had followed, keeping her pale form in his beam, never letting her get too far ahead, yet never striving to close the gap between them.

Now Aldon Hill was a black bulk to the south, the sounds of the continuing chase no more than noise fading on the light wind. He had her, he was sure of it. Linnet, a tiny woman, well under five foot and naked, could never outrun him. He had the torch as well, its beam enough to light his way and to blind her if she turned. She may run, but it would only add to the thrill of the chase. He would catch her, and when he caught her he would take his revenge.

It would be good. He would take his belt to her first, across her tight little arse, her legs and her back while he held her by the hair, teaching her the lesson she needed to learn, that nobody, but nobody, messed with him. Once he'd had enough and she was mewling on the ground, out would come his cock. He'd toss over her face, letting her know what was going to happen. She'd be spread, naked and bruised, plenty of material to wank over. He'd give her a facial, a spunk face scrub, just as he had to Ed's Lil, and when he had come in her face he would rub it into her features.

213

Again he flashed his torch, and this time he saw her, her eyes reflecting green like the eyes of the cat. He started forward and heard the rustle of the hedge as she darted away. He followed, crashing through a gap in the hedge and vaulting the fence at its heart. The field beyond was a sheet of liquid gunmetal in the moonlight, Linnet a pale ghost, already halfway across and running for all she was worth.

Perkins followed with a sadistic leer, then with his teeth gritted as he forced himself to greater speed across the flat pasture. She was in plain sight, her legs flashing as she ran, her hair swirling behind her, her tiny buttocks moving in time. His muscles had begun to burn, yet he was gaining. She looked back, and cried out in despair as she saw how close he was. The waving torch beam caught her face for an instant and Perkins felt a new thrill as he saw her fear. He pushed himself harder, hoping to trap her against the far hedge with a last burst of speed.

A gap in the hedge ahead became visible, a gate closing it off. Ahead of him Linnet abruptly changed her angle, darted for the gate and threw herself over it. Perkins followed, moments behind, only to clasp the top bar and realise that it was ringed with barbed wire.

Cursing and shaking his injured hand, he scrambled after her. Again she had a good lead, and was heading towards the jagged black outline of a wood, down the slope. As he forced himself to greater speed he decided that a beating and his come in her face would not be enough. He would beat her, hard, and not just her rear but her front, too, her thighs and belly, her tiny breasts, until her whole body was red with welts. When he was done he would have a good feel, touching her up on her neat bottom and pert boobs, fingering her little cunt. Only then would he spunk in her face, and make her eat it on the threat of another beating.

He was gaining again, and she was slowing, her tiny body unable to match his fitness and male stamina. The end would come soon, that much was certain, and it would probably come before the wood, where he could then drag

214

her for her beating and spoiling. He was panting, the blood singing in his ears, but she was a mere ten yards ahead, then five, only for her to find the energy of sheer terror and once more move ahead. Perkins knew it was her last gasp of effort and kept his pace, pounding after her.

She reached the wood, scrambling over a low wall. He followed, his torch catching the green and brown of trees and foliage, then the pink of her skin, feet away. Lunging forward, he felt his fingers on smooth skin, even as he stumbled and a branch lashed back across his face. He cursed, the falling torch catching her as she skipped away, briefly showing her naked belly and the black tangle of her pubic hair before she was gone.

He rose, cursing and rubbing at his face. There was blood on his cheek, which brought new anger. As he set off he knew he would have to take it all the way, to beat her and feel every part of her body, to force her to suck his cock and finally to fuck her, down in the grass or leaf mould, her little thighs spread wide, his cock working in her tiny cunt as she whimpered out her misery and defeat.

She was ahead, darting between the trees, her small size now an advantage. He pressed on, dogged, determined that she would never get the better of him. Again and again he lost sight of her, only to catch a glimpse of pale flesh or reflected green eyes. She was stupid, or too scared to think, never hiding but always trying to get further away, the reaction of blind panic. Twice he came within an ace of catching her, but both times she slipped away, always a hair's breadth out of reach, until at length he reached the far side of the wood.

Beyond was another field, Linnet standing not twenty yards away, panting, with her body bent and her hands resting on her knees. As she saw him she ran and he followed. His hat was gone, his face and hands were bloody with cuts, his muscles burning with the strain. None of it mattered, only the need to catch her and to teach her a lesson, to thrash her and fuck her, to ruin her and rape her.

Ahead she was limping, missing steps with her right foot, and slowing. She had angled to the right, making for a dim line beyond which the spire of Abbotscombe church showed black against the night sky. Perkins pushed himself, realising that she meant to find a house, to seek sanctuary. Doubtless she had guessed what he intended, or at least feared it, and knew that if she could not avoid arrest she might at least avoid violation.

She was yards ahead, but still running, seeming to go a touch faster each time he forced himself on. The far side of the field was coming closer, a low wall, beyond which was only the black of the night, distant trees and the church. He clutched for her and missed, his foot finding something soft and slippery with the next step. For a moment his balance was gone, but he regained it even as the rich, pungent scent of cow dung reached his nose. He could feel it on his leg and cursed her, telling himself that a mere cock in her cunt was not enough. No, he would fuck her, and make her suck, but when she thought her degradation had reached its depths he would bugger her. He would make her kneel and hold her little cheeks apart. He would make her grease her anus, as Ed had made Lil grease hers, but for Linnet it would be with juice pulled from her own cunt. He would bugger her, ramming his erection home into the tight sheath of her rectum. It would be tight, so tight, tighter even than Lil's. She might split, and he wouldn't care, he would come in her dirt box and make her suck the come and mess from his cock . . .

He hit the wall, moments behind her. She was over, vanishing and he followed, vaulting high, out and into nothing. Panic hit him a moment before the ground. His ankle caught something hard, twisting and sending a jolt of agony the length of his leg. He screamed in pain as his shoulder struck hard earth, then his head, jarring his whole body. Rolling on to his back, he clutched his leg, his teeth gritted against the burning pain. The scent of cow dung and sour milk filled his nostrils, his body sinking into the filthy mud as he moved. Above was sky, and the wall, rearing a good twenty feet above him, and on the wall was Linnet, outlined black against the moon and laughing.

'Bitch!' Perkins hissed and scrabbled for the torch.

He shone the beam up, finding her body. She was standing wide legged, the pink of her cunt visible in the light, her hands on her hips, her impish face set in an expression of cruel mirth. He cursed, trying to rise, only to collapse at the agonising pain in his leg. She laughed again, a shrill, high-pitched peal of delight. He lay back, panting, trying desperately to think what to do. Once more he shone the torch up, illuminating Linnet.

'Look . . .' he began, only to stop.

There was no mercy in her face, no fear, no uncertainty, only a demented, evil glee. He drew his breath in against the pain, determined not to show weakness, but in response her mouth twitched in obvious derision.

'Is this what you wanted, Sergeant?' she asked, and her hand went to her sex, spreading the damp pink lips to show off the centre, her hole wet, her clitoris a gleaming bud where her tiny inner lips joined, the centre bulging. She sank down, squatting, her spread sex directly above him, and as he watched in horrified anger, a stream of golden liquid erupted from her vulva, spraying out in a long arc to splash down on him in tune to peal after peal of demented laughter.

Thomazina sank down to the sand, going to her hands and knees in exhaustion. Beside her Nich also came to a halt, slumping full length on to the beach.

'We're safe, I'm sure,' he panted.

She nodded a response, thinking of the safe embrace of the sea and then deciding against it. In the darkness and chaos of the raid she had made for the cliff path, confident in her knowledge and the bright moonlight. She had made it, but found she was being followed, first with fear, then relief as she had recognised Nich's naked body. They had gone as fast as they dared, moving down into the shallow valley that cut Aldon Hill from the Ness, then to the tunnel mouth and so the beach. Her tension was draining, slowly, the lights and sounds still coming from Aldon Hill now seeming distant.

'Who else made it?' Nich asked.

'I don't know, it was too dark, too confused.'

'I lost Violet. She was holding my hand but someone jostled us.'

'I'm sorry. She was fine, so fine. You also.'

'Thank you.'

'I . . . we had hoped to talk with her, as she dreams, but tell me, why did she call that name?'

'Sigodin-Yth? The explanation is not simple, but in essence I wish to promote belief in gods other than the Christian. It is my life's work.'

'You know of him, then?'

'I have read of him, enough to believe and enough to hope his essence is not wholly spent. He is the barrow god, a pre-Celtic deity of succour and fertility. I had hoped to reinforce his worship and so give him new force. Had it not been for the cursed police I might have. And they have doubtless taken my octopus head.'

'It is odd for a man to be called. Did you dream?'

'No. My belief derives from innate certainty. But what of you? You are a worshipper, a handmaiden, to Sigodin-Yth?'

'That is the Celtic name. The true name is Txcalin.'

'You know this? How?'

'As you say, I am a worshipper.'

'There is a cult? Is that how his vitality has been maintained across the centuries?'

'Yes, in a way.'

'And the cult takes the dreamers as worshippers?'

'Yes, but few. We are only four.'

'Hence you sought to revive interest at the party, drawing in dreamers for initiation?'

'Yes. Was it not wonderful? Every woman there felt his call, and the men responded to the women's lust in turn.'

'The lust, then, derived from Sigodin-Yth, from Txcalin?'

'Yes, but it was stronger than before, and had far greater effect. People seemed more open, more receptive. I think, maybe, Christianity is weakening, dying even.'

'It is. Look, let's walk. You never know, they might search the beach.'

Thomazina rose, taking his hand, which he accepted. Memories came back to her, of walking the same beach, hand in hand with other young men, but never one in whom she felt she could confide in such depth.

'The last time it was not so,' she told him. 'We tried, but the girls were staid, closed in on themselves, the men little better. There was a dreamer, a pretty girl called Rose, but the police came and took her and spoiled it.'

'Rose? Rosemary Evans?'

'That was her name. She went away afterwards. You know a great deal.'

'I know Rosemary Evans was arrested after a party at the Wythman in 1957.'

'She was. She was fine, in a way, but we could never quite break through to her. Even Juliana could not seduce her.'

'Juliana was there, but ... The man Hobbers, he called you Thomazina Keeley when he left. I know of her. She was a dreamer, or so it seems, and used to visit the barrow by night. Was she a cult member? Have you taken her name in her honour? Do the same names pass down between members?'

Thomazina shrugged, unsure if he could see the gesture and uncertain how to answer his question. Nich continued. 'She vanished on Midsummer's Night 1853, when the temple stood open. The Reverend Wilmot had opened it.'

'Wilmot? The Reverend Clerebold Wilmot. Now there was a man who might have taught poor old Mr Hobbers how to fulfil his dirty needs.'

'You know of him, then, and doubtless more. Tell me, please, you won't find my mind closed.'

'I will tell. You may believe, you may not.'

'I will believe.'

'So you say. So where should I start? There are many beginnings, but mine was a still night in summer when I woke from a nightmare. There was a bright moon, and from my bed I could see up to the hill through the trees, with the barrow bathed silver in the light. I'd been there in my dream, and I was scared, but confused, too. What I had dreamed had been awful, or it seemed to be at the time,

219

but it had also made me feel protected, and at the time I
needed protection more than anything.'

'From who?'

'Wilmot, the wonderful, godly –'

'Wilmot? He's been dead over a hundred years!'

'I said you wouldn't believe.'

'No, continue. I confess scepticism, but my mind is not
shut. Wilmot was molesting you?'

'He intended to. Yes, the Reverend Clerebold Wilmot,
who everybody said was so kind and so, so fatherly. To me
he was the Devil. Each Sunday he held classes, teaching
reading and studying of the Bible to the local girls and boys.
He said that I was slow and stupid, also stubborn, and
offered to help, keeping me for extra lessons when the others
had gone. My parents thought this was wonderful, him, a
learned gentleman, making time for their silly daughter.'

'The abuse of priestly power. It is a common wrong.'

'Men of the church seemed very high to us, beyond
reproach.'

'Such is innocence, and without innocence there would
be little abuse.'

'Oh, I was innocent in my way, but not like that. There
was nothing I liked better than to go down to the woods
with a boy and trade a suck for a lick of my cunny. If
Wilmot had wanted to feel my titties or have me touch his
man I'd have charged him sixpence and been laughing as I
walked home. No, he was far worse, a true monster, a
torturer.'

'How so?'

'He wanted pain. Not pain that comes with pleasure, but
pure pain, both in my head and my body. From the start
he said that if I didn't learn well I would be punished. I
thought he meant he'd smack my bottom, and only felt
bad because I knew I'd get a wet cunny and thought he
would see. That wasn't what he meant.'

'No?'

'No. His trick was to tell me I was to be punished, but
that it would happen the next week. He had this horrible
machine, with a handle he could turn and bits of wire

220

sticking out of it. He made me touch it and it stung me, then he told me he would tie my hand to it, the next Sunday.'

'Some sort of electrical device?'

'I suppose so. I didn't even know the word electricity. All week I was terrified, but when the time came he said it was not enough. The punishment was to be postponed, and made worse, with wires fixed to both hands.'

'Didn't you tell your parents?'

'How could I? It would have been my word against his, and he was the vicar. I didn't dare.'

'I understand, I think.'

'It was awful, and I knew he would do it in the end. I began to dream about him and his machine. First it was just that, then about being rescued, by something I could never see, and with that came a compulsion to go up to the barrow. That scared me too. Mother had told us the barrow was a bad place, that pixies lived there. If I went at night they would drag me down under the earth. It had happened before, she said, long before, to a girl who had lived in the same house. When I told her she was scared for me, and of course she went straight to Wilmot, to ask his advice.

'He said it showed wilfulness in me and that he would give me more time each Sunday. When I went, he said that the next week he would put the wires across my stomach, and it would make me lose control of my bowels. That night the dream came again, stronger, and when I called out for help he was dragged away by a huge tentacle. That's when I woke and saw a figure standing on the mound, against the moonlight.'

'And you went to her?'

'She came to me, the prettiest little thing, so funny and so playful. It was impossible to imagine her doing harm. She said I should go with her, to the mound, and then I would be safe. I didn't dare. The mound was open, then, and I'd seen the hole, a gaping black mouth into the earth. I was so scared, but each night she came back, and she was sweet and kind, and Sunday was getting closer.

'I began to go with her, slipping out of the house and up the hill. She would touch me and stroke my hair, and it excited me like nothing else I had ever done. On the Friday I let her make love to me, on the barrow in the moonlight. When I came back I was caught by Mother.

'They were worried for me, and I told them I'd been sleepwalking, so once again they sent me to talk to Wilmot. He told them about the machine. He said I needed what he called electrotherapy. They agreed. They didn't know any better. It was to happen the next week, and when he had me alone he said what would happen, and that there would be no more delays. I was to be fixed to a table, my hands, feet and belly bound with straps. I was to be naked. He would put the wires to my head, to my stomach, to my arms and legs. When he wound the handle it would cleanse me in mind and body. My bowels would open and I might faint from the pain, but it would be for my own good, and it would stop the dreams. While he spoke he tried to be serious, but I could feel his lust and his pleasure in my fear.'

'So you went with the girl?'

'Yes, on Midsummer's Night.'

'What happened?'

'That I cannot tell you.'

'I understand. The girl was Linnet?'

'Her name is Elune. Do you know how Wilmot died?'

'He was an old man, I have seen a photograph from 1879.'

'Old and spry, and still teaching Sunday classes. In 1881 he decided my sister Emily's eldest girl needed extra class. They found him wired to his electrotherapy machine, I won't say how.'

'You did that?'

'Oh, no, I would never have the heart. Juliana did.'

'Who I made love to earlier?'

'The very same. Do you believe?'

'I do. At least I will try. What of Linnet . . . Elune that is, and the others?'

'Elune is old, older than she knows herself. She was the priestess here when the Celts came. At first they left the temple be, treating it as a sacred place. Later they grew bolder and destroyed it, setting fire to it while she was still inside. She went down into the earth.

'Alice's true name is Aileve. She was the girl my mother knew about, although she didn't know when, or why. The story had lasted nearly six hundred years by then and even the names were forgotten. Aileve was the daughter of the reeve who kept Abbotscombe manor for the monastery at Buckfast. She is clever and sensitive and was a dreamer from a young age. The monks came to open the barrow, looking for treasure, and she tried to stop them. They said she was a witch and would have burned her, but she ran and Elune took her down.'

'Juliana is older?'

'She is Roman, a settler's daughter. The villa was on land down by the estuary. The barrow was still a sacred place then, and the slab could be lifted. When men pulled it open she began to dream, and to worship. Christianity was rising, but she refused to convert. They tried to force her but she just laughed at their cruelties. At last some soldiers threw her on a midden by the Exe and threatened to bury her alive if she wouldn't deny her faith. He came for her, and took the soldiers down under the water.'

'The god, then, has corporeal form?'

'How could it be otherwise?'

Ten

Lily awoke to bright sunlight and the pleasant cool of a summer dawn. She felt stiff and still tired, after a night of fevered dreams, of the party on the barrow, of marrying Ed, of the embrace of octopus tentacles and more. Her anus hurt, too, and her vulva was sore. Ed had buggered her, beaten her and buggered her. The strapping had been for wanting to go to the solstice party, so he had said. She had put on a peephole bra and crotchless panties, in scarlet, lewd, tarty garments that had filled her with shame. He had tied her hands to the bedstead and put her in a leg spreader he had bought in a sex shop, leaving her helpless. He had whacked her with his thick leather belt, over and over until her bottom was a mass of scarlet and purple weals and the juice from her sex was trickling down her thighs. He had spat on her anus and opened her with a finger, then rubbed her own juice into the mushy hole. He had buggered her, sticking his cock to the hilt in her anus and rubbing her off to make it clench on his shaft. He had come in her rectum and made her suck his penis afterwards.

She climbed from the bed, walking to the window. Ed made no move, but slept on, snoring gently. Outside the sky was pure blue, the sea calm. With quick motions she pushed off the tawdry panty-and-bra set and pulled his dressing-gown around herself. Leaning forward, she turned to see Ness Head and Aldon Hill beyond, the barrow outlined against the sky. A few shapes could be seen, and a single, dark figure against the light, renewing the regret she felt at not having been there. The girls had wanted her to go, badly, and especially Alice Chaswell. She had wanted to go herself, yet as usual she had let Ed rule her, breaking her will.

He had even insulted her intended profession, and as she remembered his words she wondered if he would let her attend the opening of the barrow. The answer was almost certain to be no. It was Saturday and he was off duty. He would probably want her to himself, to make his lunch and clean his house, things she was sure he would consider more important than her being with the archaeologists. It was too much, yet she was trembling even as she tiptoed quietly across the room, thinking of his threats to hit her and how he would undoubtedly take out his anger up her bottom.

She dressed, willing herself despite her fear and the feeling that she was betraying her man. He would own her, she knew, but the barrow opening meant too much to her, and minutes later she was slipping quietly from the house, feeling bad, and disobedient, but also triumphant.Tawmouth was quiet, the streets empty but for a police car and two milk floats. Only at the beach did she realise that the river ferry would not start running for several hours, and with mixed feelings she sat down on the sand.

Violet stretched and yawned, happy despite herself as she waved the desk sergeant a cheerful farewell through the glass doors of Tawmouth police station. She had been cautioned, as had Juliana, who was waiting for her at the bottom of the steps, clad in an ill-fitting print dress. Yasmin and Joe were still inside, having been taken actually in the middle of sex and with cannabis on them.

After losing Nich she had not run, realising that her purple hair and body jewellery made her an easy target. Nor had she wanted to stumble about on the dark cliff top when she was both drunk and high. Instead she had dressed and done as she was told, behaving as sweetly as possible in the hope of avoiding charges relating to stripping off and having sex in public. It had worked, with the police reluctant to do more than give cautions when so many had been naked. If they had seen her having sex, then none had mentioned it.

Juliana had been unlucky, dashing blindly for cover only to run full tilt into a policeman. She had fallen and hit her head on a bottle and been taken before her senses recovered, ending up sitting with Violet in a van. Yasmin and Joe had been caught hopelessly intertwined in each other. Topher Knight had vanished, but eventually been found, at dawn, sitting quite casually on the grass near the cliff edge. There had been no sign of Nich, Tammy, Alice or Linnet, all of whom she now hoped had got away.

'Cautioned?' Violet asked.

Juliana nodded and held out her hand, which Violet took.

'You can borrow some decent clothes if you like,' she offered, 'and have some decent coffee – that stuff tastes like dirt. Nich might be back, if he's managed to get some clothes.'

'Thank you. Nich is your boyfriend?'

'Yes, sort of. He understands me. He lets me be myself.'

'You are very calm for a dreamer. What threatens you?'

'Nothing, now. I always hated the church, because my parents wanted me to be a good little Christian girl, to have a white wedding and all that. I'm free of it now, but in my dreams it's always some workmen and an old priest, Wilmot, the guy who opened the barrow in the nineteenth century.'

'Wilmot is dead.'

'Sure. I suppose he just represents the Christian church to me, while the workmen are in response to my fear of rape.'

'I imagine it is so. And he comes for you?'

'The god? Yes.'

'You have seen him?'

'Yes. Nich based his image for last night on my dreams, the green man with the head of an octopus.'

'That is the Celtic image, and you called out the Celtic name. It is strange. You are a Celt perhaps, by origin?'

'No, I don't think so. My mum and dad are both from Colchester. I don't know of any Celtic ancestors. Nich explained the image to me: it's the same image that inspired the Cthulu stories, and he says the god was worshipped in Egypt, too, under some other name, but in the same image.'

'The image then, does not come from your dreams?'

'Yes, no, not really, the other way around if anything.'

'We will speak to Linnet. For now, clothes and coffee and, if you would be kind, honey and ice cream on those sugary pieces of wheat they make.'

The barrow stood open, the mouth an uneven rectangle of blackness leading into the earth, the greying wood of Wilmot's props visible within. Professor Cobb stood to one side, watching as photographs were taken and sketches made. Others waited behind him, ready with modern shoring to support the roof when the time came to enter. They had arrived early, after hearing of the police raid, determined to take advantage of their excavation permits before any officers could decide that the site needed to be closed off for their investigations.

'The Victorian construction appears remarkably solid,' he remarked. 'Still, it is best not to take chances.'

'There seems to be a faint breeze coming from the opening,' Lily remarked, leaning forward. 'Do you feel the cool air?'

'Alice Chaswell has speculated that a subterranean passage may exist,' Cobb answered. 'Wilmot does not mention one, but he does remark that the air in the excavation remained fresher than he had expected.'

'How far in does this passage go?'

'Nearly to the far end. It finishes at a slab with a symbol similar to the one in Brittany carved on it. A starlike emblem with octagonal symmetry, supposedly meant to represent an octopus, although that is not certain.'

'I've seen drawings of it. Is it not supposed to be the god, Sigodin-Yth?'

'Again, largely speculation. Without written records it is hard to be sure. Alice is more confident, and feels there may well be more carvings. Speaking of Alice, it is unlike her to be late, most unlike her.'

He turned back to the sketch, remarking on the symmetry of the mound. Lily moved back, glancing nervously towards the path, half expecting to see an angry Ed Gardner striding towards her. Nobody was there, and she turned back to watch the first shorings put into place. The archaeologists worked fast, with practised ease, adjusting the equipment and scanning the floor and walls for objects of interest as they went. Lily stayed back, fascinated, yet troubled by thoughts of Ed and a sexual feeling that refused to be pushed down. Her nipples were stiff, embarrassingly so, and the crotch of her panties was wet, while the wild fantasies she had created, of sex with octopus, kept intruding on her thoughts.

Two other members of the team were female. One was helping with the shoring, and facing away. The other was standing, sketching, and, although she appeared deep in study of the barrow, it was impossible not to notice the straining points of her nipples showing through her light summer frock.

A voice called out her name, a male voice, and Lily's heart jumped. She turned, expecting to see Ed. Relief washed over her at the sight of Nich, striding briskly towards her, Violet beside him, Tammy and Juliana close behind. Nich was dressed as usual, in black, as were Violet and Juliana, Tammy making an odd contrast in brightly coloured beach shorts, an overtight halter top and sandals.

'I hadn't realised you were starting so early,' Nich announced as he joined them. 'How is work progressing?'

'As you see, we have opened the passage,' Professor Cobb answered. 'Currently we are shoring it and making preliminary notes. You have missed little.'

'Good,' Nich answered and moved to beside Lily, the others moving further back to sit down in the grass.

The work continued, the team pushing deeper into the interior of the barrow and bringing up lights, illuminating a long passage of red-brown earth with grass roots growing from the roof and walls. Lily found her excitement rising,

228

also her arousal, while the dank tunnel gave her the same feelings of sanctuary and protection she had known in her dreams. Glancing back, she found Violet, Tammy and Juliana chatting happily, animated, perhaps aroused, but not overtly so.

Linnet arrived to join the others, not from the main path but from the track that led down the hill to the north. She was in a summer dress, a loose white cotton smock that showed the contours of her body beneath, apparently naked. As she approached she turned a handstand, proving she was nude underneath with a brief flash of pubic hair and pert bottom. She laughed as she landed, and put her hand to her mouth as if on the sudden realisation of what she had shown. Lily smiled and waved back at her greeting, wishing she herself could feel the small woman's simple, unrestrained happiness.

As Linnet sat down one of the team appeared in the tunnel mouth, announcing that they had reached the slab, and that the last of the shoring would shortly be in place. He disappeared again and Lily glanced to the stile, praying that Ed would not appear before she had at least had a chance to look at the slab. Her need was urgent, stronger even than her normal curiosity for ancient sites. If Ed came she knew she would go, and that as his fiancée she would get no help from the others. Ed did not appear, but Alice Chaswell did, hurrying over to them and apologising for her lateness.

'Your timing is, in fact, remarkably good,' Cobb answered. 'In a moment we can go in.'

'Excellent,' Nich remarked. 'I trust I may accompany you?'

'Yes, yes,' Cobb answered, 'in due time, the way is narrow. Alice and myself should, I think, be first.'

The shoring team returned and Lily watched with mounting impatience as the initial investigation of the slab was completed. At last her turn came, and beside Nich she ducked low and entered the passage. It was well lit, stretching through the red earth. The floor was soil, then broken rock and at last hard sandstone before they reached

229

the slab. She was sweating, despite the cool, fresh air and the undeniable draught. A lump rose in her throat as she focused on the slab, a great piece of granite, set at a low angle, her own height or more and nearly as wide. Marks showed on the surface, smooth, flowing curves, eight arms spread around what might have been eyes.

'Beautiful,' Nich breathed, reaching out to stroke the smooth surface of the stone.

Lily was trembling, her heart hammering in her chest, her nipples agonisingly stiff, her panties and thighs wet with juice.

'There's a breeze,' Nich went on. 'I can feel it. Beneath is a hollow. We must persuade them to lift it, we must.'

He moved back, making a salute to the image on the slab. Lily nodded and followed him, finding it hard to draw herself away. Outside, Nich's efforts proved unnecessary. Alice had already persuaded Cobb that it was crucial to lift the slab without delay. Again she glanced nervously at the stile, then at the group of girls, finding Linnet looking back at her with a knowing smirk.

Heavy equipment was brought up, the shoring team sent back down, and after a wait of agonising frustration they returned, reporting that the slab had been moved and what appeared to be a natural opening into the rock revealed beneath.

'You said it from the first,' Cobb addressed Alice. 'I admit I was sceptical of your famous intuition, but I take it back. Now let us see what we have found.'

He went down, Alice also, again leaving Lily in a state of nervous frustration. Alice alone returned, highly excited, telling the others to follow. Again Lily entered the passage, her feelings stronger than ever, leaving her weak-kneed as she finally reached the end and peered into the gap where the slab had been pushed aside. Two brilliant arc lamps illuminated it, a gaping cavern running with the low plane of the strata, widening from the hole. The roof was marked, figures cut into the sandstone, writhing, flowing curves of tentacles and the soft contours of female bodies, entwined together, caressing, copulating.

Lily tried to stifle her cry as she came, involuntarily, without so much as a touch to her clitoris. Embarrassment welled up inside her, but if Nich or anybody else had noticed they gave no sign. He was staring at the carvings, his mouth wide, then squeezing into the gap and shuffling crablike down the slope to join Alice and Cobb.

Nich nodded and went back to his examination of the carvings, his eyes wide with wonder and delight. Lily stayed close to him, her body in his shadow, sure that her sexual arousal would be all too obvious. It was impossible not to look at the carvings, and looking at them was bringing her rapidly towards another orgasm. All were in the same, smooth, flowing style, unlike any art she had ever seen. The human figures were undoubtedly feminine, some petite, more with the opulent curves she had seen in early carvings of the Earth Mother. One near her showed a girl kissing the bulbous head of an octopus, another a more rounded woman kneeling with the creature on her back, a thick arm disappearing between her thighs and clearly into her vagina. More showed women wrapped in tentacles, the octopus on their bellies, the sperm arms curved back to probe their vaginas. Some of the women were kneeling down to lick the bodies of the beasts, others squatting, wrapped in tentacles, or to take the sperm arms into their mouths, between their breasts, even into their anuses.

Her urge was to strip naked, to stare at the pictures and let her mind run with dirty fantasies, of being mated by huge octopus, of doing the same things as the women in the carvings, of being held in eight firm arms, of being penetrated, her vagina filled with sperm arm, then with the sperm itself, of her nipples being pulled up under suckers, of her breasts being enfolded, of the taste of their skin in her mouth, of her anus being opened by a tentacle tip, of coming as a sucker pulled on her clitoris . . .

She had come again, crying out and slipping on the sloping rock.

Violet sat cross-legged, her eyes fixed on the black hole in the front of the Wythman. Linnet, or Elune, had finished talking, leaving her dizzy with emotion. What had been said was compelling, yet frightening, also hard to embrace. Nich's concept of the god Sigodin-Yth, or Txcalin, had been easy to come to terms with. It was essentially metaphysical, something she understood, a being that could be sensed, that could influence humanity, but could never be seen, nor touched. Elune had explained that this was merely an echo of her Christian upbringing, and that a god could animate a solid form, yet it was difficult to accept.

So was the thought of entering the earth and dedicating herself to the god, especially when the girls refused to explain the process in detail. To revel in the freedom of pagan belief was one thing; to crawl into a dark hole and down to whatever might lie in wait for her was another. She was also sure her dreams had come not from the god, but from Nich, by suggestion. Certainly they differed from those of the girls, and, although she had felt the same overriding sexual urge at the solstice party, the same was true of every other female present. Finally, and perhaps most importantly, as it was Nich who had brought her to her new level of belief and awareness, she felt it was to Nich that she owed her love. Her chain of thought broke at the sight of movement in the barrow mouth. Aileve emerged, supporting Lily, with Nich following.

'She was overcome,' Aileve announced as she helped Lily to the ground.

Thomazina nodded, Juliana moving to place an arm around Lily's shoulders. Nich squatted down beside Violet, kissed her and put an arm around her waist.

'It's magnificent,' he said, 'beyond anything I could have imagined. There are carvings, and what Professor Cobb thinks is a form of writing. The carvings go far beyond anything Laverack even dared to speculate . . .'

'Laverack?' Aileve broke in.

'Yes,' Nich replied. 'He wrote a treatise on the octopus in erotic imagery. He knew of Sigodin-Yth.'

'I knew him,' she went on. 'Theo Laverack, he was my lover in '57. We went to Brittany together, and I told him some of my dreams.'

'You affected him strongly,' Nich replied. 'Thomazina has explained to me. You may speak openly.'

'You are a man,' Juliana stated. 'Still, you have rare sympathy. You seem to have induced dreams in Violet, as hers do not come from the god, or not entirely.'

'No?' Nich answered. 'But she called on him and he came.'

'You came,' Juliana went on. 'A green man with the head of an octopus, the image the Celts gave Txcalin, mingled with your own image. I am impressed, I wonder, but she is not a true dreamer.'

'Suggestion,' Violet added.

'You may still go down, if you wish,' Elune said.

Violet shook her head, unable to answer, or to meet the girl's eyes.

'I'll go,' Lily said softly.

Elune rose and walked to Lily, taking her hand. Violet felt herself shivering and leaned closer into Nich. For a moment there was silence, broken by the sound of voices from the direction of the barrow. Aileve rose and walked to where Professor Cobb was emerging from the hole, talking excitedly to his colleagues. He was grinning, his whole body animated, and he greeted Aileve with a hearty handshake. They spoke for a while before Aileve returned to the group.

'They are going down to the Ferryboat for lunch,' she announced. 'I've said I'll stay here and keep an eye on things. Now is our time.'

Violet stood, responding to the gentle pressure of Nich's arm. Lily rose with Elune and Juliana, her expression dazed, her eyes wide and damp. They walked forward, Thomazina and Aileve linking arms to either side, Violet and Nich following. At the tunnel mouth they stopped. Elune spoke, a tumble of words in the same, quick sibilant language she had used when mounted on Nich. At the end Violet caught a word that may have been Txcalin. Elune advanced, with Lily's hand held in hers, into the tunnel, the white of their dresses fading in the blackness, then gone.

* * *

'We must celebrate!' Thomazina declared. 'Come down to Abbotscombe, we'll get drunk on cider and go into the woods for sex.'

'A new handmaiden,' Juliana answered, 'and so lovely. Come, then, there are nettles in Rocombe Woods, I hope.'

'We must celebrate, yes, but not in Abbotscombe,' Aileve put in. 'Elune and I were there this morning. There is likely to be a fuss.'

'Why?' Violet asked.

'She stole clothes for us from a washing line,' Aileve explained. 'Her dress and a great big baggy thing so I could get back to my hotel and change. A woman saw her and chased her. I think she saw me, too. Also there is your policeman, Thomazina, who you need not worry about meeting in the town.'

'What did she do to him?'

'She led him over a wall on the slope, four feet on one side, twenty on the other. She was still laughing about it when I met her in Rocombe. We can go into Tawmouth: the bar in my hotel serves a cider like your father used to make.'

'I agree, I need the drink,' Violet put in. 'But what about Elune and Lily?'

'They won't be back, not for a while,' Juliana answered. 'Meanwhile, Nich and yourself may join us.'

'You do us honour,' Nich answered. 'Is there some ritual we should complete, some sort of abasement to Txcalin?'

'Even you think like a Christian,' Juliana laughed. 'There is no abasement. He feeds on joy and sex, not fear or subordination. Elune's people would drink and couple until they passed out, even the Celts, those who worshipped. I used to join them, and mock the prudish Christians in the street!'

She jumped the stile, breaking into a run on the path, the others following, down to the shore, where the ferry was about to leave. Thomazina came last, letting Nich pay her fee and trailing her hand in the water as they crossed the estuary. She felt happy, blissfully so, revelling in their success and her part in it, knowing that her efforts would bring new love and respect from Aileve and Juliana.

At the hotel they chose seats in the garden, overlooking the sea, deep blue and sparkling with reflected sunlight. Aileve had chosen the Royal, as always, allowing them to watch the sea and the crowds on the front. She and Aileve ordered strong cider, Juliana and Nich heavy red wine from the south of Italy, Violet gin punch. They were quickly merry, drinking and toasting their success.

A waiter arrived, bowing unctuously and suggesting a salad of baby octopus and fish. Thomazina found herself laughing at Juliana's indignant refusal and realised that she was already drunk. Aileve placated the waiter with a tip and ordered Dover sole, mackerel and salmon, then chocolate cake, ice cream and honeycomb. They ate, becoming increasingly drunk and in ever better humour, even Violet losing her sombre mood.

As Thomazina began her second helping of chocolate cake, with melted ice cream and honey already running down her chin, Juliana nudged her and pointed to the front. A man was walking in their direction, his grey suit and angry expression very out of keeping with the generally happy atmosphere.

'Lily's boyfriend,' Juliana said, 'the one who drove her to the god.'

'Ed Gardner,' Nich added, 'a customs officer and a regular bastard. I only wish we could tell him.'

'You can,' Aileve answered. 'He won't believe you.'

Ed's anger, already high, grew as he saw the drunken group. Nich Mordaunt was there, flaunting his weirdness, along with his freakish purple-haired girlfriend, a fat girl whose beach shorts could barely contain her bottom, some vicious-looking, busty bitch and one of the female archaeologists, which showed that they were all the same: freaks and parasites. Worse still, Mordaunt was looking at him, an impudent, taunting stare.

He walked on, intent on finding Lily. She had been gone in the morning, leaving no note. He had been to her flat, and to everywhere else he could think of, until he had decided that she must have gone up to the barrow.

Returning to his house, he had waited, intending to teach her once and for all who was in charge when she came back to make his lunch. She had not done so, and his intentions of slapping her face and perhaps taking his belt to her backside and legs had grown to a determination to give her a full-blooded beating.

'Ah, Officer Gardner, looking for your fiancée?'

'Yes,' he snapped, stopping. 'Was she with you?'

'She was,' he answered coolly, then hid a sudden grin behind his wine glass.

'Well where is she now?' Ed demanded.

'Gone,' Nich answered. 'Gone beyond your reach, Mr Gardner, gone to her god.'

'What the fuck are you talking about?'

'The truth, Ed, even if you could never accept it. She has left you, dedicating herself in preference to Txcalin.'

'Look, you weirdo, I don't know what you're going on about. Where's my Lil?'

'Lily has left you, as I said.'

'Where is she, you little shit?'

Mordaunt laughed and took a sip of his wine. Ed clenched his fists, tempted to drive one into the grinning face. Holding himself with difficulty, he addressed the archaeologist, whose name he struggled to remember.

'Right, then. Dr Cashwell or whatever your name is, perhaps you've got a bit more sense than your weirdo friends. Did Lil go up to Aldon Hill this morning?'

'Yes, and it's Chaswell, Dr Alice Chaswell.'

'Right, so what I want to know is, where is she now?'

'As Nich said, she has had a change of heart, and of religion. You cannot follow her.'

'Bollocks!' Ed spat. 'She's my girl. I want to know where she is, now!'

'Temper, temper,' the plump girl said and giggled.

Ed closed his eyes, trying to fight down his rising fury.

'I will tell you,' he heard, looking round to see that it was the busty girl who was speaking.

'The tide is approaching low,' she continued. 'If you hurry, you might arrive in time.'

'Juliana!' the plump girl hissed.

'No,' Juliana continued. 'Don't worry, Thomazina, he wants to know. I shall tell him.'

'Get on with it,' Ed growled.

Juliana reached out, taking the bottle of wine and pouring a slow measure into her glass. The plump girl was staring, round-eyed and frightened. Dr Chaswell looked worried, then suddenly calm, as if reaching a decision. Mordaunt was grinning, his girlfriend merely puzzled.

'Cross the ferry,' Juliana said, 'and go through the tunnel to Ness Beach. Walk out to the Aldon Head and around the ledges of rock until you come to a big sea cave, if you can. Enter the cave along the ledge, then wade and climb until the space opens into a cavern with a sandy floor. There you will find Lily, with her new lover.'

'I'll kill the bastard!' Ed hissed. 'And bollocks to you, Mordaunt, you freak, with all your crap about gods. I ought to break your arms!'

'I told the truth,' Nich answered. 'Lily's lover is no mere man. You will find Txcalin in the form of a great octopus, and Lily in his tentacles.'

'What?' Ed snapped. 'You bullshitting little freak!'

Nich said nothing, but shook his head and sipped his wine. Ed's grip tightened on the wall of the hotel garden, his nails digging into the paint.

'It's true,' Alice Chaswell said quietly. 'Believe what you like. Lily has tired of your brutish, controlling ways. She has left you for Txcalin.'

'An octopus! She's left me for a fucking octopus!' Ed yelled, then caught himself, realising that several diners from nearby tables were staring at him.

'It's true,' the plump girl said. 'See for yourself.'

'I will,' Ed grated, 'and if it's true, which I don't believe for a minute, I'll be back here for dinner, fried octopus, and I'll make Lil eat it, you lot too, if you've the guts to hang around!'

He moved away, his face hot with his anger, his fists clenching and unclenching as he walked. They were taunting him, they had to be, but there had been a certainty, a conviction about their words that made it impossible to be certain. Walking fast, he made his way to the beach hut of a friend and borrowed a torch, also a spear gun, reasoning that while Lily was probably just with a man there was no harm in being armed. For one thing he could shoot the bastard in the leg and pretend it had gone off accidentally.

The ferry was in mid-channel and he was forced to wait a frustrating ten minutes before crossing. On the far side he strode ahead, through the tunnel and on to the beach. It was empty, but there were tracks in the sand, twin tracks, leading towards the headland. His mouth set in a savage grin and his grip tightened on the spear gun. Doubtless Juliana thought whoever was with Lily would be a match for him, letting him know where they were in the hope of his getting a bloody nose. She was wrong: it was not his blood that was going to be spilled.

He came to the ledges, his anger and determination building as he climbed each. Two girls were sunbathing on the fourth slope, one topless, one nude, but he ignored them, climbing quickly to the next ledge. The seventh was tricky, and at the eighth he was forced to wade a little way into the sea, his feet slipping on the weed-grown boulders before he found a place where he could pull himself up.

Something moved on the slope, a small seal, sliding into the water and quickly diving in a swirl of black-green weed. Ed had moved the spear gun towards it, eager to kill something, and cursed at its sudden disappearance. For a moment its head appeared at the surface, oddly bright, green eyes peering at him, and then it once more dived. He turned, the animal forgotten. The cave was before him, a great gash in the face of the cliff. He paused to load the spear gun and went forward, cautiously now, with the safety catch off, into the dim interior of the cave. Ahead of him was blackness, the only sound the gentle splash of the waves among the weed and boulders on the cavern floor. He moved on, to where the ledge merged with a sheer wall, across slippery rocks and then on to sand. His eyes had begun to adapt, and he left the torch off, climbing a slope

238

of wet rock to a ledge. Beyond was blackness, and silence, but as he strained he caught a sound, a wet, smacking noise, then a low moan. His thumb went to the torch button and he brought the spear gun up, aiming it into the blackness, then turned on the torch.

Light flooded the cavern and Ed froze, his mouth falling open in shock. On the broad, sandy floor was Lily, naked, her body entwined in the tentacles of a colossal octopus. In colour it was yellowish green, its eyes huge, vermilion discs in a great, bulbous body the size of a truck. Its giant tentacles stretched out, each as thick as his body, three anchored to the ground, five busy with his future wife. Two wrapped her body, holding her immobile, the third was pulled back, as was the fourth, the tips only touching her body, one caressing her breasts and belly, the other her back and bottom. The last was different, longer, and swollen, with a pale tip, a good deal of which appeared to have been pushed into Lily's vagina, with more pressed out to coil over her open sex. She had not seen him. Her eyes were shut, her expression one of utter, undiluted bliss. Her body was twitching, shivers running through her flesh, the same climactic spasms she went through in orgasm, only running on and on as she came over and over in her lover's embrace.

He could do nothing, only watch, horror-struck as the monster fondled his girlfriend, and as he stared he realised that it was pulling her in, beneath the bulbous dome of its body. Her feet were already hidden, the curtain of flesh that separated the creature's tentacles moving slowly up her legs, drawing her under. She made no resistance, staying in her blissful dream state as she was drawn up under its mantle.

Her thighs vanished, and as the mantle edge crept towards her sex the sperm arm burst, spraying white fluid across the golden down of her pubic hair and up over her belly and breasts. Lily gave a groan of unparalleled ecstasy as the sperm ran out around her vagina, and then her sex had been drawn up under the mantle edge.

The beast's arms began to tuck up under its body as Lily's middle was engulfed. Green, resilient octopus flesh

239

crept up over her belly, her chest, her breasts disappearing from view, and still she was coming, half engulfed, but in the throes of orgasm after orgasm as the grotesque thing consumed her. At last her head was gone, her hair trailing behind as a massive arm squeezed her in beneath the mantle.

Ed finally found his senses, bringing up the spear gun and pulling the trigger with an inarticulate cry. The spear shot out, catching the monster between the eyes and sinking deep into the turgid flesh. He wrenched at the line, meaning to tear the barbs through the awful creature's head. Instead the spear came back without resistance, nearly unbalancing him, and the wound closed over the hole he had made.

Catching up the spear, he struggled to reload. The beast was turning, its great eyes fixing on him, a tentacle snaking towards him. Again he fired, hitting an eye, but to no effect, the line slack as he pulled, the eye undamaged. He backed, slipping on the rock. A tentacle lashed out, catching him, wrapping around him and pinning his arms to his sides. He struggled, using the strength of desperation, but to no avail. Another tentacle caught him, and a third, around his legs, and he was being drawn in, dragged inexorably towards the bulk of the monster.

He screamed, the sound echoing from the walls of the chamber. The beast reared, exposing its underside, the opening to the mantle from which Lily's blonde hair still hung, and the central mouth, with the parrot-like beak opening, then shutting with a horrid, clacking sound. Again he screamed, gripping uselessly at the sand. The torch flew from his hand, sending a beam upwards, to briefly illuminate a high red ceiling, carved with symbols and pictures. Blackness engulfed him as the torch burst on rock. The weight of the monster came down on him, crushing him, even as the beak closed on the muscles of his belly and tore into his squirming flesh.

Epilogue

Joe drained the last of his coffee and stood up. The throb of the engines came up through the deck, making the ferry shudder as she turned away from the dock. From the window he could see the Roscoff terminal, bright in June sunlight. It had been a long drive, hauling Spanish tractor components up from Barcelona, and he needed sleep, but he was determined to at least scan the beach for a glimpse of nubile female flesh as the ferry pulled clear of port.

Clutching his binoculars, he made his way to the upper deck. It was hot, and crowded, including more than a few French schoolgirls of seventeen or eighteen in tight, bottom-hugging jeans or even shorts that left slices of creamy cheek showing at each side. He smiled to himself, wishing he had more hair left and less of a paunch.

Going to the rail, he steadied the binoculars, indifferent to the attention of those around him as he focused on the beach. Several girls were visible, sunbathing, bikini-clad or topless, one on her back, fine young breasts bare to the sun. A boat blocked his view as the ferry swung round and he changed his angle, focusing on the Ile de Batz. A couple caught his eye, the girl shamelessly topless, walking beside her man without the least trace of self-consciousness. With a pang of jealousy he followed them, watching the gentle sway of the girl's hips and the movement of her breasts. An outlying rock cut off his view and he clicked his tongue in frustration, moving his view, only to move quickly back.

There were two people on the rock. Girls, standing, and not just topless, but stark, totally naked. Both were black haired, around twenty, one full-figured, one small-breasted but with a fine, cheeky bottom. His eyes locked to the bigger girl's breasts, huge globes of flesh, yet extraordinarily firm, breasts he had seen before. With a start of surprise he realised that the girl was Tammy, could only be Tammy, the wonderful girl he had met in Tawmouth, years before, while her companion, for all her long dark hair, was Lily Tompkins.

Nexus

NEXUS NEW BOOKS

To be published in May

INTIMATE INSTRUCTION
Arabella Knight
£5.99

Hot on the trail of a young, aristocratic credit-card defaulter, Emily Wyndlesham visits Laments Hall – an institution to which the privileged consign their wayward daughters for discipline under the stern governance of Dr Flint. Groomed for a future within the institution, Emily quickly comes to put her new skills into practice. But painful lessons must be learned if Emma is to demonstrate her devotion to discipline.

ISBN 0 352 36618 8

CAPTIVES OF THE PRIVATE HOUSE
Esme Ombreux
£5.99

Amidst the vast acres of the Private House estate live the forest dwellers. Led by the beautiful Talia, these pleasure-seekers live a bucolic life. But Talia is enthralled by a newcomer to the forest: a whipmaker to whose discipline she readily submits. As the regime in the forest becomes ever more severe, the whipmaker and his minions exert their perverse control over Talia and her people. Talia and her friends must suffer extreme indignities in order to defeat the whipmaker's scheme. The latest in the popular *Private House* series.

ISBN 0 352 33619 6

SISTERS OF SEVERCY
Jean Aveline
£5.99

The villa at Severcy is a place of extremes. Here, innocence and love vie with experience and cruelty as young Isabelle is led into perversion by Robert, the handsome young Englishman who visits the villa one summer. As Isabelle is introduced to the dark pleasures of Severcy, so her sister aids in the sensual education of Charlotte, Robert's bride in England. Only passions as strong as those shared by Charlotte and Isabelle can survive these dark tests. As they are enslaved, so they enslave all who use them. A Nexus Classic.

ISBN 0 352 33620 X

To be published in June

DRAWN TO DISCIPLINE
Tara Black
£5.99

Student Judith Wilson lands a job at the Nemesis Archive, an institution dedicated to the documentation of errant female desire, under the imperious Samantha James. Unable to accept correction at the hands of the Director, she is forced to resign. But one manuscript in particular has awoken her guilty fascination with corporal punishment, and leads her to its author and his obscure Rigorist Order in Brittany. The discipline practised there brings Judith's assertive sexuality into a class of its own, and she returns to the Archive to bring her wayward former co-workers to heel.

ISBN 0 352 33626 9

SLAVE REVELATIONS
Jennifer Jane Pope
£5.99

The third book in Jennifer Jane Pope's *Slave* series continues the story of the bizarre pony-carting institution hidden from prying eyes on a remote Scottish island. Those who seek to investigate befall some curious fates: Tommy is now Tammy and Alex is – well, still not at all happy with pony girl slavery. And who or what has given the pony-girls their genetically re-engineered pain thresholds?

ISBN 0 352 33627 7

PLEASURE ISLAND
Aran Ashe
£5.99

The beautiful Anya, betrothed to the prince of Lidir, has set sail for his kingdom. On the way, her ship is beset by pirates. Captured and put into chains, Anya is subjected to a harsh shipboard regime of punishment and cruel pleasures at the hands of the captain and his crew. When landfall is made on a mysterious island populated by dark-eyed amazons, Anya plots her escape, unaware of the fate that awaits anyone who dares to venture ashore. A Nexus Classic.

ISBN 0 352 33628 5

If you would like more information about Nexus titles, please visit our website at www.nexus-books.co.uk, or send a stamped addressed envelope to:

Nexus, Thames Wharf Studios,
Rainville Road, London W6 9HA

NEXUS BACKLIST

This information is correct at time of printing. For up-to-date information, please visit our website at www.nexus-books.co.uk

All books are priced at £5.99 unless another price is given.

Samplers and collections

NEW EROTICA 4	Various ISBN 0 352 33290 5	☐
NEW EROTICA 5	Various ISBN 0 352 33540 8	☐

Nexus Classics

A new imprint dedicated to putting the finest works of erotic fiction back in print.

AGONY AUNT	G.C. Scott ISBN 0 352 33353 7	☐
BOUND TO SERVE	Amanda Ware ISBN 0 352 33457 6	☐
BOUND TO SUBMIT	Amanda Ware ISBN 0 352 33451 7	☐
CANDY IN CAPTIVITY	Arabella Knight ISBN 0 352 33495 9	☐
CHOOSING LOVERS FOR JUSTINE	Aran Ashe ISBN 0 352 33351 0	☐
CITADEL OF SERVITUDE	Aran Ashe ISBN 0 352 33435 5	☐
DIFFERENT STROKES	Sarah Veitch ISBN 0 352 33531 9	☐
EDEN UNVEILED	Maria del Rey ISBN 0 352 33542 4	☐
THE HANDMAIDENS	Aran Ashe ISBN 0 352 33282 4	☐
HIS MISTRESS'S VOICE	G. C. Scott ISBN 0 352 33425 8	☐
THE IMAGE	Jean de Berg ISBN 0 352 33350 2	☐
THE INSTITUTE	Maria del Rey ISBN 0 352 33352 9	☐
LINGERING LESSONS	Sarah Veitch ISBN 0 352 33539 4	☐
A MATTER OF POSSESSION	G. C. Scott ISBN 0 352 33468 1	☐
OBSESSION	Maria del Rey ISBN 0 352 33375 8	☐

------ ✂ ----------------------------

Please send me the books I have ticked above.

Name ....

Address ....

....

....

.... Post code ....

Send to: **Cash Sales, Nexus Books, Thames Wharf Studios, Rainville Road, London W6 9HA**

US customers: for prices and details of how to order books for delivery by mail, call 1-800-805-1083.

Please enclose a cheque or postal order, made payable to **Nexus Books Ltd**, to the value of the books you have ordered plus postage and packing costs as follows:
    UK and BFPO – £1.00 for the first book, 50p for each subsequent book.
    Overseas (including Republic of Ireland) – £2.00 for the first book, £1.00 for each subsequent book.

If you would prefer to pay by VISA, ACCESS/MASTER-CARD, AMEX, DINERS CLUB, AMEX or SWITCH, please write your card number and expiry date here:

....

Please allow up to 28 days for delivery.

Signature ....

------ ✂ ----------------------------